TYRANT

R.K. LILLEY

ISBN: 978-62878-057-4

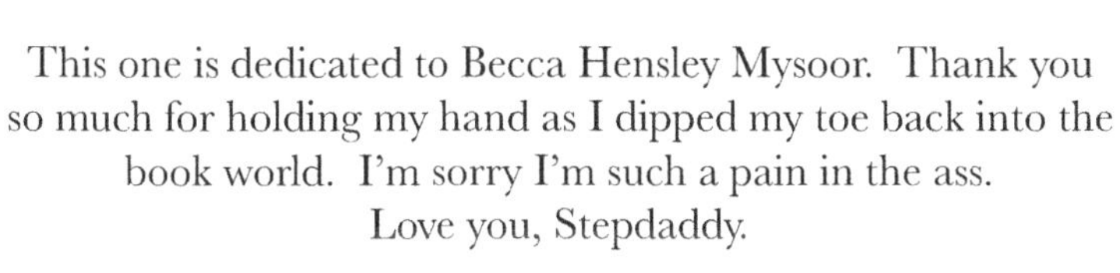

This one is dedicated to Becca Hensley Mysoor. Thank you so much for holding my hand as I dipped my toe back into the book world. I'm sorry I'm such a pain in the ass.
Love you, Stepdaddy.

TURNER THE TYRANT HAS MET HIS MATCH

I was done for. Profoundly screwed.
The issue, of course, was my assistant, Devereux.
She was slowly but surely driving me crazy.
It wasn't supposed to be like this. Hiring her was supposed to bring order to my life.
Instead, she'd brought disorder.
Chaos. Irritation. Malaise.
Comfort. Exuberance. Delight.
I was obsessed with her.
Truly, irrevocably obsessed.
She was stubborn. Standoffish. Painfully honest.
Take no prisoners efficient.
In summary, a termagant -- much too young for me.
And even I, oblivious bastard extraordinaire, was aware in some corner of my mind, of every well-laid plan I'd ever had slowly crashing down and exploding into dust.
I was simply no match for Devereux Laurent.

PROLOGUE

I was fucked.

Done for.

Profoundly screwed in the head.

The issue, of course, was my assistant, Devereux.

She was slowly but surely driving me crazy. I was literally going to lose my mind.

It wasn't supposed to be like this. Hiring her was supposed to bring order to my life.

Instead she'd brought disorder. Chaos. Vexation. Irritation. Malaise.

Joy. Fun. Comfort. Exuberance. Delight.

I was obsessed with her.

She was stubborn. Standoffish. Painfully honest. Take no prisoners efficient. In summary, a termagant.

And even I, oblivious bastard extraordinaire, was aware in some corner of my mind, of every well laid plan I'd ever had slowly crashing down and exploding into dust.

I was simply no match for Devereux Laurent

It all started with one innocent conversation with my good friend Dair.

"Iris found someone that she swears would make the

perfect assistant for you. She's organized, meticulous, and highly intelligent. She has management experience, but evidently has decided that she'd like a change, and is extremely interested in learning more about the literary world."

I had assistant issues. It was a notorious and long standing problem of mine. I needed someone to pick up all of the loose ends in my life. Instead, I had a history of hiring the wrong people and then allowing that to blowup in my face.

I needed to hire someone I wasn't attracted to, but more importantly, someone who wasn't attracted to me.

My goal was to find an assistant I didn't want to, and wouldn't, fuck. Someone who would actually stick around and do their job.

"I'm listening," I told him pleasantly. "Please tell me she's fifty years old. No wait, sixty."

"She's young, but not at all your type, though she is actually Candy's cousin. You remember Candy? She was your assistant a few years ago."

I rolled my eyes at that, because he knew as well as I did that my memory was excellent, but I found myself confused. "How does Iris know Candy's cousin?" I tried to wrap my mind around that strange connection.

Dair's smile was beyond fond and into sappy. "You know Iris." He said his wife's name like she was the key to the universe, and I totally got it. The woman was off the charts hot and crazy enough to keep his life interesting. "She makes friends with everybody. She went out dancing with Candy and they hit it off, and they've remained friends. Recently, Candy invited us to a family barbecue where she met your new assistant, Devereux, who was visiting from out of town."

"You make it sound like a done deal."

Dair glanced around my disastrous office pointedly. "What have you got to lose? This place is a mess, and you're behind on everything, right? Your emails, your social media, your deadlines, God only knows what else. She's available to start right away."

"Explain what you mean by not my type," I said, interested. I really did need an assistant, especially one that would do some actual work.

"Not like Candy. Or the ones that have followed her. Devereux is smart. And wholesome. She's not interested in you, she's interested in learning about the book world, and having a job."

My nose wrinkled up in distaste muddled with a bit of reluctant fascination. "Wholesome," I tasted the word. It didn't taste bad. Just utterly foreign. "*That's* not something you see every day."

Dair laughed. "No, my friend. It's not something *you* see every day."

CHAPTER ONE

Our first meeting was a bit awkward, for her more than me, but I figured it was necessary. Best she knew up front just who she was working for.

I answered the door for her myself. It was early for me, ten a.m. on the dot.

Had I told her to come this early?

Dammit, I had. What had I been thinking?

Well, I hadn't intended for the party to go so late the night before. Or to keep on going once most of the partygoers had left.

At least I was awake. And clean. In fact, I was barely dried from a shower wearing nothing but the damp towel I'd used to dry off tucked haphazardly around my hips.

I grinned at the sight of her.

At first glance I knew she'd do. "My new assistant, I presume?" I inquired.

"Devereux Laurent," she said stridently, pushing up her glasses and holding out her hand. "Nice to meet you, Mr.

Thorn."

I shook her hand, tilting my bemused head to study her.

She was cute, with a very nice face, which wasn't good. She had clean, neat features, and big brown Bambi eyes that were probing to the point of disconcerting. Not the best-case scenario.

But she'd do.

She wasn't a dime, just based on her figure and wardrobe alone, which I gave a point in her column.

She was wearing a long, dark green, bulky skirt that nearly dragged on the ground, a loose, black turtleneck blouse that covered her entire throat, and a boxy blazer that hung well past her hips.

She wouldn't stop traffic with two red lights strapped to her ass.

Perfect.

I couldn't see her shoes, but I just assumed they were as hideous as the rest of it. Good. Nothing sexy to see here. She'd come to do a job, and that job was not to seduce me.

Still. It wasn't summer, but it was an unseasonably warm autumn day. "Aren't you hot in that?" I asked her.

"Aren't you cold in that?" she asked back, deadpan, her eyes staying on my face, never drifting down once to openly check out my tanned, ripped to shreds, barely covered body.

I smiled. A bit of sass never went unappreciated by me. Another point in her favor.

I flexed my abs and her eyes shot down for a brief second before shooting back up at me and glaring.

My smile grew. I wasn't like my friend Dair, some humble, unassuming hunk.

I knew exactly how appealing I was. I was big, built, hot, and used it shamelessly at every opportunity. Good looks were a weapon just like every other asset a person carried around, and I made a point of using my assets at every opportunity.

It didn't hurt that I was a shameless hedonist.

I continued to study her blatantly.

Her hair was brown bordering on black, and must have been thick going by the size of the chignon she had it wound into at the back of her head. She wore those square framed glasses that were so in right now. Normally I didn't like them, but on her they looked adorable. Point against her.

She wasn't wearing makeup, which was a point in her favor.

But her lips still looked soft and were naturally pink. That was a point against, since that color made me think of her nipples, and I looked at her breasts under her baggy blouse. They were well covered, but I could still tell that there was something substantial there. You couldn't hide a big chest, not from a connoisseur like me.

She was petite, which was a point for her. I usually liked them tall and leggy, with outrageous curves, like her cousin Candy, who incidentally had been my short-lived assistant a few years prior.

Devereux didn't even reach my chin, and though I couldn't see her legs under the awful skirt she was wearing, I was confident that they weren't long enough to wrap around me properly.

She'd do.

"Come on in," I said, moving aside to let her pass. "I'll give you the tour."

"Go ahead and get dressed first," she told me briskly. "I don't mind waiting."

My brows shot up in intrigued surprise. I couldn't remember the last time a woman had asked, no ordered, me to put my clothes *on*.

"I'm fine," I assured her. "The essentials are covered." I started moving, motioning for her to follow me. "Right this way."

I led her straight to my office. The back wall was lined with my book covers. I explained this to her.

"Yes, I can see that," she said wryly. "Red Twin is my favorite, but Red House is a close second."

"You've read my books?" I tried to recall if any of my former assistants had ever read my books.

No.

I tried to recall if any of my former assistants could read.

Who knew?

She raised a vaguely insulted brow at me. "Well, yes. Of course I did," she said. "I've read them all. I'm looking at this job as a mentorship. I want to enter into the field myself at some point."

"You want to be an author?" I asked with no surprise.

Everyone thought they wanted to be an author until they realized how fucking hard it was to write an entire book without hating it, the world, and yourself by the end.

"Yes. And an illustrator, though I know that's not in your wheel house."

My brow furrowed, "An illustrator? What genre are you interested in?"

"All of them. I read everything."

"No. I mean, which genre are you going to write in?"

"Guess," she said with no expression.

So she was playful, with a dry sense of humor. I liked that. "Fiction?"

"Yes, but I'm not impressed by your guessing skills. Don't you think you can narrow it down?"

I studied her. "Perhaps some sort of graphic novel? Manga? I'm trying to get a feel for how the illustrating ties in. Nothing in the horror category. You're not crazy enough."

"You don't know me that well."

"True. But I'm still eliminating it."

"That's fair," she said blandly.

Damn, she had a good poker face. "Not romance. No offense, but you don't look like you have a romantic bone in your body."

"Fair enough," she agreed.

"Not erotica. No one could write good sex and dress that way. No offense."

"Offense taken," she shot back, looking not at all offended.

Oh, God. So she was sarcastic and good at it. I *really* liked that.

"Historical. No," I kept musing, almost to myself, answering my own questions as I went. "Sci-Fi. No."

"Definitely not fantasy," I said with conviction. "You're too level-headed to have your head in some other world all the time."

"God, you're terrible at this," she told me with a small smile.

I got a kick out of that, because she was right, and because, even on her first day on the job, she had no problem giving me shit.

"Children's books," she put me out of my terrible guessing misery. "I want to write and illustrate children's books with a focus on ages four to eight."

I couldn't help but laugh at that, it was so unexpected.

And it was adorable. "Well, I hope you know that's not what *I* do," I warned. I wasn't sure how I could help her on that particular path, but I was game to try if she was.

"I'm aware. Your books would give children nightmares and probably put them in therapy, but it's not about the genre. I believe I can learn a lot from you. Like I said, I've read all of your books, and you're clearly competent at the many nuances of your craft."

She said it with no expression, none of the fan enthusiasm I was used to, but I somehow found myself more flattered because of it.

I was trying to think of a proper response, a thank you maybe, but that was when a half-dressed redhead leaned in the doorway, sending me a very pointed smile.

I'd flat out forgotten about her, which was kind of sad, since I'd left her sleeping naked in my sex room mere hours before. "Oh, hi," I told her pleasantly. "You're awake. Well, I'm working, but help yourself to whatever's in the kitchen before you leave, and feel free to make an extra for me if you decide to cook."

A throat cleared not so subtly behind me, and I turned to grin at Devereux. "Oh, sorry. How rude of me. Glasses, this is . . . Red. Red, meet my new assistant, Glasses."

Devereux shot me a less than friendly look, approaching the other woman, who towered over her. She held out her hand exactly as she had to me, and the redhead let her shake hands, looking confused at the exchange.

"My name is Devereux," she told the other woman pointedly. "Nice to meet you."

"Oh, um, nice to meet you. My name is Jennifer." She shot me a friendly grin. "Though Red works fine, too."

I smiled blandly back. That was good, since I had no intention of remembering her name beyond this moment. There was only so much space in a brain for one-night stands.

"Okay, back to the emails," I began when Red/Jennifer had left.

I was sidetracked by another figure promptly filling the doorway. I smiled warmly. It was the blond with the mad oral skills from last night that I'd left naked in my sex room a few hours prior... in bed right next to the redhead. How could it be I'd already forgotten there were two?

She was wearing one of my T-shirts, and I was assuming not much else. "Hey," she said in a soft bedroom voice.

"Hey, erm, Blondie," I said back. "New assistant, this is Blondie. I'm working, but feel free to feed yourself breakfast before you take off." I turned away, trying to get back to business.

Devereux wasn't having it, rising again, shaking the other woman's hand. "Nice to meet you. I'm Devereux," she told Blondie.

"I'm Sara," she replied, eyeing Devereux up with less than friendly eyes. I, for one, thought the hostility was uncalled for.

Blondie/Sara looked pointedly back at me. "Do you *have to* work right now? I'm in the mood to spend the day in bed." She was using her best bedroom voice and her best bedroom eyes.

She was good, but I was done. "Not today. I have your number though, right? Maybe I'll text you sometime." I turned my attention back to my computer, putting the whole thing from my mind.

It would have stayed off my mind if a persistent little voice hadn't said archly, "Red and Blondie, really? You could at least remember their names."

It was probably for the best that I hadn't gone with my first auto-names for them. If she took offense with Red and Blondie, she'd have had a conniption if I'd just cut to the chase and called them the first thing my filthy mind had come up with: Spit and Swallow.

"They didn't mind. I just met them yesterday. How can they possibly be offended?" I was standing in front of her, looming over her tiny form, and I didn't even remember how I'd gotten there.

That should have been my first warning that she was going to be trouble, but I was so distracted that I didn't wonder at it.

She looked up at me like she was looking down. I was a

full head taller than her, but it didn't feel like it. She was the only person I'd ever met that treated being short like it put her *higher*.

Infuriating little termagant.

"Don't be so judgmental," I told her with my most charming smile. It was a smile that let me get away with a lot. Usually. "I'm sowing my wild oats."

"Well, you're an over-achiever. But did it never occur to you that you'd have to reap what you sow?"

"That sounds like a threat."

"Not from me, but life tends to find a way."

"You know, I'd bet they don't know my name, either."

"Is that what you tell yourself, to make it better?"

I squinted at her. It was a bit early on for her to be giving me *this* kind of shit, but I was twisted, so I found it somewhat entertaining, enough so to gamely shout at the redhead to come back.

She seemed the more easygoing of the two.

She came back smiling. "Can I get you something? I'm making eggs for you. And coffee. Devereux, would you like some?"

"No, but thank you, Jennifer," Devereux replied politely.

"How sweet of you," I told Red, "but before you get back to it, we had a question for you. Actually, she did. Ask away, Glasses."

"Do you know his name?" Devereux asked her.

Red grinned wickedly. "His real name or the one we gave him? We'd heard he likes nicknames."

Devereux shot me a look that tickled me. She didn't have to roll her eyes for me to see that she wanted to.

"His real one," Devereux answered.

"I'd like to hear the one you gave me," I answered at the same time.

Red was sweet enough to answer me first. "Tall boy."

I caught the reference the second she said it, but Devereux seemed confused to the point that Red felt the need to explain it to her. "You know, like a tall can of beer," as she spoke she gestured comprehensively, and obscenely, with her hands.

Devereux blushed. *Blushed.*

I felt myself getting hard.

That was my first inkling that we might have a problem.

I went and sat behind my desk.

"What about my real name?" I asked Red, an attempt at changing the subject, and my current, unproductive, filthy thought process.

"Turner Thorn," Red spouted out promptly and cheerfully.

Well, dammit. I hadn't even proven my point.

"Thanks, Red. I like my eggs fried."

"How many do you want?"

"Three, please and thank you. Now back to these emails, Glasses."

"No," my new assistant said firmly, hands on her hips, trying to look intimidating, all five foot three inches of her. "You're not doing that. It's dehumanizing. I have a name."

I rolled my eyes. "Fine, whatever, Dev."

"Devereux. I don't like Dev, either."

"Who has a name like that and doesn't shorten it? *And* you won't let me give you a nickname?" I didn't look at her as I spoke, eyes on my computer.

"If you need to shorten it, call me Ro. Dev is trite." The first few sentences were said in a deadpan tone, but when she got to the *Dev is trite* line, I could hear the clear amusement in her voice.

My eyes shot to her and widened. God, she tickled me, like every word out of her mouth was designed for my specific entertainment.

Oh, this is going to be fun, I thought with wicked glee.

That was my second inkling that we might have a problem.

I shook it off, forcing myself to be professional.

As professional as a guy could be while wearing nothing but a towel and calming down a hard-on.

"Dair told me you had management experience that qualified you for all of the random duties attached to this job," I told her, "but that you wanted this job because you wanted to shift fields. What field was your management experience in?"

She blinked at me in a way that seemed to imply she thought I was possibly insane. "You didn't ask him what the experience *was*?"

"I didn't care then. Dair's a close friend and colleague with a good brain, and I trusted him to make a solid recommendation, but I'm curious now."

"I helped manage a nursing home."

I laughed, and laughed, and laughed. When I finally caught my breath, I couldn't hold in one snarky comment. "Well, that explains your wardrobe."

I got a glare for that, but it seemed half-hearted to me. She had to know she was a terrible dresser.

As we began to work, I quickly realized that I'd need to rearrange my office. I'd become too accustomed to working alone. "I'll get a corner in here cleared out for when we need to work together sometime today, but in the meantime, let me show you your office, where you'll spend most of your time."

She simply nodded and followed, but I got the distinct feeling that she was actually paying attention, listening to and absorbing what I said.

Taking me seriously.

I was encouraged.

It was a new experience. Usually my assistants were too busy putting on makeup or taking selfies to ever acknowledge that there was a real job to be done. I, of course, took full responsibility for that, as in the past I'd tended to hire women with all of the wrong qualifications, and all of the right measurements.

The second office was directly next to mine. It was smaller, but still large, and its current state was one of mayhem.

"What on earth happened in here?" she asked, sounding more judgmental than worried, which perversely made me happy.

I scratched my chin, looking at the bastard stepchild office. It was stacked floor to ceiling with boxes full of who knew what work crap to the point that I couldn't even see the furniture that I was fairly certain the room contained. "I don't really know. I haven't had an assistant for a while, and I guess this room just got away from me. There are bookshelves, a desk, chair, and a computer in here somewhere. Hell, I'm pretty sure there's even a sofa and a TV."

"I won't need a sofa or a TV," she said briskly, pulling up the sleeves of her hideous, oversized blazer.

I liked the determination in her eyes. It made me think, before I ever had any evidence, that she might be up to any task she set her mind to.

"Obviously, this needs to be my priority," she stated in a no-nonsense tone.

"Sounds good to me. I'll hire some guys to help you move this stuff around."

She sent me a look of pure affront. "Not necessary. I can move some boxes on my own. You go back to work. I've got this. When I finish, we'll touch base on what I should make my next priority."

"I'm almost certain that most of those boxes are full of books and very heavy."

"I'll handle it," she said mulishly.

"You're tiny. I didn't hire you to do any heavy lifting; I hired you to make phone calls and work on a computer—"

"You hired me to handle the things that need to be handled so you can finish your work in progress. Go work on that book, Mr. Thorn. Like I said, I'll handle this."

And just like that, I was dismissed.

I took it with good grace. No way could she handle that disaster of a room on her own. When she figured it out, she'd come to me and ask for the help she so obviously needed. I was content to wait her out.

"Suit yourself," I said blandly and walked away. "If you have any questions, I'll be in my office, racking up some word count."

"Good luck," she said in a tone that implied I'd need it more than she would.

She was a stubborn one. That suited me just fine. It would make it all the sweeter when she realized that I was right and she was wrong.

I got dressed (even I couldn't wear a towel *all* day) and tried to get back to writing, but I felt almost antsy with delight. I couldn't say why, but I was really looking forward to the moment when she caved in to the overwhelming impossibility of tackling that office on her own and came to ask me for help.

I blamed my penchant for instant gratification, but three hours later I was nearly out of patience.

Red and Blondie had long since left, gamely feeding me an abundant breakfast first. Red had prepared me eggs, coffee, and sausage. Blondie had attempted bacon, fresh squeezed orange juice, and toast.

They'd done it almost competitively, as though I'd pick a favorite between the two based on what they prepared. It was nearly charming, even after realizing after a few bites that they were both beyond dismal cooks.

Still, I'd eaten every bite of the undercooked bacon, overcooked, unseasoned eggs, lukewarm sausage, burnt toast, weak coffee, and pulpy orange juice as they both looked on with varying degrees of satisfaction, making a lot of noises about how delicious it all was.

It was the least I could do.

I politely walked them both out after I was done, but only because I wasn't sure they'd leave unless I saw to it firsthand.

After that I felt very in control as I passed by the stepchild office without so much as glancing inside. All in good time.

But it wasn't long before smug anticipation had turned to impatient irritation.

What the hell was she doing? Was she still working on that damned office? Did she really think she could move all of those boxes on her own? Some of them were *heavy,* and sassy as hell Ro had to be more than a foot shorter than me and small-framed to boot.

The thought made me unreasonably irritable, enough so that I'd risen from my chair more than once to confront her before I'd realized what I was doing and made myself move to the pull up bar mounted into the wall in the corner to do a grueling round of reps before sitting back down.

No. She'd already decided to engage me in our first battle of wills, and I sure as hell wasn't going to be the one to cave.

A few more hours ticked slowly by, my word count sluggish but determined, my mind more than halfway directed at the new girl and what she was doing with the room next door.

I went through three cups of coffee from the Keurig machine in my office. It wasn't my favorite way to caffeinate, but the espresso machine in the kitchen went too temptingly past the room I was so resolute to ignore.

CHAPTER TWO

I was mid round of pull-ups when my new assistant finally appeared in my office doorway.

It was after five p.m.

She looked exactly as she had before, completely composed, not a hair out of place, so I deduced right away that she couldn't have gotten much accomplished in her new disaster of an office.

I lowered myself back down to the ground and smiled blandly at her. "Give up yet?"

One of her eyebrows shot up. "Of course not. It's just one room, and it's coming along nicely. Though I realized I should get a tour of this house… and figure out where to put my suitcases. I still haven't unpacked my car."

I'd forgotten about all that, nearly forgotten that she'd be staying at the house.

The assistants had always been live-in since I worked all hours of the day and night, and my place was huge. They stayed out of my wing when I wanted a break from company or needed privacy for whatever reason.

It had been so long since I'd filled the position that I'd forgotten to bother showing her where she'd be sleeping.

"Of course," I told her and began to lead her to what was now her side of the house.

I couldn't help but steal a peek into the stepchild office as we passed it.

I stopped in my tracks, swiveled on a heel, and leaned into the room, eyeing every corner.

"How the fuck did you do this?" I asked her, tilting my head around and down to get a proper look at her smug face.

"It's just a room. And you were right. Most of the boxes were full of books, and every wall is lined with bookshelves. It wasn't hard to do the math."

I looked back at the nearly cleared space. The walls were a nice pale blue color, the built-in bookshelves a soft gray. It had been so long since I'd seen them that I'd forgotten. Nearly every shelf was lined with books now, most of them mine. The room was brighter, windows uncovered now, blinds opened wide to let in the sun.

I glanced down at the floor. It was a dark gray wood, like the majority of the house, but I hadn't seen it in so long that it was startling.

"I guess I was wrong about the TV and the sofa," I mused, still taking it all in. "Just a chair and desk. Hmm. Don't worry, I'll have that fixed by tomorrow."

"Don't bother. I don't want a sofa or a TV. I don't plan to do anything but work in here. I will, however, need some kind of computer."

"Of course," I murmured, back to studying her. She was a determined little thing. I decided that I found that endearing. "What did you do with all of the empty boxes?" I asked her.

She curled her pouty upper lip, and I could tell I'd offended her. "I broke them down and put them in your garage. It wasn't hard to find, and I'm fairly confident I'll be able to successfully navigate any future recycling. How about that tour?"

I thought about reminding her who the boss was here, but decided against it.

For the moment.

"Right this way," I told her blandly, leading her to her side of the house.

I took her to her room first. Or rather, rooms.

It was set far away from the center of the house, on the second floor, for optimum privacy, and it was designed as a master, almost as large as mine. She had her own sitting room, mini-kitchen, a king-sized, four-poster bed, and a closet that belonged on Cribs. Her en suite bath was obscenely huge, with a Jacuzzi tub, all the amenities, and marble everywhere you looked.

Frankly, I expected some reaction. It was a hell of an assistant's pad.

Her response was less than gratifying. "Hmm," she hummed after I'd shown her everything. "It's a bit large. I have no idea what anyone could ever do with all this space."

I'd had no intention of giving her a detailed tour, I knew she could explore her way around, but the way she was so obviously unimpressed had me showing her every detail of my house.

Every room, every piece of art, every expensive toy.

Perversity had always been a good fit for me.

I was nearly finished not impressing her with her wing of the house when I noticed the expression on her face.

She wasn't just unimpressed. She was *bored.*

Now that, I could fix.

I showed her *my* wing of the house, starting with my favorite part.

It was near the front door, for obvious reasons.

"This is the sex room," I explained, waving my hand around at the twelve hundred square feet of hedonistic delight. "Conveniently close to the kitchen and the front door, so no one goes hungry and no one gets lost on their way out."

A giant bed dominated the space, but it wasn't the beginning and end of the versatile room.

Several bookshelves lined the walls. They were full of every kind of sexual literature, from Kama Sutra to modern erotica. And of course there was no shortage of sex furniture, all attached to a bathroom with a shower most school gyms would envy in size.

"Your sex room?" she repeated back, but she didn't look bored now.

She looked perturbed. Disgusted. Riled. So much so, she wasn't even blushing.

"I don't sleep where I fuck," I explained. Reasonably, I thought.

"You won't even let them into your real bedroom? I think you've taken your promiscuity to a disturbing level," she said every word with quiet revulsion and with just enough conviction to make me feel suddenly uncomfortable.

"Perhaps. What does it matter, anyway?" I asked shrugging it off. "Whether I fuck my way around the world, or lock myself away, we're all just dust in the wind. I may as well enjoy myself."

"Self-absorbed nihilist," she muttered under her breath as she walked away.

Well, hell.

"You don't know me well enough to get me this much." Her insults were possibly my favorite thing about her so far. She was just too spot on accurate, and the delivery was the chef's kiss on top.

I shook it off, showing her the en suite bathroom, or as I'd more appropriately named it, the bath hall.

"There's the orgy shower," I pointed out, watching her face. If anything in here was going to get another blush out of her, I figured that was it.

It worked. Her face flashed bright pink at the cheeks, the corners of her mouth went down, and she turned on her heel, her small form pacing out of the bathroom, and then the sex room, in record time.

I grinned. This was going to be fun.

"I feel sorry for them," she said quietly when I joined her. She wasn't looking at me, but I was studying her like a scientist would study a particularly odd specimen.

I was offended, I realized. That was hard to do. But I wasn't accustomed or prepared for a female that felt sorry for the women I hooked up with. In general, I tended to encounter an opposite reaction.

"You shouldn't feel sorry for any of the women I fuck. Trust me, they know the score, and I take good care of them."

She just met my eyes, and shook her head, her expression managing to convey both condescension and pity.

The deluded girl thought *I* was the clueless one.

It was a bit infuriating, but I shrugged it all off.

It's for the best, I told myself. Because of course it was. A prudish, judgmental girl that looked down on my unrepentant debauchery was hardly likely to tempt a guy like me, which was just what I'd been looking for in an assistant.

I showed her the kitchen next, though it was in the center of the house, impossible to miss, so I didn't really need to. Still, I gave her thorough instructions on how best to make my coffee, because nothing's more important to a writer on a deadline than caffeine, and I was very picky about just how I liked to take mine.

"I like to start the day with a cappuccino. After that, I tend to stick to espresso shots, usually doubles, though some days that varies with my mood. Pay very close attention to these measurements," I said, pouring milk into the steamer. "A writer's best weapon is a perfect cup of coffee, and the first cup of the day is the most critical."

"Got it," she said with confidence.

I nearly rolled my eyes. Everyone seemed to think coffee was so easy to get right, but I'd never had an assistant that didn't botch it to the point that I ended up making it myself more often than not. Still, this one seemed more competent than my usual, so I'd give her the initial benefit of the doubt.

I showed her the outside of the property, as well. I never missed a good opportunity to show off the things I had earned for myself.

I showed her the pool, which was massive. It was closer to three pools, really, with a slide, diving board, and hidden grotto. It was made for parties, lined top to bottom with glass tiles that sparkled in the sun.

She didn't seem impressed, so I just kept going, showing her my oversized garage full of cars and motorcycles.

That didn't get a reaction, so I took her along my property line, letting her get the full scale of just how much land I owned.

"Those are some high walls," she stated mildly as she followed me around the perimeter of the estate.

"I like privacy. If I want to take a walk naked on my own land, it's my prerogative. One of the perks of having money."

She snorted and it made me smile. "Yeah . . . walking. I'm sure that's the naked activity that you were thinking about when you built this place."

She was a wiseass. Thank God. We'd be spending a lot of time together, and it would have been torture if she didn't have a personality.

After a much more extensive tour than I'd planned, we moved her into the house. She didn't like it, but I insisted on carrying her things in from her car.

I was shocked to find that she only had two suitcases.

"Didn't you come from Kansas?" I asked her. "Is a moving company sending the rest? Let me know the cost of that. I'll reimburse you for all of your moving expenses, just like we agreed on—"

"This is everything. I'm a minimalist. I've never needed much."

I just stared at her for a beat, wondering if she was messing with me, then shrugged it off and took her things inside.

CHAPTER THREE

"Another one of your duties is attempting to help me stay on task," I told Ro as she brought me my morning coffee the next day.

"Got it," she said instantly. "How do you propose I do that?"

"Well, I have a deadline right around the corner, a few short months away. I need to complete 2k words a day between now and then. I need you to remind me of this often, and every time you see me, I'd like you to ask me what my word count is for the day. Also, if you see me doing anything other than staring off into space, deep in thought, or actively writing, I want you put me in check."

"How do I put you in check?" she asked reasonably.

"Bribery. Coercion. Threats."

"I think I could get on board with the threat part."

"Of course you could."

"One problem. I don't know you well enough to know what to threaten you with."

"You'll think of something."

"You know, you're not exactly the tyrant I've been made to believe. Tyrants don't usually ask their assistants to threaten them."

"Oh just you wait, little girl. See what happens the first time you try."

She bit her lip to keep from smiling.

It was at that moment that I realized two things, neither one of them good for my peace of mind.

One: Ro had about the sexiest mouth I'd ever seen. Just my motherfucking luck.

Two: She was growing on me *fast*.

"Go get yourself some breakfast," I told her almost affectionately, "We're going to run some errands in a bit."

"What errands?"

"I like to go to Office Max about once a week," I explained. "I know, I know. I can get all of this stuff online, but I enjoy browsing office supplies."

"You enjoy browsing office supplies?"

"I'm always trying to reinvent my office. Think of it as a brainstorming session for that. I feel like, if I tweaked this office just a bit, it would make me write faster."

"Aren't you supposed to be writing all day?" she asked pointedly.

"Hush," I said, "don't talk back, and go eat some eggs."

I was ready to go when I tracked her down in the kitchen.

She was chatting with my hook-up from the night before. Real friendly like.

I did not like that.

First of all, I'd forgotten that I *had* company. Veronica was a regular, a tall, busty, insatiable redhead who was down for any damn thing, and she'd shown up the night before (without invitation) at booty call hours. I'd accommodated her, because I was an accommodating kind of guy, but I was surprised to see her still at the house. She usually didn't stick around after.

And I didn't like the way she was looking at Ro, like she thought Ro might be a particularly delectable dessert.

No. Uh uh. Ro was off-limits, for me and especially everyone else. I realized right then that I might have to readjust some of my patterns for her. I'd never shared a house with anyone who wasn't cut from the same cloth as me.

"Let's go, Ro," I said impatiently. "Have a good one, Veronica. I trust you can find your way out."

Ro started moving toward the door.

Veronica just smiled, not moving an inch from her perch on the counter, so I decided to leave her to it. Sometimes women came and decided not to leave for a bit. My policy on this had always been to ignore the issue until it went away. I figured she'd be gone by the time we got back, and if she wasn't, we'd just go about our business as usual until she did.

We took my Harley, just to shake up Ro's composure a bit.

She didn't like it.

"I'll follow you in my car."

"That's silly. Hop on." I handed her a helmet.

She wasn't happy about it, but she did it, pushing the helmet on and straddling the bike awkwardly in her too-long skirt.

She thought she could hang on by barely touching my shoulders, but the second we started moving her little arms snaked around my waist and held on for dear life.

I felt the problem right away, or should I say problems.

It was one thing to speculate about nice breasts under a thick, ugly, unflattering shirt. It was another thing entirely to feel them pressed firmly against your back.

Yep, her tits were nice. I could tell for sure. Soft and pliant. Big and bouncy.

And her shapely little thighs gripping my hips were almost

as distracting.

Fuck.

I spent way too much time in Office Max. I was on deadline, so of course I was going deep into procrastination mode.

And the fact that I couldn't glance at Ro without my eyes dropping to her tits after that ride was not helping me to be one bit faster.

I'd swear I could picture just exactly what they looked like after that ride, but it didn't stop me from wanting to see her body firsthand.

On the contrary.

"So this is how you shop for office supplies?" she asked me after about a half an hour of aimless wandering. "You didn't even bring a list?"

I shrugged. "I'll know it when I see it."

"Aren't you supposed to be writing right now? This feels like a colossal waste of time."

"Hush. Procrastination is a key component to the writing process."

"Your process maybe."

"Yeah, that's exactly what I meant."

"Didn't you tell me that part of my job was to keep you on task? This is the opposite of on task."

"Hush," I said absently, playing with a random pen. "Look at this pen." I was drawing on the display I'd pulled it out of. "Isn't it cool? I'm pretty sure I need a pen exactly like this."

"It's a pen," she said flatly. "Are you messing with me?"

I kind of was. Also, I was trying not to look at, or obsess about, her tits. "Define messing?" I asked, still drawing on the display.

With a sigh, she grabbed a pen and started drawing with me.

After a while, I had a very shitty looking stick figure with big boobs. I looked over at hers.

She'd drawn a small, detailed unicorn, and it was actually quite good.

"These pens *are* cool," she said, still drawing. "We should get some."

I threw a handful of them in the cart.

"So I have a question for you," I asked her abruptly, trying and failing to make it sound casual.

She straightened, studying my face. She caught on right away that what I was about to ask was going to be awkward for us both.

I cleared my throat. "I was told, erm, I mean, I heard that you're, um, wholesome. Can you tell me exactly what that means?"

She blushed. Flat out blushed bright pink.

It was not helpful. I wasn't sure why, but seeing her blush got me hard at a glance.

She fidgeted, looking down at her feet.

That also did not help.

"I, um," she started, sounding as uncomfortable as I felt. "I'm not like you. I'm not experienced. I don't take sex lightly."

"What exactly does that mean?"

"Well, for example, all of the women coming and going from your sex room is nothing I've ever been exposed to before. As a matter of fact, the idea of a separate room for sleep and sex isn't something I've ever even *heard* of. I'm not completely ignorant about that stuff, but I guess you could say I'm somewhat innocent."

She'd said *somewhat* innocent. I found this encouraging, because it meant that she wasn't *completely* innocent.

And those weren't the only words she'd spoken that had gotten through.

"I'll try to keep that stuff away from you," I said solemnly. I could work out other arrangements that didn't involve Ro having to entertain a parade of different women in my kitchen every morning.

Because, all jokes aside, I hated to think that my dissolute bed habits might negatively affect her.

Corrupting Ro was not on my agenda. Ever.

I intended to keep repeating that to myself until my dick got the message.

I wasted another half hour looking at office supplies before we headed home.

I grinned when I saw cars parked in my driveway upon our return. I didn't recognize all of them, but I spotted Dair's Tesla right off the bat.

He got out of his car and waved at us as I parked my Harley and helped Ro get off.

She looked as terrified from the return trip as she had on the one going. Motorcycles weren't for everyone.

I gently took off her helmet and patted her on her cute little head. "Chin up, Ro. We lived."

She glared at me, but the glare turned to a smile when Dair greeted her.

"How are you settling in?" he asked her.

"It's an adjustment, but it's going well, all things considered." At the all things considered, she sent me a less than friendly look.

Dair grinned. "Have time to sit down and talk some shop?" he asked me. "I'd like to shoot some ideas off you."

"Always," I replied. Dair was another author and had been one of my heroes since I was a teenager. He was a decade older than me, and he was one of the reasons I'd started writing in the first place. I considered his friendship to be a privilege. Growing up, I'd never dreamed I'd one day become his colleague. We usually had a coffee and book talk session at least twice a week.

Ro coughed, staring pointedly at me. "Remember telling me something about staying on task today?"

"Hush," I said, patting her on the head again. It seemed to drive her crazy when I did this, and I got a kick out of that.

We went to grab coffee first. The good kind, not the basic stuff in my office.

The three of us walked into the kitchen and stopped dead.

Two naked women, Blondie and Red from the day before, were sixty-nine-ing each other on my kitchen counter.

CHAPTER FOUR

"What the *fuck*, Thorn?" Dair burst out, sounding disgusted.

"What?" I shot back, sarcasm coming out on auto-pilot. "Look how generous they're being with each other."

And then I remembered Ro.

My hands clapped over both of her eyes exactly one second later.

Fuck. I was doing a hell of a job of not corrupting Ro.

Fuck. Fuck. Fuck.

With my hands still over her eyes, I guided her away from the kitchen down, down, down the hallway and into my office.

Dair was hot on my heels like he couldn't get away from the flexible nymphos fast enough. Which was fair, since he had a smokin' hot wife at home that put both of those women to shame.

"I apologize for this unfortunate incident," I told them both solemnly, and for some reason I had a hard time so much as looking at a blushing Ro as I said it. "I'm not sure what's going on in there, but I'll see to it right away."

I started to leave and noticed Ro was following me.

"What are you doing?" I asked her.

"Don't you need help?" she asked back.

My eyes tried to bug out of my head. "You should have never seen that. I'm very sorry that you did, and I don't want you to see any more, okay? So sit tight. I'm going to ask them very nicely to leave, and then I'll be right back."

She didn't try to follow me when I left that time, and I did exactly as I said I would.

The naked women, predictably, tried to talk me into joining them.

For some reason I wasn't even tempted. Perhaps because I was a bit mortified by what my house had turned into, and how it made me look in front of Dair and my new assistant.

I couldn't even blame this on these random women. I had no idea why or how they were there, but it was a fact that I'd fucked both of them together and separately, and they had every reason to believe I'd enjoy the little show they'd staged for me.

When they realized that I wasn't going to play today, they left with reasonably good grace, even getting dressed first.

I walked them politely to the door, waving goodbye.

"How did you get in here?" I asked their backs.

"Veronica let us in before she left," one of them said. Their backs were to me and I couldn't even tell which one said it.

Good to know. So I didn't need to change the locks. I just needed to quit letting random women come inside in the first place. Noted.

I made a quick call to my housekeeper, and she agreed to come sanitize the kitchen as soon as humanly possible.

No one should have to eat in there after that, particularly Ro.

"They're gone, and the kitchen is going to get a good scrubbing," I told Dair and Ro as I re-entered my office.

"That's reassuring," Dair said dryly.

Ro was behind my desk, sitting in my chair like she owned the place. Dair was lounging in one of my comfy leather chairs. I sprawled out on the room's biggest sofa.

"Sorry Ro, I hope you don't quit on me now," I said with mock solemnity. "I'll do better, I swear."

"I find you exceptionable for too many reasons to list," she said flatly, not looking up, "but I'm not quitting."

"That's not even a word!" I told her.

That clearly tickled her. She looked at me and smirked. "I'm sorry to burst your bubble there, English boy, but perhaps your command of the language isn't what you thought it was."

I shook my head. "Nope. Not a word."

She grinned. "Look it up."

"I don't need to look it up. I know."

"If you're so certain, look it up."

I looked at Dair. "Back me up, man."

He shook his head. "I can't. Look it up."

With a sigh, I did.

"Oh, now I recall," I said as my search quickly proved her right. "It was the way you pronounced it that threw me off."

"You're full of it," she said smugly.

I pointed at Ro. "Look at her, Dair. She already thinks she runs this place. This isn't even her office. That's *my* desk."

Ro, working busily on my computer, looked up at that, arching a brow. "You know you asked me to work on your emails, right? And my office doesn't have a computer yet."

I cursed. All the ways I'd been goofing off today, and I'd completely forgotten to get another computer. "Do you want a desktop or a laptop?" I asked her.

She appeared pensive for a moment before answering.

"Let me look online. I'll find something, and you can tell me if it'll work."

I shrugged. "Whatever you want. In the meantime you can work there, and I'll work on my laptop over here."

Ro went back to work, and I turned my attention to Dair.

He waved a hand between me and Ro. "This seems to be going well. It's already the most productive working relationship I've ever seen you in.

I realized he was right. Hands down, Ro was killing it compared to her predecessors.

"I could do with less naked people having sex on counters," Ro piped in.

Unhelpful, I thought.

"I said I was sorry," I told her sullenly. Saying sorry was hard enough. I hated repeating it.

"Hostile work environment," she muttered, not looking up from the computer.

"I'll make sure it doesn't happen again!" I told her.

Dair was shaking his head at me. "How do you not get sued more?" he asked me, sounding like an exasperated parent.

"Fuck if I know. Ro, are you going to sue me?" I asked her.

"Not today," she replied.

I sent her an affectionate smile that she didn't look up to appreciate.

When I turned back to Dair, he was studying me with an odd look, like I'd done something out of character. I ignored it. "So tell me about your WIP," I said, staring up the ceiling. "Shoot some ideas off me."

We brainstormed for about an hour. I watched Ro while we worked, but she never glanced up once. Little miss professional.

I started sharing some detailed, juicy, shocking gossip with Dair just to get her to react. "They have to go to strip clubs so he can get hard enough to fuck her," I finished telling him a random story about a dysfunctional couple I knew.

Dair was shaking his head as I watched Ro for a proper reaction.

Fourteen seconds passed while she completely ignored me.

Yes, fourteen. I counted.

When she finally looked at me, I could see her internal struggle not to say something.

"Yes?" I asked her with an innocent smile.

She shook her head and went back to work.

"You look at me like you've thought of the worst insult possible and you're just choosing not to say it," I observed.

She smiled blandly. "Self-control is easier for some than others," she noted.

I studied her. "What does that mean? Is it just me, Dair, or is she plotting my murder? Behave yourself, Ro."

"Perish the thought," she returned without missing a beat.

I grinned.

My phone dinged a text at me. It was a video sent from *me*, from my laptop messages to my phone messages.

I squinted my eyes at her. "Did you just send me a video from my own computer?"

"It's very important; you should watch it right away."

I played the video. It was of a gray cat with folded ears hugging a stuffed pink bunny.

Aww. Wasn't that sweet? How strange and random. Why would she send me something sweet right now?

Aha! There it was. As the video kept playing, the cat's hugging turned into a solid maul. I watched, bemused, as it proceeded to tear the pink bunny's head clean off.

"Tell me how you really feel," I told her.

We shared a smile.

Oh, she was just too much fun. I was tickled.

Dair was looking at me strangely, and I ignored it.

Nothing to see here.

When he left, I hit my home gym. I made Ro workout with me, staying close to take notes if I thought of anything.

"You know you can get voice to text software for this, right?" she asked. "You don't need an actual extra human here to jot things down for you."

I waved off that bit of sass. "Don't mess with my process. Your workout gear is the most hideous clothing I've ever seen, by the way.

She was on the bike beside my treadmill, plodding along sedately while I busted my ass.

She glanced down at herself. Her oversized gray sweatshirt and sweatpants made her look like she'd gained fifty pounds instantly. Even her shoes were hideous, dingy white and clunking. "I got a really good deal on them. Five dollars for everything I'm wearing, can you believe it? I'm a sucker for a bargain."

I cringed. I couldn't. I honestly couldn't believe that she thought that atrocious ensemble was worth five dollars. "Oh my God," I burst out. "Well, stop it. I'll give you a clothing allowance if you'll just burn everything you own in a fire."

She laughed.

It was a very nice laugh, rich and bright. Something in my chest grew warm at the sound.

"I don't mind my clothes," she finally answered, "but I do mind being wasteful, so no thank you."

I was onto weights when my workout brainstorming finally bore fruit.

"Sanguine," I told Ro.

"Sanguine?" she repeated back.

"Yeah. Just write down that word. It will trigger the rest of the idea I just had."

"Are you sure?" she asked me. "Want to give me a few more details?"

"Nope. Sanguine."

"You don't want me to write anything except for the word sanguine?"

"Trust me," I said with complete confidence.

It was a few hours later, and I was shooting hoops in my indoor basketball court when I asked Ro to read my brainstorming notes back to me.

"You only had one," she told me.

"Okay. Read it."

"Sanguine."

"Sanguine?" I stopped dribbling the ball. "What the fuck does that even mean?"

Her reply was expressionless and absolutely perfect. "I guess you were pretty sanguine about only having me jot down this one word note."

"Smartass," I muttered, but I couldn't stop smiling.

It was a few hours later, and I was swimming laps while she watched me, her hands on her hips.

"You know," she laid into me when I came up for air, "the first thing you said to me today was that you weren't supposed to be doing anything but writing, and everything we've done today has had *nothing* to do with writing."

"That's not true. I brainstormed with Dair, and again when we worked out."

"That's right. I forgot about sanguine. I'm pretty sure we've reached the part of the day where you've procrastinated enough that I'm supposed to be putting you in check, right? With threats and such?"

I was intrigued. I tilted my head back to look at her straight on. "Yeah, probably. Whatcha got?

"If you don't get five hundred words written in the next half hour, I'm going to make you watch an entire episode of Fuller House."

Oh, she was good.

CHAPTER FIVE

It was remarkable how well Ro settled into her new job in just a few short days. She seemed to learn everything on the first try. I never had to tell her anything twice, even when it looked like she wasn't listening. Hell, half the time I didn't even have to tell her once. She had a much better idea of her job duties than *I* did.

It had only been four days, but I could already feel my life becoming less chaotic, my work life more productive.

Also, and much more importantly, more fun.

I woke up and went straight to the kitchen, where she was just finishing up with the coffee.

She'd prepared me a perfect cappuccino, but I didn't reach for it, instead I took a long drink of her too sweet latte, grimacing as I set it down.

"You want some coffee with that sugar?" I asked her.

"That wasn't yours." She pointed at mine.

"Oh," I grabbed mine, playing dumb.

"You knew that was mine. Why do you love stealing the first drink of my coffee when you know it's too sweet for you?"

I didn't tell her that it was because of the way her nose wrinkled up when I did it. Annoying her was fun for me. I got way too big of a kick out of it.

I grabbed my cup, taking a long swig of it.

"Your cappuccinos are life-changing," I told her appreciatively, "I'm hooked. Totally addicted."

"Addiction isn't funny," she said in her perfect deadpan way.

"Sure it is."

We shared a smile, mine big, hers just a slight upturn at the corner that showed her amusement with me. I really liked that smile.

"How did you know I'd just woken up?" I asked her.

"I didn't. I got lucky. I was just about to take off, and I figured I'd leave you a cappuccino in the hopes that you'd come down before it got cold."

My eyes narrowed on her. "Take off? Why would you take off?"

"It's Sunday."

"Is it?" I asked. I wasn't that great with days of the week. "Okay, what's that got to do with anything?"

"I need Sunday mornings off. I thought we went over this when you hired me."

I just kept looking at her, brows drawn together in confusion. "That thing about church? I thought that was a joke."

"Well, it wasn't. I have church on Sunday mornings, and I don't like to miss it."

Well, hell. "How long does church take?"

"Around an hour."

I noticed for the first time that she was dressed somewhat differently than normal. She was wearing a dress. It was hideous, but it had flowers on it, and it did look vaguely like something a person might wear to church.

"Um, well, good luck with that," I told her. "Hurry back."

She laughed. "Why? Will you miss me?"

I scowled. "No. There's work to be done."

"You know I need days off, right? No one works seven days a week."

"I do," I shot back.

"The amount of procrastinating you do nullifies the fact that you attempt to work every day," she pointed out.

"Bullshit. Even with all of the goofing off, can you honestly tell me I don't work at least ten waking hours every single day?"

She mulled it over. "Yeah, that's true. You do manage to spend a surprising amount of time working considering how much time you spend doing the most random things I've ever seen, and all without ever wearing a shirt." She smirked as she said the last bit.

"Are you ever going to let that go?"

"Probably not. As a matter of fact, if you don't get 1k words done while I'm at church, I'm going to make you wear a shirt for the day."

"What's up with your obsession with me putting on clothes?"

"Why do you hate clothes so much?"

I glanced down at my bare chest. I worked my ass off to get as lean and muscular as I was, and I'd literally never had a woman complain about seeing it before. "Can you honestly tell me you don't enjoy the view?"

"I'm not sure your ego could handle the truth," she retorted, heading for the door.

I couldn't hold in a laugh, but I didn't believe her for one second. She could say whatever she wanted, but I'd caught her stealing looks at my built chest and shredded abs more than once. Perhaps that was why I'd taken to wearing a shirt even less than usual since she'd moved in.

I walked her out to her car, opening the door for her.

She shot me an odd look. "Bye," she said, reaching for the door handle.

"God bless!" I called out, waving. She tried to hide her smile at that, but I saw it.

I watched her car drive away, wondering what the church thing was all about. Maybe I should have gone with her, I mused. For *research*.

My phone dinged a text at me, and I glanced at it.

My eyes widened, rolled, and I put it away. I hoped to God Ro never got a look at some of the things women sent to my phone on a daily basis. It'd be the kitchen sixty-nine thing all over again. Another stain on her innocence. Another crack in her wholesomeness that I didn't want on my conscience.

She was gone for four hours, not that I was counting. And I wasn't waiting for her in the front drive when she finally made it home. It was totally a coincidence that I was out there.

"Welcome home," I said casually as I opened her car door for her.

She eyed me suspiciously. "What are you doing out here?"

I glanced around. "I was plotting a complete overhaul of my shrubbery. I think my curb appeal is off."

"I don't think that term applies when your house is hidden behind huge walls and no one can see it."

"*I* can see it. It's curb appeal for *myself*."

"I can't tell if you have too few hobbies or too many. Or maybe you just need different ones."

"It's not just for me," I said defensively. "I'm having a big party soon," I improvised on the spot. "I want things to be just right. How was church?"

"It was good."

"Why were you gone so long? I thought you said it was only an hour."

One of her brows went up in question, her eyes squinting at me adorably. She was like a curmudgeonly old woman trapped in a twenty something body.

"Were you timing me?"

"Of course not. I just happened to notice. So where'd you go for four hours?"

She gave a long suffering sigh. "I have family that lives in town. I stopped by to see them."

I recalled. "Oh. Your cousin Candy, right?"

She rolled her eyes but nodded. "Yes, her and her sisters and my aunt and uncle. And she has a name, you know."

I did know, but I couldn't for the life of me remember what it was. "Yes, of course she does. How is she?" I asked. Not because I cared, but more because it felt like something I should ask.

Her cousin, Candy per my naming habit, had worked for me a few years back. She'd been a horrible assistant, and we'd had a brief fling after she quit, and oh yeah, she still liked to send me naked pictures out of the blue, but I really had no clue (or cared to know) what she was up to these days.

"She's fine. She didn't want me working for you. In fact, she was adamantly against it."

I couldn't help it. I was offended, and I didn't try to hide it. "Why the hell not? We're getting along great and you're gaining plenty of insight into the book world." I didn't miss the fact that I had no real right to be offended, Candy and I were hardly friends, but that wasn't stopping me.

Ro shrugged. "It's nothing to do with the job. She just doesn't like you."

"Oh, well," I couldn't argue with that. "I guess that's fair. She's no peach, either, you know. But what does that have to do with you? She doesn't have to deal with me anymore."

"She thinks you're going to corrupt me."

She said it blandly, and I threw back my head and laughed. "That is rich. Is she trying to say that I corrupted *her*?"

I got a small smile for that bit of sass. "No. You can say a lot about her, but she's never pretended to be an angel. I just don't think she believes that you and I could work well together, but I'm going to prove her wrong. Whatever you're lacking in moral fiber—"

"Hey!" I said, trying to muster up some righteous indignation.

She mowed right on, "—will not affect the fact that you need an assistant with my focus and efficiency, and I need a creative workplace, not to mention the perk of a mentor with your mastery of the field."

Well I couldn't, and didn't particularly want to, argue with that.

We fell into a nice pattern quickly. I knew I was a challenge to work for and with, but with Ro it was actually quite effortless.

I was chaotic and had a tendency to leave jobs half done. She was organized, neat, and never left any damn thing unfinished. She cleaned up my messes and added periods to my unfinished sentences.

Relinquishing my work load was the only potential snag in our seamless flow, but she cut right through even that, taking things over before I could so much as protest.

"Hey! Ro! Have you seen that Brazil contract I signed a few days ago? I'm supposed to mail it out by today!"

She poked her head into my office. "I sent it out less than five minutes after you signed it. Who do you think you're talking to?" She disappeared.

"You complete me!" I called after her.

"Name a better duo," her sarcastic voice drifted back at me.

I couldn't stop smiling. That was happening a lot with Ro around. I got a kick out of her sense of humor, and she seemed to get mine before I finished the joke. She didn't even mind when I harassed her about every random little thing for no reason whatsoever. I think she actually liked it.

It was mid-afternoon and I was just coming down from a record breaking word count roll. She set a double espresso on my desk like she was reading my mind.

I studied her.

She was wearing a pleated plaid skirt, which, in my experience, was usually sexy and always trashy.

Not so with her. What the hell? This thing was a tent, covering her from waist to calf, stockings pulled up to cover every inch of skin. One was failing at that, having rolled down into a bulky clump at her ankle.

The entire thing was ridiculous. Her wardrobe was a caricature of a wardrobe. It was what someone would put together for a movie about a mousy secretary that had no clue about her own sex appeal.

And somehow, it was driving me slowly insane.

"My God," I started in on her for the sport of it. "Those little knotted blouses... what's wrong with you? Do I need to implement a dress code? You're not eighty-five, and this isn't a fucking funeral."

"Coming up with a dress code would involve you doing something besides procrastinating or doing pull-ups and looking at your own abs," she began dryly, "but hey, maybe something that superficial and shallow will keep you entertained long enough for you to actually *finish* a task today."

I blinked at her little tirade. It took me a solid minute to muster up a response. "I like your sass. You know this, but for future reference, you shouldn't talk to any boss you ever have that isn't me like that."

She didn't miss a beat. "I wouldn't talk to anyone but you, boss or not, like this, trust me."

That appeased me a little. "Once you start handing out sass, it's hard to change your ways."

"Don't I know it," she shot back, turning to leave.

"I'm not shallow. Can we agree on that, at least?" I called to her retreating back.

"You're so deep, I can see Adele rolling in it," she called back, deadpan.

I was dying. This girl entertained the hell out of me.

CHAPTER SIX

Everything was going just great until a problem arose around week two. A very big problem.

I discovered her phone voice.

I didn't realize it was her speaking at first. I heard the voice from a few rooms away, pitched just so, and thought it might be a stranger in Ro's office. I went to investigate. Maybe we had company. Company I could fuck. I was going through a very rare and inexplicable spell of abstinence recently.

But no, it was her. My wholesome Ro. Everything she was saying was perfectly innocent. But the strangest thing happened when she spoke into a phone. Her voice was pitched softer, lower, more airy. She was full-on sex kitten seductress. And those things added to her normal, familiar voice were a recipe for destruction. Namely, mine.

The sound of it was like velvet running along the nape of my neck.

I practically ran away.

In bed (by myself) that night, I tossed and turned all night, the sound of her phone voice keeping me up, my mind racing, my body aching.

Eventually I took a cold shower. It was miserable.

And worse, it didn't help.

It was the first night I jacked off thinking about her.

Not the first time I thought about it.

The first time I couldn't stop myself from doing it.

Three times.

The first time: Her voice, in phone sex mode, telling me to touch her, to feel her, every filthy detail of what she wanted from me, which in my egocentric fantasies, just happened to be exactly what I wanted to do to her.

The second time: She wasn't talking. Her mouth was busy. It was a visceral image, what her soft lips felt like. How they tasted. I could almost feel her obstinate jaw cupped in my hands as I devoured her mouth. Eventually the fantasy had me pushing her head down, lower, lower.

I didn't last long in my own hand after that.

The third time: I dozed a bit and woke up humping my randy cock against my mattress. I'd been dreaming she was moaning underneath me, and I was fucking her good, pounding mindlessly away, stroking, fondling, groping at those curves she was hiding under those hideous clothes. My face was buried in her hair. Her soft, silky hair that smelled completely randomly like a tropical breeze.

I came on my twelve hundred thread count Italian sheets with a frustrated groan.

It didn't help. None of it helped.

I was understandably grumpy the next day.

"You're in a foul mood," she eventually pointed out.

I was pleased she'd noticed.

"Do you know what you sound like when you talk on the phone?" I asked her when she handed me my second espresso.

Her adorable brow furrowed. Her delectable lips pursed. "What?" she asked, clearly perplexed.

"I heard you talking on the phone yesterday. Do you know what you sound like?"

"I try to sound professional. Was I not professional?"

A professional what? I barely kept myself from asking her. And then I realized what I'd done. I'd never used a filter between my thoughts and my mouth for *anyone*. What was making me use one now? Was it her? Her innocence? Her blasted *wholesomeness*?

"You sound like a professional, all right," I told her. "You know how in old-school porn—"

"I've never watched porn," she interrupted.

I stared. "Never?"

"Not once. But go on."

I tried to move past that. "Okay, well picture a porn star answering the door to a handyman with a ten inch cock and saying, 'Can I help you?' in her breathiest, sluttiest voice."

"I'd rather not."

"That's what you sound like."

She was turning pink. "Excuse me?" she squeaked in the most timid voice I'd ever heard come out of her.

"A porn star at her filthiest. That's you on the phone."

She was blushing beet red, shifting where she stood, adjusting her glasses, not meeting my eyes because she was so embarrassed.

I got an unholy thrill out of it.

"Behave yourself," she muttered quietly.

I grinned. "Perish the thought," I said with relish.

"You're out of control," she told me and promptly left.

She came back an hour later and promptly took her revenge.

"I was added to that Facebook group they made about

you. They made me an admin, in fact."

I raised a brow at her. She was standing in my doorway, looking awfully sassy considering she'd run away blushing not long ago. "The Turner the Tyrant group?" I asked. I'd heard about it. It amused me.

She nodded. "The one with all of your ex-girlfriends."

I raised a finger, wagging it at her as I shook my head. "Wrong. None of those women are my ex-girlfriends."

Her nose wrinkled up and she glared. It was way too adorable. "Your ex-hook-ups then."

I shrugged. That was close enough.

"I was wondering something," she added. It sounded like a set up. A trap. I walked into it anyway.

I liked her traps.

"What were you wondering, curious Ro?" I asked her.

"I mean, it's just odd to me, your nickname."

"Why's that? Some of them worked for me at one point or another, and they thought I was a tyrant as a boss."

She snorted. "No way."

"Excuse me?"

"They were being sarcastic when they named you that."

"Excuse me?"

"You're not a tyrant."

My brows shot up. I could tell by her tone that our conversation was about to turn interesting.

Interesting and a touch volatile.

"I'm not?"

"No. They call you that because you're bossy, but even your bossiness is half-assed. You can't be a tyrant because you don't take anything or anyone seriously. You know what you really are?"

"Do tell.

"You're a coward."

I felt my smile freeze on my face. Leave it to Ro to surprise me with a gut punch like that. "How so?" There was a bite to the question.

"You talk a lot of shit, that's a fact. But that's all it is. Talk." And with that, she left, the little termagant.

She was half my size soaking wet, but she'd just wiped the floor with my ego.

CHAPTER SEVEN

Another significant problem arose when I found her tiny body curled up on the couch one lazy Sunday afternoon, sleeping like a baby kitten.

It did something to me, to see her like that. I couldn't put my finger on what it was, but it was dangerous.

It made me feel wild and alive, like even *I* couldn't predict what I'd do next.

It was delightful and a bit terrifying.

She'd asserted that her day off would be on Sunday, and so it was. It drove me a little crazy as she proceeded to leave the house for hours for church and 'family time,' and laze around the house. On top of that she completely ignored all of my orders and pleas throughout her declared day of rest.

And now here she was, sprawled out on the sofa in my rec room, a dog eared Alasdair Masters paperback flung above her head.

I got a kick out of that. I'd be sure to tell him his latest release was putting people to sleep, but even that thought wasn't enough to distract me from Ro's luscious little body writhing around restlessly in sleep like it was looking for something.

Namely, to ride my cock.

I'd caught sight of her earlier heading to church. She'd been wearing one of her church lady floral atrocities and that had been just fine. Now was another matter. She'd changed into her Sunday lazies sometime after she'd come home, and it was just too goddamn much for me. My mind had burned a lot of calories feverishly trying to imagine what was under all of her horrendous polyester, so when I got my first real confirmation that I might be right it was all I could do not to come in my pants.

Her outfit wasn't meant to be sexy. Just the opposite. It was an ugly, oversized gray T-shirt, but it was riding up high enough to show her flat little tummy. Her belly button was an innie. I knew it!

On her bottom half all she was wearing were some men's boxer shorts. Two thoughts assailed me at once. 1. Where the fuck had she gotten those boxers? Were they from some ex-boyfriend? And 2. Why did she hide those legs? They were gorgeous, shapely but trim and topped by a perfectly plump little ass.

Damnit. I just knew it. I could have some real fun taking that hot little body for a ride on my dick.

I bet she'd fuck with a purpose, getting off like it was on the day's agenda.

Her feet were bare. They were so tiny, which made sense, because she was tiny.

What didn't make sense was how much those little bitty feet turned me on.

Even her face resting in sleep was another, softer, sexier version of her. Goddammit, but she was prettier than I'd let myself see before.

She also looked painfully young. She was such a force of nature it was easy to forget she was still in her early twenties.

I didn't like them that young. Under twenty-five and they

weren't quite all the way cooked, usually.

I was *well* into my thirties, and she was just too fucking young.

My dick *emphatically* didn't care about that.

She shifted, turning and hiking a leg up, revealing more smooth skin with each movement.

It was too fucking much. I cleared my throat.

She rolled onto her back, blinking up at me.

"Morning, lazy buns," I told her. My voice came out all funny. Throaty and soft with a thread of something worrisome.

She blinked some more. "Morning?" she yawned.

I smiled down into her confused face. "It's four in the afternoon. You're taking your lazy Sunday to a whole new level." I sat on the coffee table in front of her. My knees were almost brushing her bare legs.

She shrugged, unconcerned, sitting up slow as you please, smoothing her T-shirt down to cover skin as she went. Was she not wearing a bra? Jesus Christ. "Are you wearing a bra?" I asked. Damn lack of a filter again.

Her face screwed up into a cute little glare. "Not that it's any of your damn business, but I am."

I studied her some more. "Not your usual kind. Whatever you're wearing has little to no support."

She glared harder, grabbing her glasses off the coffee table and perching them onto her face. "For your information, it's a bralette, and no, it's not supportive, but it's comfortable. Now can we stop talking about my underwear?"

I nodded at her legs. "Where'd you get those boxer shorts? An ex-boyfriend or something?"

She looked caught off guard. It was a talent of mine. "Noooo," she said slowly. "I bought them. They're comfortable to sleep in."

"You bought men's underwear to sleep in?"

"Like I said, they're comfortable."

"Well, if you ever need to borrow any of my underwear, let me know. It'll save you the trouble of shopping in the men's underwear section."

She was blushing. It didn't take much. Yummy.

"So this is what you're doing with your whole day?" I asked her, trying to sound judgmental. "Reading?"

She looked intrigued. "Don't you *write* books? I'd think you of all people would understand the appeal."

"Point taken. I just don't catch many people reading around this place. There's so much else to do on the property."

"Maybe try dating a girl that knows *how* to read."

My brows rose. "Is that an offer?"

"Not remotely. But anyway, I've done more than read today. I went to church and got some work finished too. Some illustrations."

"Can I see them?" I asked. She hadn't shown me any of her work yet.

"Do you really want to?" She peered at me.

"I want to see absolutely everything you have to show," I said instantly, raising my brows suggestively.

She took it how I meant it. She rolled her eyes. "God, you're such a sex pervert!"

"Isn't that redundant? Did you really need to put the word sex before pervert?" I grinned at her. God, she was adorable.

"No. You can pervert anything."

"Hell yeah, I can. Show me those pictures."

"They're in my room."

I stood up, waving toward her wing of the house. "Lead on."

I followed close behind her as she walked. A little too close. Had her hair always been that shiny? I leaned forward slightly and sniffed. Dammit, it did smell like something tropical, like my fantasies were coming to life. Coconut mixed with passionfruit was suddenly my favorite smell.

Was it out of line to ask her to change her shampoo just for my peace of mind?

Her room was spectacularly orderly, just how I'd have guessed.

I started instantly snooping through her drawers while her back was turned. I hit jackpot on the first try. When she turned around, I held up a pair of lacy black panties, feeling betrayed. They weren't at all wholesome. I wished I'd never looked.

"Does all of your underwear look like that?" I asked, eyes narrowed on her.

"Except for my Care Bear panties," she said without expression.

"Do you know how much this discovery is going to mess with me?" I asked her. "Do you even have a clue?"

She smirked. She liked that bit of sass.

She'd never cop to it, but she fucking liked it.

It didn't help. "If you don't want to know these things, don't dig through people's underwear drawers," she pointed out the obvious.

"I refuse to take responsibility for this! You're the one with lacy black panties you have no business owning, let alone *wearing*," I declared. "It's shattering all of my illusions about you."

She wanted to laugh, I could tell, as she said, "You know you have a ridiculous notion of how the world works, right? You've spent too much time in fiction land. I think some part of you never comes out of it."

"Hey! This is my house! I'm the one defining reality around here!"

"Put the panties back and walk away slowly," she said, laughing.

I tossed them back toward the dresser and threw myself on her bed just to mess it up, rolling around and undoing her covers. As I was still rolling I said, "This room is so neat and tidy. It doesn't even look like anyone lives here."

"I like things organized. Are you surprised? Now quit playing in my room. Do you want to see my drawings or not?"

I sat up, noticing the sketchbook she was holding for the first time. I held out my hand. "Gimme."

I leafed through it.

The subject was an adorable lavender unicorn. The designs were simple and charming. Many were still black and white, but some had been inked with bright, pure colors. There were a lot of sketches, all of the same unicorn in different settings. She was talented, and that talent was a perfect match for her target audience. "It's… nice." It was. I meant it literally, with the true use of the word. It was the essence of clean and good. Endearing and unexpected.

"That's all you have to say?" she asked stiffly.

Fuck, I'd hurt her feelings.

"No, I mean that I like it. It's *really* good. I think you've got something here," I said sincerely.

"Really?"

"Yes. She's cute. What's her name?"

"It's a he. He's supposed to look like a badass. His name is Mayhem the Unicorn."

"I like it. What's Mayhem up to?"

"He stands up to bullies."

I stared at her. "Stop being so adorable. I mean it."

"Never," she returned instantly. "Adorable is how God made me."

"Pride is a sin, you know."

"I know," she said wistfully. "It was always my favorite one."

"Oh! Oh!" I liked this game. "Guess mine!"

She rolled her eyes. "That's too easy. I'm not going to encourage you."

Fair enough. "You seem pretty far along here. Do you have a story in mind? I have a friend that works in a children's division at one of the big publishing houses. Want me to give her a call?"

Her nose scrunched up in that cute, sexy way it did when she was thinking too hard. Finally she shook her head. "Not yet. I'm not quite ready. I need to come up with more story first."

I shrugged. "Suit yourself. Let me know when you change your mind. So what else were you planning for your lazy Sunday? Going to take another nap or want to try something more interesting?"

She eyed me. "What did you have in mind?"

She let me think I talked her into it.

I was a lamb to slaughter.

I should've known. Before we ever broke out the cards, she'd shown me her poker face, and it was the best I'd ever seen.

"You're just lucky," I told her as I shuffled the deck for the third time. "It's a game of luck."

"If it's a game of only luck, why do I always win?"

"You always win? Against everyone?"

She hesitated. "Well, not with Iris, but she cheats."

"I knew it! Can you prove it, though?"

"Well, I mostly meant she cheats because she has a genius IQ. It's really not fair. She's hacking life."

I nodded emphatically. "It's *not* fair, is it? And wrapped up in that bombshell package. No one sees her coming. And she doesn't always use her superpowers for good."

Ro laughed. "She's one of the sweetest people I know. She's wouldn't hurt a fly."

"Did no one ever tell you about that time she ether-tapped Dair?"

She looked shocked. "You're making that up. That damned fiction brain of yours is spinning tales again."

"I'm not lying! She did that. Ask Dair. She's terrifying."

My eyes widened as Ro shrugged as though it was all no big deal. "Even if that is somehow true, he must not have minded too much. They're one of the happiest married couples I've ever seen."

"Yes, because she *plotted* it that way."

Ro shrugged again. "She can help me plot out my life too, if that's the result."

It boggled the mind. Those two conniving women together made me shudder in dread. Oh the schemes they could concoct if they teamed up. "What can I bribe you with to make sure that never happens?" I asked her archly.

She just laughed.

The next morning I found a picture on my desk of a small pink unicorn stomping another, much bigger blue unicorn into a rainbow puddle on the ground at its feet while Mayhem watched with glee.

"A bit violent for children, don't you think?" I shouted.

"Oh that's not going in a book!" she called back from her office. "That one was for you to keep. Don't you like it?"

I loved it.

I had it framed by the end of the day and hung it directly across from my desk where I could look at it constantly.

That bit of mischief was going to be worth money someday.

CHAPTER EIGHT

I practiced violin a few days a week. I'd played since I was a child. While I didn't take it as seriously as I used to, I still kept up with it so I wouldn't lose all mastery of the craft.

It was a natural stress reliever for me and I often played in my office when I got stuck on a part of a novel and just needed to step away.

I noticed pretty quickly that Ro was enamored with it. When I'd play she'd hover nearby, close her eyes, and listen.

As soon as I caught on to that I was practicing more than ever. I liked to watch her like that, unguarded and peaceful. She looked different, her face wiped almost clean of everything but innocent pleasure.

It reminded me rather pointedly that I'd like to see what it looked like filled with the other kind of pleasure.

"How can you play like that when you're... you?" she asked me one day just as I was putting my instrument away.

She'd wandered into my office while I played that time,

even sitting on my couch, leaning her head back and closing her eyes to listen. I'd practiced longer to keep her there.

"Play like what?" I asked, already half-smiling at her potentially ornery answer.

"Like you're a romantic," she said promptly. "When you're a cynic down to your *soul.*"

I laughed. She wasn't wrong but the way she said it was so judgmental that I could tell she was looking to get a rise out of me.

"Don't look too much into it. Just sit back and enjoy."

"You're really good," she pointed out.

She was talking about the violin, of course.

I purposely took it wrong. "You have no idea."

She wrinkled her cute little nose at me. "It's hard to take all of the pieces of you and make sense of you as one person. You're a lot, Turner."

I was pleased. "Why, thank you."

"I'm not sure I was complimenting you," she said but even that was a compliment from her. I'd take an almost compliment from Ro over gushing praise from anyone else, any time.

"What made you want to write books?" she asked, chewed on her lip, then added, "How did you know, or when rather, that you were *really* an author?"

I thought about that. It was a good question, and the way she'd asked it, not idly but seriously made me try to answer honestly.

"I was shaped by fiction," I explained. "It made me who I am. Words, sentences, prose." I paused. "Lies." I paused again, got back on subject. "Reading never felt like anything so much as a necessity to me. I couldn't stop once I realized what was in books. The magic they could contain. I was reading everything I could by the time I was ten, and I had very strong opinions about it—what I liked, what I hated.

"Dair was my favorite author from the moment I discovered him. He is to this day. I thought for a long time I'd write like him, that my books would be some sort of homage to his, that his career would be a prototype for me, down to its root, but once I really started writing that just didn't fit me.

"It just so happened that I liked writing the gory stuff best. Actually, writing sex is my favorite, gory stuff second, tragedy third, if I had to choose. Did that answer your question?"

I liked how she was looking at me then, like I'd pleasantly surprised her.

"It really did. Thank you.

"You're stubbly today," she told me one morning as she handed me my perfect cappuccino.

I rubbed my jaw. "Do you like it?"

"Do *you* like it?"

"Sure, why not? But do *you* like it?"

She shrugged, barely looking at me. "Sure, why not? It suits you. I need you to sign some books today, and a—"

"Touch it," I interrupt.

She paused, looked up, imperious brow raised. "Excuse me?"

"Touch it." When she just stared, I moved closer and brought her hand to my face, rubbing my stubble against her palm.

"Give me two words to describe the way it makes me look," I told her. "This is part of your mentorship. More in-depth descriptions.

She didn't miss a beat, glaring at me. She tried to pull her hand away, but I held it there. "Dastardly. Rakish. You look like you're about to captain a pirate ship or deflower a young maiden just for the hell of it. How's that?"

I was grinning. "It was good. I like the way your mind

works, Ro. Less and less wholesome by the hour."

I let her go, and she was striding away as she said, "Maybe you *are* corrupting me."

Unaccountably, that made me hard.

"Everybody loves a scoundrel," I called after her.

"Says a scoundrel," she called back.

That afternoon she returned with several copies of my book *Red Door* for me to sign for some promotions.

It was after five, and I was sipping at a small glass of straight Scotch, the really good shit, as I grabbed a pen and started signing.

"How do you write books like that and sleep at night?" she asked, more curious than judgmental. "I had nightmares for weeks the first time I read this one."

"Oh, that's easy," I said as I signed. "Most of my books have a supernatural element, and I'm a complete skeptic. It's hard to be scared when you don't believe in anything."

"You're crazy, you know that, right?"

"Of course I do. Do you know why writers are crazy like this?

"Why?"

"Because there's magic in chaos. We need to find you yours."

"Maybe or maybe you'd reach your deadlines on time if you were a bit *less* chaotic."

"That's it," I said dramatically, throwing down the pen. "I'm going to quit writing, give away all of my money, and start delivering pizzas. Are you happy?"

"It could work. I mean, you don't need much money for clothes, being that you're only half dressed most of the time, but how would you keep yourself in Scotch?"

I was so turned on by that, I almost chased her out of my office.

Luckily she didn't seem to notice.

I didn't recover.

The rest of the day passed in distracting snapshots of Ro: An oblivious Ro bending over her desk to grab a contract for me to sign. Ro with her head down, focused on work, her thick eyelashes falling into dramatic shadows on her cheeks. Ro reaching her arms up to smooth loose strands of baby soft, dark hair back into her chignon, the motion outlining her spectacular tits under her ungodly ugly sweater.

Ro, Ro, Ro. Obsessing me. Amusing me. Driving me wild. Making me enjoy each day thoroughly.

I couldn't seem to stay in my wing of the house one night. I found myself in the kitchen, a shared space, eating her yogurt of all things, at three in the morning.

"That's my yogurt," she said, her tone sour.

I turned to watch her as she moved toward the counter. She was wearing an oversized shirt that hid her curves, but it didn't keep me from obsessing over what might be underneath.

My eyes were locked tight on her as she grabbed an apple, sat down, and started eating it.

"It's three a.m.," I pointed out. "What are you doing still up?" As far as I knew, she normally went to bed much earlier than this.

She chewed her bite of apple and swallowed before answering, her tone sardonic, "I wasn't aware there was a curfew."

"I can't sleep, it looks like you can't either, and I'm taking a breather from work. How about we watch a movie?"

She shrugged. "Why not? Can I pick?"

I was fascinated with what she'd choose so I answered easily, "Be my guest."

She picked Jojo Rabbit.

I'd seen it, it was a good movie, and I watched her face as

much as the screen.

We shared a sofa but sat on opposite sides of it.

For her safety, though she didn't know that, thank God.

When we got to the part with Jojo's mother's shoes, she was crying like a baby, her big Bambi eyes leaking like a faucet.

It was just about too much for me. I was close to my limit.

I wanted to hug her, to pull her into my arms to comfort her, but I was certain that if I did I'd try to fuck her on the spot.

I was, somehow, becoming even more perverse than usual.

When the movie was over, I was just staring at her as she wiped her cute little cheeks.

"Okay, let's hear it," I said, trying to distract her without touching her, trying to distract myself. "Tell me some more about your Mayhem books. What is it that you have in mind? The drawings are stellar, now you just need the story. Need some help plotting it out?"

"Not just yet. I'm still bouncing the particulars around, but the gist of it is, I want to make something that makes lonely kids feel less alone."

Well fuck me if that wasn't endearing and adorable as hell.

I needed to get away from her. Fast.

I practically ran away.

The next morning I asked her, "Was I high last night?" It was an honest question.

She pushed her cute glasses up her sexy little nose, and her eyes narrowed at me. "You tell me."

"No," I decided out loud. "So we really did watch Jojo Rabbit in the middle of the night and you really did cry like a baby."

I didn't get the reaction I was trying for. I'd wanted a blush, some embarrassment, maybe. Instead she raised a brow and said, "Your point?"

I was getting close to meeting a big deadline when I told her to set up an appointment with my masseuse to celebrate.

"She comes here?" she asked as she typed in the information I'd given her.

"Yes."

"I'll set it up ASAP."

I studied her. "You know what? Tell them to send someone for you too."

"Excuse me?" she asked, looking genuinely confused.

"Have them send a masseuse for you, too. You could use a little loosening up."

She blushed. "I'm fine."

She was so stubborn that I set up the whole thing myself, calling the parlor and booking my usual girl and whoever they recommended as their second best for Ro.

I didn't think it through properly, and I regretted that the second I saw who they sent.

My usual girl was a petite blond named Mary. She was smoking hot but faultlessly professional.

Standing next to her when I opened the door was a big, muscular dude that my mind took way too long to gather was going to be massaging Ro.

It was the least relaxed massage I ever had.

Ro was one room over, getting the same treatment I was with some strange dude touching her body.

At one point I heard her moan through the wall, and I came up off the table ready to fight.

Mary blinked at me, her oiled hands held palm up. "Something the matter?" she asked, looking genuinely confused.

I shook my head like I could shake the pictures out of my head. Pictures of a sweet, innocent, naked Ro with that big burly guy's hands all over her.

I lay back down on the table and forcibly restrained myself until the very end.

When it was done, they left and I shrugged on my white spa robe and moved quietly to the door.

I peeked into the room that Ro's massage had been set up in.

She was still lying face down on the table. She'd fallen asleep. At least one of us had had a relaxing experience.

There was a cloth covering only her ass, her back and legs bare.

I approached her. I couldn't help myself. Her back was lovely and naked and still covered in oil.

I touched her shoulder to shake her awake. In spite of myself, it became a caress.

She mumbled something and moaned.

My brain short-circuited for one intense moment. I was enthralled.

I stroked her silky hair, leaning closer to her.

"Wake up, sleepy head," I breathed into her ear. "The massage is over."

"Don't wanna," she mumbled, clearly still half asleep.

I smelled her hair in one long inhale and resolutely shook her awake.

"Go away so I can sit up and get dressed!" she finally snapped at me.

"You sure you don't need a hand with that?" I asked.

"Get out!"

"You're no fun," I told her as I left.

"Slytherin," she muttered not quite under her breath.

"Hufflepuff," I shot back.

"I'm obviously a Ravenclaw," she retorted.

Of course she fucking was.

I began to hate Sundays. She was gone too much. For too long and leaving me no notion of when to expect her back more often than not.

When she was gone, every time I'd think of something amusing there was no one to share it with.

I'd think, *Ro would get the humor of this.*

It was just no fun without her. Nothing was.

It was one of the reasons I found myself planning a pool party on a Sunday right after my most recent deadline.

Well, I didn't plan it. I had Ro to do that.

I did give her a guest list and attempt to brainstorm it a bit with her.

"It's a lot more women than men," she noted as she looked at the list.

"Well, yes," I said, frowning.

"I didn't think you liked parties. You haven't had anyone but Dair come over almost since I started here.

I frowned harder. She had a point, and I didn't like that. "I consider myself to be a social recluse. I like people, but I also like to stay in my house a lot. I actually have these parties fairly often, I've just been on deadline."

She took that without comment, though I was curious to see what she thought, as usual.

"What about food?" she eventually asked. "Anything in particular you want to cater?"

"Whatever sounds good."

"Does it have a theme? Anything special you want to do or to celebrate?"

"Let's have a party entrance fee: Tops."

She just rolled her eyes and took charge of the whole thing.

CHAPTER NINE

Problem number I'd lost count was that fucking pool party.

A pool party that was supposed to be fun and completely free of stress. It was an afternoon to decompress after being locked away for months in my writing cave.

It wasn't even one problem. It was a whole new slew of them. All under the category of problematic Ro.

She organized the whole thing without a hitch, I'd give her that. She went above and beyond. She usually did. That wasn't the issue. The real issue was her. Her behavior and her attire.

Also an issue: It'd been way too long since I'd gotten the fuck laid.

It wasn't that big of a deal, I told myself. I was a writer. My schedule was a bi-polar nightmare. Sometimes I got caught up in a book and didn't get laid for months . . . Well, probably more like month as in the singular.

But it'd happened before. Certainly this latest bout of abstinence wasn't *unheard* of.

Certainly it wasn't because of *her*. That would be a

significant problem. Unthinkable, really. So unthinkable that the second the thought hit the edge of my brain, I shut the door firmly in its face.

Not today, Satan.

The party didn't start until two, but the house was flooded with activity by noon. A few were early partygoers, but mostly it was various service staff: caterers, waiters, bartenders, and the like. Ro handled most of it without a word to me, but occasionally she had to seek me out to ask my personal preference on something or other.

One such time I was in my bedroom and had just changed into swim trunks.

She barely knocked on my door before charging inside, the bold little minx. Luckily for her, I'd covered all the essentials first. No use putting a picture in her head.

I slipped my thumbs into my shorts, resting them there, but more importantly, pushing the waistband down to expose more skin, watching her face the entire time.

Her eyes followed my hands, and I watched with smug satisfaction as she flushed, looked away, then dragged her eyes back like she couldn't keep them away.

"Hey, eyes up here, cupcake," I told her mock sternly.

Her big Bambi eyes glared at me.

She got her revenge for that soon enough.

"Come here," she said to me sometime later as I walked into the kitchen. Her hands were behind her back.

I was instantly wary. She was up to something.

"You're fucking with me," I pointed out.

She pointed at herself, one hand still held behind her back, her face a mask of innocence and sarcasm that only she could pull off. "Me? Nooo."

"I don't trust you," I said.

"This won't hurt, I promise." Her voice was mostly neutral, but there was another thread to it, one I was only beginning to recognize now, as I learned to read her better.

"I don't believe you," I told her, glaring. "That's your bad girl voice."

"All the good girls go to hell anyway. At least, that's what Billie Eilish says."

"Who the hell is Billie Eilish? Is she coming to the party? She doesn't sound like someone you should hang out with."

She just laughed and laughed. She was mocking me.

And I liked it. A little too much.

Way too much.

"You really don't know who that is?"

I just shook my head, smiling at her, bemused.

"She's a singer. Have you been living under a rock?"

"More or less."

"Well, she's really good. You should listen to her while you write."

"Okay," I told her. "I'll look her up." I meant it. Ro had impeccable taste. She didn't recommend anything unless she genuinely thought I'd like it. "Now tell me what you have behind your back there."

"I'll show you. Just close your eyes first."

I finally gave in out of sheer curiosity for what she'd do next.

I felt her move close to me and stopped breathing as she brushed against me to drape something light over my neck. She grabbed one of my hands, moving it, and I felt the tips of my fingers go a bit numb with the effort not to grab anything forbidden and conveniently within reach.

It was done in a flash, which was a mercy.

"Okay, look."

I looked down at myself, at what she'd placed on me. It was a sash, and it took me a moment to realize reading it upside down that it said Birthday Bitch.

I stared at her, genuinely amused.

Absolutely tickled. "What the fuck, Ro?"

She beamed at me, and I almost jumped her on the spot. "I saw in your calendar that your birthday's in a few days so I planned accordingly. Surprise."

I started laughing, and I couldn't help it, I grabbed her and pulled her soft body into a hot, affectionate hug.

Luckily she didn't take immediate exception, her little arms wrapping around my middle as she laughed along with me.

"Birthday bitch, though? Really?"

"I saw it at Party City, and I just couldn't resist."

"So long as you know you're wearing this on your birthday, too."

I nuzzled the top of her head and she pulled away, shooting me a disgruntled look.

"What? I'm an affectionate guy."

"Affectionate like a horny puppy."

"A horny puppy? Really? That the best you can come up with?"

Her soft, pouty mouth was twisted thoughtfully. "Ridiculous, perverted, narcissist," she tried.

"Hey!" That one hit close enough to home to actually sting a bit. "I'm not ridiculous."

She was walking away. "I'm too busy for this, you gorgeous asshole," she muttered under her breath.

"That one was practically a compliment!"

She ignored that.

"Now, listen," I told her, following her persistently, going into my boss lecturing tone, "you've organized everything. The catering company and wait staff can take it from here. Why don't you just relax and have fun? It's a party. Enjoy yourself for once. Hell, put on a swimsuit." She was still wearing some of her hideous work attire, as usual.

She stopped walking, turned and smiled at me. "I'm glad

you said that. That is just what I was planning to do. It *is* my day off."

"You don't have days off."

"Yes, I do."

"Whatever," I shot back. It was a longstanding debate and neither of us had ever conceded more than a whatever in defeat. And by that I meant me. There'd been no whatever from her. She remained consistently stubborn on the point. On all points, really. The adorable little shrew.

It was a few hours later when I caught sight of Ro. The party was in full swing when I noticed her and something strange happened in my brain.

Something vital disconnected.

Or maybe it snapped.

I started behaving strangely, in a way that I couldn't account for.

She was standing across the pool, flanked by my friends Lourdes, Frankie, and Iris, and she was laughing at whatever Iris had just said.

I didn't recognize her at first. I'd never seen her wearing so little clothing. The itty bitty black bikini that barely covered her essentials was wholly uncharacteristic for her.

Which was why I immediately blamed the three wicked women she currently found so fucking funny.

Troublemaking females, I thought with a huff.

Her figure wasn't boxy. On the country, she had delicate, shapely shoulders, world class, *natural* tits, and a tiny waist that shaped into some very grabbable hips.

She had a knock 'em out and kill 'em, figure, and she'd been hiding it like her life depended on it this entire fucking time.

I'd strongly suspected, but having it confirmed was not helpful at all.

I watched the women huddled together, gimlet-eyed. Iris, Devereux, Frankie and Lourdes and several other party girls I vaguely recognized.

I was lounging in the shade under a cabana, Dair next to me, Heath on the other side of him.

I sent Dair a look, and he nodded silently. He saw what was happening.

I sent Heath the same look, but he just glared at me and kept sipping his beer. Even with the soothing influence of his lovely wife Lourdes and their cute little son, he was still the scariest motherfucker I'd ever met.

"Seriously?" I asked the men. "No one else is worried about this? Look at them. They're planning world domination over there. We should be frightened."

Even Heath laughed at that one.

"Iris likely is," Heath said, laugh dying, serious again. She was his sister, so he knew better than anyone how diabolical she was. "She could pull it off, too."

"See? My God, she is scary. Do you understand how scary she is, Dair?"

He was smiling fondly at his much younger wife. She saw him, winked, and shook her barely covered, perky ass in his direction.

He was so far gone, I didn't know why I bothered.

It was like he'd totally forgotten her scorched earth campaign to take his soul. She'd pursued him like a detective on a hot case and upended his whole life in the process.

My eyes narrowed when I saw what they were doing then. "Do you see this?" I asked loudly.

"See what?" Dair asked good-naturedly.

"What they're doing!"

"Shots? What's the big deal?"

"Tequila shots!"

I watched them all down the tequila feeling somehow

helpless. I was certain that it was not a good idea for inexperienced Ro to be doing stuff like this, but I had no clue, and no right, to stop her.

Lourdes broke from the other women and moved toward us with a smile. Well, not us. Toward Heath, her very scary husband.

She was a stunning woman, sex on a stick from the top of her black wavy hair, her bedroom eyes, down her tanned, toned body to her pastel pink toenails.

I remembered all of this mostly from memory. I tried not to look at her directly these days. As I've said, her husband was a scary motherfucker.

Not that she'd given me a shot even *before* she'd met the man, but I'd at least been able to *look*.

Lourdes joined Heath on his lounger. He pulled her between his legs, her back to his front.

They made a striking couple, him huge, tall, muscular and blond with a golden tan. Her a few shades darker, graceful, lithe, long limbed and just lovely all over. She was some fifteen years older than him, but no one would have guessed it. The woman took care of herself and had some stellar genes to boot.

She murmured something to her husband in her sexy as sin accent. Heath started kissing her neck, his big hands on her toned stomach.

I tried not to notice. I also didn't bother to tease them about it. He was a little too scary even for that.

Dair had no qualms. "Get a room, Heath," he said cheerfully.

Heath growled at him. *Growled*. Like he was a pit bull and Dair had just gotten between him and his food dish.

Lourdes laughed, a low, rich, sexy sound.

I couldn't help it. "You're one to talk," I told Dair. His PDA with his wife was quite notorious. They'd desecrated several rooms in this very house.

I was distracted from my thoughts when a movement caught my eye. The music was loud, Ro had hired a decent DJ for the occasion. Lots of people were dancing, but only one person stood out to me.

Ro was wiggling in her tiny bikini, shaking her ass like it was a Polaroid with Iris and the girls.

"No." I shook my head. "No."

I kept watching. She was practically unrecognizable. Her luscious dark, silky hair was down and hugging her curves, her glasses replaced with heart-shaped shades. She was barefoot, hands up in the air while she pulled off some pretty sultry moves.

"Don't look at her," I growled grumpily at no one in particular.

It was possible, likely even, that I was talking to myself.

Dair's head whipped around in surprise. He studied me. "Who could you be talking about?" he asked.

I scowled. "Ro. In that teeny tiny bikini.

"I wasn't looking at her," he pointed out. "I was looking at Iris. But why don't you want me looking at Ro?"

"She's *wholesome*," I said the word with the gravity it deserved. "She should not be acting like this."

"Acting like what?"

I waved my hand around at her. "She's drinking tequila! Shaking her ass like she knows what she's doing! I didn't even know she drank alcohol! How has she stayed so innocent this long looking like *that*, moving like *that* and drinking *tequila*?"

Dair was laughing. So was Heath. So was Lourdes.

"What is *wrong* with everyone?" I asked the world. "Is it *me*? Have I lost *my* mind?"

"Yes," said Heath succinctly.

"Absolutely," Dair agreed.

Lourdes just kept laughing.

Ro did a little move just then with her hips that filled my veins with a heady, electrifying rush.

Why couldn't I fuck her again?

Just then I simply could not remember.

I snapped.

CHAPTER TEN

I was moving before I'd even realized it was happening. I was on her in a few long strides.

"A moment, if you please," I said tersely, grabbing her arm and tugging her determinedly around the pool and back into the house.

I took her straight to my office, shutting the door behind me before I said another word. It was an act of utter restraint, when restraint was the last fucking thing I was known for.

She was in front of me, and I pushed her straight to my desk. She was stiff and quiet.

Very, very quiet.

I took a step back, my eyes raking her body, top to bottom.

With a curse, I turned her around, grabbing her hips to perch her outrageously cute, shapely little bottom on the edge of my desk.

I set her precious little heart-shaped shades up on her head so I could see her eyes.

I loomed over her, glaring down.

"You're not just cute." My voice was an accusation. "You're *sexy*."

My breathing was labored, like I'd just been running miles instead of walking a short distance through the house.

"What are you wearing?" I asked her pointedly.

"A swimsuit," she said in that deadpan way of hers. "It's a pool party. You told me to participate."

"You do realize it doesn't fit you, though, right? There's clearly not enough material to cover your—" I couldn't even say the word, just waved in the direction of her generous chest. "Where did you get it? It's indecent! I thought you were modest!"

She huffed. "It fits fine, and Iris let me borrow it. I didn't have any two-piece suits, and the girls convinced me that I'd stand out if I wasn't wearing a bikini."

"Well you shouldn't listen to them. If I don't get to corrupt you, they shouldn't get the privilege either! It's not fair."

She was smirking at me. I wanted to bite her in some very creative places. "You're twisted. Unhinged. Out of control."

I ignored all that because she was right, and there was nothing I could say about it. "And what was so fucking funny out there? You and I joke all the time, but you never laugh like that for *me*."

"Sometimes I do. And girlfriends are different. Besides, your humor isn't the laugh out loud kind. You're a *different* kind of funny."

She was trying to appease me.

I wanted to shake her. And fuck her silly.

My eyes were on her chest. Her not at all hidden, glorious chest. I was studying it with abject disapproval.

She was a tiny little thing, from her itty bitty hands to her petite feet, which made her abundant, over-spilling breasts and perfectly shaped, plump ass seem all the more disproportionate.

"Did you even bother to put on sunblock? Look at your skin. You're so fair, you'd burn in ten minutes flat, sunblock or no."

"Of course I put on sunblock. I know my burning potential better than anyone."

I looked at her lips, licking mine. Hers were shiny pink, glossy in a way they'd never been before. "Are you wearing makeup?" I asked her, tone disgruntled.

"Just lip gloss. Iris gave it to me. It barely has any color, but it was SPF 15, so I figured why not?"

Without asking permission, I grabbed a tissue and began to rub it off.

Instead of taking exception as I'd expected, as she damn well should have, she started giggling. She was drunk, or at least well on her way to getting there.

It did terrible things to me, head to toe. It was all I could do not to drag her by her silky, fragrant hair to the nearest bed.

Something was happening to me, and it was crazier than any damn thing I'd ever experienced.

Seeing her like this had set something off inside of me, set something fundamental askew, and I didn't know how to put it right again, didn't even know how to make myself want to.

I couldn't put my finger on how it had even happened, this budding—blooming—overripe obsession. It had just creeped up on me, grown through all its stages while I'd been struggling to convince myself that it had never been planted at all.

I leaned back, eyeing up her barely covered body as she convulsed with laughter. Her magnificent tits were bouncing up and down so perfectly, they were dribbling like perky basketballs and her joke of a bikini top was hardly containing them.

It took everything I had not to outright palm them.

I felt a bit dizzy with the effort.

"Come with me," I told her sternly. "We'll find something more appropriate for you to wear."

I took her gently but firmly by the hand, and she came along without protest. I lectured her all the way to her wing of the house, straight up to her room. She was being surprisingly silent for my deranged tirade. It wasn't like her. Usually she couldn't keep her mouth closed when I was acting halfway normal, and now that I'd lost my mind… she was shockingly amenable.

But every time I glanced back her eyes met mine, and they were telling me something, studying me curiously, like she'd just learned the answer to a very significant question.

I set her firmly on her bed, went to her closet, and started rifling through it without permission, searching until I found a long, baggy muumuu that I'd previously seen her wear when I made her go out to the pool with me. I tossed it at her.

She caught it, but made no move to put it on.

I wasn't deterred. I threw it over her head, dragging her arms through the generous holes.

Just like that she was covered up. I wanted to sit down, I was so relieved.

"No one else out there is dressed like this," she pointed out, one of her perfect, sassy eyebrows raised.

"Well, they're all sinners," I said, tone deadly earnest. "Hedonists. You aren't like the rest of us. You're wholesome." That word tasted different suddenly. More dangerous. A barbed-wire fence in my path, and me with wire-cutters already in hand. "And that's not going to change on my watch. Your meddlesome friends need to stop tampering with your clothes. They would probably think it was funny if that itty bitty top had gone askew and let a nipple slip out. They'd think it was no big deal."

"It's not that big of a deal. They're just nipples, and it's mostly women out there, as I'm sure *you* noticed."

I sat down hard on her bed the moment the word nipples left her mouth, swallowing hard as I looked up at her. "Put on a hat, too. The sun is brutal out there for skin like yours. I'm warning you now, I'll be pissed if you burn yourself. You won't hear the end of it. I'll turn into a total nag, worse even than you."

"I can't be a nag," she told me.

I squinted at her. "Why's that?"

"You *ride* a nag." She started laughing as soon as she said it.

My mind went to filth for a few tense moments. "You're too much," I told her, wanting to kiss her, wanting to ride her *raw*. "Seriously though, *please* wear a hat. I worry about your skin."

Her lips pursed, and she gazed at me out of her clear, glasses free, Bambi eyes, no barrier between us for a moment. I didn't know if it was my imagination, but if I'd had to describe it I'd have said she was affectionately exasperated.

But for some reason she did listen to me. She grabbed a big straw hat out of her closet and moved toward the door.

"Wait," I said to her.

She stopped, but didn't turn around.

"May I use your restroom?"

She turned her head enough to let me see the confused furrow of her brow. "It's *your* house. Knock yourself out. "

If beating off angrily over her pretty little vanity sink could be considered knocking myself out, I sure as hell did.

I palmed my stiff cock through my shorts. It was thick and throbbing with need. I pulled it out, looking around for anything, any sign of Ro in the bathroom.

I used her lotion, even grabbed a bottle of her shampoo, smelling it while I gripped my rigid shaft, giving it a few half-hearted tugs before fully committing to the sad, angst fueled jerk off session. It didn't take much before I was jacking off with gusto, eyes closed, taking deep breaths, hand pumping my dick in a hard and steady rhythm. I had a crystal clear picture of her spectacular body in my head as I spurted my viscous frustration into the air.

I found her in the kitchen eating some sort of premade ice cream cup I hadn't seen before. She was slowly taking my kitchen over with *her* preferred foods, and I always had to try them when I saw a new one.

"What flavor is that? Can I try it?"

"No," she said, no hesitation.

"I want to try it," I cajoled.

She shook her head, looking like a smug little brat. "It's just vanilla," she told me.

"*Just* vanilla?" I exclaimed. "That's such a disservice to the flavor of vanilla. Everyone loves vanilla flavored anything."

"I'm basically the human equivalent of vanilla," she said wryly. "No one is clamoring for a Ro flavored anything."

I couldn't help it. She'd walked right into this one. "I beg to differ. *No one* is a strong term."

She studied me with narrowed eyes for a moment, rolled them, and went outside without another word.

Huh. No comeback Ro was a new experience.

I ran into Iris on my way to the pool. She was coming inside, and I was right at the back door. I'd just gotten a look at Ro and what she'd done as soon as she rejoined her evil friends. She was practically naked again.

"She was supposed to keep her hat and cover up on," I said almost absently but with no little frustration.

"You seem to have taken an unholy interest in your new assistant," Iris said like it was the most delightful thing she'd ever seen.

My eyes widened in horror as I studied my closest friend's

dime of a wife. She was petite, blond, and drop dead gorgeous. The definition of a bombshell. She also happened to be a literal genius. And an actual evil mastermind. "You! You're planning something, aren't you? Plotting again." A terrifying thought struck me. "You're doing it to *me*, aren't you? Whatever you did to Dair."

"What did I do to Dair?"

"Brainwashed him into believing in love."

She moved toward me suddenly, eyes narrowing, a sharp finger jabbing into my chest. "Brainwashing is what turned you *off* of love. Maybe you're just getting a much needed *reprogramming*."

I warded her off with my hands, giving her a wide berth as I maneuvered around her and stepped outside. "Stop it! Begone, thot! My head is not your playground!"

I left her laughing behind me as I made my way to Ro. If my stubborn assistant wouldn't behave, I'd just have to stick closer to her.

She was in the water with several other women, and I moved in right beside her like she'd been saving me a spot.

She hadn't, I was just more willing to crowd her than anyone else. Personal space was taking a vacation until she was dressed and sober again.

She had a plastic cup in her hands and when she was listening to some crazy story Frankie was telling, I took it from her and set it down on the side of the pool.

Without comment, she found it and picked it up again, taking a long drink.

The next time she was distracted, I took it again and downed it in one gulp. I grimaced. It was a too sweet but still boozy as hell berry margarita. The perfect recipe for the world's worst hangover.

I wasn't worried about a hangover for myself. I was built big enough to take a lot of just about anything without consequences. But her tiny body combined with rarely drinking then drinking too much concerned me greatly.

Ro wrenched the cup from me and stared into it like she could will her drink to come back with thoughts alone.

Ro was drunk. It was stressing me out.

I waved down one of the waiters. She leaned down and I said, pitched too low for Ro to hear, "This one doesn't need any more strong drinks, okay? She's had enough."

I thought that was settled but shit-stirring Frankie smiled at me as she handed Ro her own, still full cup.

I glared. "I always knew you were a bit evil," I told her.

She shrugged, looking very amused. "No one ever implied that I wasn't."

"Where's your girl?" I asked her.

"She'll be here any minute. Why, you going to get her drunk as revenge?"

I glared harder. "Maybe I should."

"Give it your best shot. She could drink everyone here under the table, I guarantee it."

Frankie shouted for another round of shots.

I shouted for another round of waters.

I took Ro's shot for her and made her finish her cup of water down to the last drop.

I had my arm around her to keep her steady as she drank but pulled away the second I could.

Frankie slapped her own arm like she was killing a bug and looked at me pointedly. "I think you've got a bite there, Turner."

My brows drew together. "Mosquitos? I haven't noticed any."

"I didn't say it was a mosquito. I think you've been bitten by the *love bug.*"

Everyone in earshot laughed like that was hilarious. I pointed at her. "You stop that." For some reason they all just laughed harder.

Sure enough, Frankie's girlfriend Estella showed up a few minutes later and took a few shots straight off without missing a beat.

Frankie tried to turn it into a drinking contest, but I nipped that in the bud right away. I was not getting drunk when Ro was like this. I needed to be sober enough to take care of her if she couldn't take care of herself at the end of the night.

Just about everyone ended up in the pool as the party raged on, and when I was distracted, Ro even managed to get a few more drinks in.

I was worried about her. She was laughing a lot but not saying much, which was the opposite of her real personality.

Drunk Ro made me miss sober Ro.

It was dark out by the time my friend Carter made it to the party.

Carter was another author, a successful and prolific one, but much like me and Dair, no one would have guessed it by looking at him.

He was built huge, he'd played football in college and even coached high school football to this day, with messy brown hair and warm eyes and a smile that made him look as harmless as a hunky teddy bear.

He'd shown up already in his swimsuit and shirtless, and he was ripped, head to toe, his abs shredded beyond all reason.

"Wow, who's that?" Ro whispered. "Oops, did I say that out loud?"

Not accustomed to being overlooked, even in favor of my hottest friends, I was highly insulted. "Wow?" I asked her in my sternest voice. "He's not more wow than *me*, I hope you know."

"Yeah, but you're crazy. He looks sweet."

"Not your type at all. Look away." I covered her eyes

when she just kept staring. "And for your information, he's as much of a slut as I am, he's just sweeter about it in the morning."

Several people were laughing at our quiet but vehement interaction.

Iris, in the pool now and standing in the circle of Dair's big arms, was laughing the loudest.

"That's Carter," Iris said, answering Ro. Ro pushed my hands away from her eyes and looked at the other woman. "He's an author and a *high school teacher.*" She giggled adorably. "Can you imagine? His female students must be losing their minds…"

Iris and her penchant for older men was well-known and even documented now in the form of a marriage license.

I rolled my eyes. "First of all, you're screwed up, but I think you know that. And second, so is he. He doesn't even need the money. He's rich. He teaches because he *likes* it."

I caught the look on Ro's face and saw that she found that charming.

Barf. "Stop that," I told her quietly. "Bad girl. If you don't stop looking at him, I'm going to send you to bed with no supper."

She looked at me like *I* was the one out of line.

Louder even than the background music was Iris laughing at me. I tried to ignore that she-devil completely.

Carter was still making his way to us, slowly, because of course every woman between us and the door stopped him for a long, tight hug.

"Poker's at your house next month," I told him when he was close enough that I didn't have to raise my voice.

I'd maneuvered myself so I was standing directly in front of Ro.

He looked around, holding out his arms to indicate the party at large. "This does not count as you hosting poker, I hope you know."

Ro tried to peek around me, but I shifted with her, effortlessly blocking her view. I could and would do this all night.

"I saw people playing poker earlier," I said. "It's not my fault you're late."

He shrugged and smiled in that good-natured way of his. "Okay, my place for poker night next time, fine."

Another round of shots came by, passed around the pool in little plastic cups on a big tray, courtesy of evil Frankie.

I dumped Ro's in the pool while she watched. She grabbed at another. I dumped that too.

Carter waved the tray away without taking one. "I work in the morning. No shots."

He was just too good. I couldn't imagine him getting so much as a parking ticket. When we talked women, he even managed to make sleeping around seem harmless. He was friends with every one of his exes. They all fucking loved him. It was unnatural.

"When you break bad it's going to be something interesting, I bet," I mused out loud.

He looked amused and unfazed by that.

"He does work at a high school," Iris threw out.

"Hey now, what's that supposed to mean?" he asked, looking much less amused.

He was flushing to the point I actually thought she could be onto something, sinister savant that she was.

"Some of the seniors have got to be eighteen," Iris added.

I shivered. She scared me just as much when her mischief was aimed at someone else.

"That is *not* funny." Carter's voice brooked no argument.

He was so serious that even dauntless Iris dropped the subject.

CHAPTER ELEVEN

In an unprecedented and shocking move, I kicked everyone out of my house before one a.m.

Ro was still drunk and still half naked, and I simply couldn't take it anymore.

It was just us and a busy cleanup crew as I carried/led/dragged her back inside the house. I stopped and she kept moving enough to glue herself to my chest. Her head was tilted back, and she was looking up at me with a glazed bedroom stare.

I tilted my head down, closed my eyes and inhaled her sweet, boozy breath, shuddering and not with distaste.

I took a significant step back, and she stood on her own without me having to touch her, thank God.

"Have you ever been this drunk before?" I asked her pointedly.

"Neverbeendrunkafore," she slurred.

"See what happens when you overindulge?" I asked her, trying my best to sound like a chiding parent. "I'm left to take care of you at the end of the night. I don't even trust you to put yourself to bed in this state."

"Oh, staaahhhp. Jus' lemme be. I know where m'bed is. Leave me 'lone."

Drunk Ro was too much for me.

I knew it, but I still couldn't keep away.

My concern overrode my natural inclination to run away from, instead of into, an obvious trap.

I was trying to keep my hands to myself as much as humanly possible, but she was swaying on her feet. I sighed. "Hold onto me, or I'm going to have to carry you up like a baby," I warned her sternly.

She gave me a drunk pout for that. "You can't carry me thafar. Thas alot a stairs, and Imma *grown* woman."

"Barely grown. You're an itty bitty barely slip of a woman, and I could carry you easily for miles. Do you *want* to be carried?"

She harrumphed. "Nuh uh. I canwalk."

"Fine. Then hold onto me."

"Where?"

I lifted up my arm and held it out. "Hold around my waist," I told her. I was so tall, and she was so small that it was the only way we fit walking side by side.

She actually listened, hugging me around the waist, her big, soft, nearly naked tits nestling into my abs.

I sucked in a breath, but quickly recovered, cupping her shoulder and moving her slowly in the right direction.

I was tempted to give her my bed as we passed my room, but quickly abandoned the idea. She'd likely get the wrong idea if she woke up alone with her first hangover in my wicked, wicked bed.

We ran into a slight problem when we hit the stairs that led to her wing of the house. She saw the first carpeted step, and it was just too tempting for her.

She pulled away from me with a grunt and parked her cute

little ass on it, elbows perching on the step behind her, thrusting her magnificent tits forward at the same time that her lovely, slender legs spread limply out in front of her. "Jus' leaveme here. Thisis good."

I sighed, hands going to my hips. I loomed over her, jaw clenched, whole body clenched, and wondered how I was going to last another five minutes with a nearly naked Ro sprawled out in front of me.

I didn't realize what the stance accentuated until her eyes traveled rather unerringly to the obvious erection that my swim trunks were never going to hide.

Her hand covered her mouth, her eyes gone wide in drunken shock. She pointed, the tip of her finger less than an inch from my pointing cock. I couldn't help it. I twitched, my tip nearly closing that one inch gap, less than a breath away from assaulting her unsuspecting, innocent finger.

"Y-y-your penis," she gasped, scandalized.

"Don't pay any attention to that," I said calmly. "It's involuntary and has nothing to do with you."

"Why?"

"Why what?"

"Why'sit hard?"

"Just blood flow. Like I said, ignore it."

"Why's your blood*flowin'*?"

She was so drunk, I doubted she'd even remember this conversation in the morning, so I responded somewhat honestly. "Because you're barely wearing any clothes, and your tits are out of this world. I can see your nipples trying to fight their way out of your top, and my money's on those nipples winning that fight. It would make any halfway healthy heterosexual man come to attention. Don't even get me started on the rest of you. That flat little belly. That tiny little waist. The thick hips and plump ass. Those shapely little thighs. Your perfect little knees. Those adorable little feet. Your tiny, delicate hands. I could nut on your cute, sassy eyebrows at this point."

As I spoke, she was looking down at her body, looking scandalized and very, very drunk. She looked up, up, up at me and pointed to herself incredulously.

"Yes, you," I told her with tender gravity.

She adjusted her top, as though trying to cover up, but only uncovered more.

I groaned out loud as she tugged the ridiculous triangle to the center and one tantalizing, rosy pink nipple popped out the side.

I thought she'd be embarrassed, but she was too drunk for that. She started giggling so hard that she forgot to even try to put that sweet little bud back under cover.

I bent down and tried to do it for her. I tugged the material over with just my fingertips, very careful not to touch her skin.

She giggled harder, adjusting the other triangle until a second nipple popped free.

I straightened, glaring at her. "Devereux Laurent! That's no help at all. This is quite unwholesome of you. Bad girl."

I wasn't going to take advantage of her, but boy was I going to give her a good talking to. "I'm very disappointed in you."

She didn't take me seriously. Who would? Even in my head it sounded ridiculous. I wasn't her father.

She seemed to read my mind. "Stop lecturing me," she gasped out between adorable giggles. "You don't look like *anyone's* dad."

"A few people have called me Daddy," I mused, distracting myself with the thought, "but that was more their kink than mine."

Certainly that didn't stop the giggling. It was worse than ever after that.

I tried again to fix her top. She tried to help *me* help *her*, and it was a very bad idea.

I let her move my hands over her flesh for a beat, two, utterly mesmerized by her, before I came to my senses, and immediately realized how fucked up that was.

It took every bit of my self-control to stop touching her.

She didn't help at all, clutching at my retreating hands with a surprisingly strong grip.

"Stop that, cupcake," I chided her softly.

She let go of my hands and stuck her tongue out at me.

I almost took her up on the offer.

Finally, with a curse, I bent, picked her up in a cradle hold, and made a quick dash for her room.

Like I was holding flames in my bare hands, and the quicker I could put them down, the less I'd burn us both.

Her heavy breasts were crushed, warm and delicious, against my chest.

I was so hard I was grinding my teeth.

I set her on the bed as gently as I could which meant I practically threw her on it.

She landed on her back and bounced a bit, her pink rosebud nipples still out and teasing me outrageously.

I watched, knees close enough to touch the mattress, hands in my hair.

It was madness.

She was looking up at me, her lush lips quirked enigmatically. "You're so funny," she told me. "I think you're secretly a nice guy."

"Oh, Ro, you innocent little thing. I am not nice at all. All of the depraved ways I could corrupt you. All of the filthy things I could do to you."

"You could talk me to death." It was a taunt, and she had the nerve to giggle after she said it.

"This isn't a laughing matter," I told her sternly.

"Sure it is."

I couldn't help it, in spite of my discomfort and frustration, I smiled fondly at that. "Even when you're being impossible, I get a real kick out of you, you know that?" I asked her. "Now do you need anything before I go? Want me to pull your hair? I mean, hold it back while you throw up?"

She was laughing, and I was still smiling as I went into her closet.

It was absolute torture but I determinedly put her into an oversized T-shirt and untied all the strings on her bikini.

I stepped back. "Now throw the bathing suit on the floor. I don't want you getting tangled up in it while you sleep."

She obeyed, but in the worst way possible, practically taking off the shirt and giving me a real show that, even trying my best, I could not look away from.

The tips of my fingers were trembling.

When the bikini was a heap on the ground by the bed, I handed her some panties.

"You're adorable," I told her softly, tenderly. "Now I need to get the hell away from you."

CHAPTER TWELVE

I didn't sleep. I paced the house, jerked off several times, and drove myself crazy until morning.

When she woke up I was there with coffee, and I got the treat of seeing her utterly hungover, paying for all of her sins of the day before.

"Do you remember anything from yesterday?" I asked her, parking myself at her hip.

She was sitting up, looking out of sorts and disoriented. She took a long draw of her coffee and just looked at me. She wasn't drunk, but she wasn't quite back to being the Ro I missed yet.

"I remember," she finally said slowly. "I drank too much, but I didn't black out or anything. You were being crazy."

I glared at her. "I was being crazy? *I* was being crazy? I saw your nipples, Ro, *both* of them."

She didn't laugh but got a vaguely amused look in her eyes, an ironic twist to her mouth that was the most Ro thing I'd seen in almost twenty-four hours.

I loved it. It was a bit worrisome how much I'd missed that look.

"Would it have been better if it was only one?" she finally asked wryly.

"Yes. Both was overkill. No more bikinis for you," I decided on the spot.

Her eyes narrowed. "You are not going to tell me how to dress."

"I just did."

"You know what? I'm not fighting with you right now."

"Hey!" I exclaimed. "Fighting is just an angry way of caring, you know."

I waited for one of her pithy comebacks.

She wasn't playing. She pointed at her door. "Give me some privacy. I need to get dressed."

I sighed and got up. "Come see me when you're dressed. We need to talk."

She took her sweet time. I was in my office staring at my computer screen when she finally showed up.

"We have a problem," I told her.

She sat down on my sofa. "We do?" she asked, sounding disinterested, like things were business as usual, and I was just going to send her on some unpleasant but relatively normal errand.

I got up and joined her, sitting right next to her and looking straight into her eyes.

I wanted to touch her. Would she be warm? Would she lean into my touch, or would she recoil?

I took off her glasses, and she tried to snatch them back.

I set them on a side table out of her reach. "You're nearsighted. You don't need them for this conversation."

I looked deep into her eyes, brushing her hair back from her face.

She looked highly suspicious and vaguely offended. It was

probably a fair reaction for what I was about to say. What I quite simply couldn't keep myself from saying.

I was shaking a bit. That's how much I couldn't keep it in.

What the hell was wrong with me?

She was driving me crazy. No design for it on her part, but that somehow made it all the more irresistible.

I couldn't seem to stop myself from harassing the poor girl.

"You can wear bikinis," I finally began with. "That was out of line, me telling you what to wear."

"Gee, thanks, I was real worried about it," she responded, exactly on brand.

I smiled. It was out of hand. I'd never wanted so much to fuck someone for their personality in my life.

I tried to keep my body calm as I searched for how to start this little headfirst dive into insanity that I had decided on over the long, sleepless night.

"We need to be face to face for this, no craning our heads sideways to look at each other," I mused out loud.

"What are you talking about?"

In answer, I picked her up and arranged her on top of me, straddling my lap.

She was wearing a T-shirt and boxers, and I was wearing close to the same thing, and the two materials together weren't thick enough to keep me from feeling her taut flesh underneath. Our lower bodies were flush just how and where they needed to be.

God, I wanted her.

She put her hands against my chest, palms almost cupping my pecs. I didn't think it was deliberate but my cock didn't care about her intentions. "What are you doing?" she asked slowly.

"You know I'm your boss," I began. It wasn't the best start, but I was having a hard time finding the right words.

Her lips parted ever so slightly, going from pursed to lush.

Her eyelids drifted down, making her eyes darken, and like a light switch going off, her entire expression went from serious to sultry.

I was lost.

I took a deep breath, then another, my need rising up to the surface until I was choking on it.

She mumbled something.

"Huh?" I said.

"Your hands," she muttered. She pushed against me and budged me not an inch.

"My hands?" Oh that. They were full of her delectable ass, keeping her flush against me, my die hard erection trying to drill its way through our clothes and into her soul.

"Your hands are on my butt, boss."

I removed them with great effort.

"See?" I said in a less than steady voice. "There you go. Was it really so hard to call me boss?"

"Not at all. I find it extremely easy to say things I don't mean." She shifted. "You're not a very comfortable seat."

"Keep moving around like that, and I'll get a lot less comfortable in a hurry." That was a joke. I was already hard enough to punch a hole through the wall.

Though I supposed it would in fact be less comfortable if I tried to stick it somewhere it didn't belong.

Just having the thought was problematic. I couldn't think about anything like that without a little involuntary shudder, a groan, a hip grab, a quick, thoughtless grind against the soft heat of her.

She gasped and climbed off my lap.

I grimaced, hand going up to rub at my temple. "I'm sorry. That was out of line and an accident, I swear. I clearly need to get laid."

"You didn't get laid at the pool party yesterday?" she asked slowly, moving away. "Isn't that the point of you inviting fifty females to get half-naked at your house?"

I glared at her. Glared. The pint-sized termagant had a nerve. "Oh, well. I'm *so sorry* that I was too busy babysitting you to worry about my hard-on."

I composed myself and tried to get back on track. "I have something to say to you, and I'm going to get it out, goddammit."

"So say it," she said with just the perfect amount of quirky insolence to distract me again. "Talk already, boss."

The way she said boss made it clear who she thought was really in charge between the two of us. "You're a little brat, you know that?" I told her slowly, trying not to clue her in on just how much she delighted me.

"Let me guess, you're going to make a short story long; what you do best." She had the gall to rub her hands together like she just couldn't wait to see what I had to say because it would prove her right, the minx. "I bet you particularly hate the quote: Brevity is the soul of wit. It's like a personal diss against your whole career."

My jaw went a little slack. I was beginning to suspect, with good reason, that her sass was my own personal kink.

"Look at you," I said slowly, my tone seductive, thoroughly off topic once again, "Even hungover, you're landing fucking haymakers before noon."

She got a kick out of that, and the way she tried not to show it, biting her lips, made me want to attack her on sight.

"I want you," I finally said it.

She froze and stared.

It wasn't my smartest idea, but it wasn't my worst one either.

So I wanted to have sex with a female who had developed very quickly into my closest friend. So what?

I stood and moved to her until I was close enough that I had to look down and she had to look up and my erection was almost touching her through my shorts. "I want you," I said thickly. "I want to fuck you, to *pleasure* you, and I can't for the life of me think of one good reason why I shouldn't."

She didn't give me the reaction I was hoping for. I hadn't been dense enough to assume she would.

I'd wanted a reaction. Period. Any reaction from Ro was foreplay for me.

"What the hell is wrong with you?" She burst out with, moving away. "Don't you remember the contract I signed? I'm not quitting. I refuse to give up a job for whatever the hell it is you think you're doing." Her every word was breathless, and pained, like she had to force them out.

"Listen, I take full responsibility for anything that happens. I'll put it in writing if you're really worried about that."

"What are you even *doing*, Turner?"

Her saying my name did something to me, and it took me a minute to recover and speak. "Just a few times, probably, then we can go back to business as usual. It wouldn't affect your job, I'm not letting you go, not ever, it's not even an *option*, but I think we need to get *this* out of our systems."

"*Our* systems? Like this isn't your idea alone?"

I shot her a level look. I was a lot of things, but I wasn't blind. Not about this. I pointed at her, making solid eye contact. "Go ahead. Try to deny this to my face. You're trembling. You're out of breath. I know the signs. You want me. And lucky you, I'm right here."

And then she said it. The thing that complicated things out of all proportion and beyond all reason.

"I'm a virgin, Turner," she said quietly, and I froze.

And stared. And stared.

Fuck, all of this was way worse than I could have predicted, because my reaction was the opposite of what it should have been.

That little technicality didn't turn me off.

Just the opposite.

It drove me wild.

"What does that mean, exactly?" I finally asked. We'd been staring each other down for an uncomfortably long time.

"You don't even know what a virgin is?" she asked, amused. "It's that foreign of a concept to you?"

"Don't make me smile right now. This is serious."

"No, it's not," she said with sheer, confident, frustrating exasperation. "It's *absolutely* not. Certainly not to *you*. You take *nothing* seriously."

"What is that supposed mean?"

She rolled her eyes.

I wanted to throttle her.

I wanted to climb inside of her and rut until she was a boneless puddle at my feet.

I tried again. "How are you a virgin?"

She looked at me like I'd just said the silliest thing on the planet, but it was just another bit, the damned little hellion comedian. "Everyone starts out a virgin. Did you not know that?"

She had the nerve to make fun of me at a moment like this?

My brain short-circuited, vision going a little fuzzy for a delicious moment. I thought I might come in my pants.

"How are you *still* a virgin?" I tried again.

We were both smiling. I had the thought then that she was my favorite person on the planet.

Ever.

It was unhinged. I should have been running away screaming just from the thoughts my own brain was producing in that moment.

"Well, you see, how that works is, I haven't had sex with anyone yet."

"Godfuckingdammit, Ro! This isn't funny!"

I could have mouthed the words with her as she said, "Sure it is, boss."

I never wanted to let her leave my sight. I wanted to keep her in my pocket for the rest of my life.

Nothing romantic, of course. These were just strong friendship feelings with a dash of healthy, powerful lust thrown in.

Romance was just chemistry plus hormones and once you knew it, it lost half of its power.

I told myself those things, hoping if I said it enough I would feel it. Feel it like I was supposed to if I wanted my life to stay sane and normal and free of that ridiculous, *useless* L word.

Luckily she helped rouse me out of my ridiculous thoughts.

"I don't want my first time to be with someone like you," she said, tone serious and free of irony, for once.

Not gonna lie, it stung when it shouldn't have. Fucking ouch.

"I'm saving myself."

My bruised ego was immediately paused. This was too fascinating for me not to explore. "Are you waiting for *marriage*?"

If she said yes, I thought I might propose on the spot.

Her cute little nose wrinkled. "Not for marriage, no. I just thought I'd be in love, the first time. I was waiting for that. For love. For something meaningful."

"Well, hear me out." I paused as I searched for a way to sugar coat it, and when I didn't find one said, voice conciliatory but assured, "Love isn't real."

She glared.

I went on, "But what is real is chemistry. And chemistry like ours, that's extremely hard to come by. You may not even like me all that much—"

"I like you," she interrupted, voice begrudging. "Sometimes. Okay. I like you at least half of the time."

We smiled at each other.

"No, that's not true," she conceded. "I don't dislike you at all."

She paused, and I could taste the jab before she even delivered it. "You're my favorite pain in the ass."

I was hard. So fucking hard.

Even her bizarre, peculiar, twisted sense of humor turned me on. Especially that.

"Hear me out," I tried again, and we were both smirking as we waited to see what kind of crazy shit would come out of my mouth. "We're friends."

She looked at me like that was debatable, but she didn't mean it.

"Who said friends can't mess around?" I continued unabashed. "So how about I get you off a few times and *then* you can decide? I'm quite good. Ask anyone."

She snorted, the ungrateful little brat, and stormed away.

"Shrew," I muttered at her very straight retreating back.

"Wastrel," she shot back without slowing down.

That did it. It may as well have been an invitation.

I moved to follow her, I wasn't done giving her a piece of my mind, and stating my case, but two steps in I remembered why it was a bad idea to chase after a delectable virgin while sporting a relentless erection that may as well have had her name on it.

God, what was I doing? She was the best assistant I'd ever had, and more than that, much more, she was my friend. I liked having her around. I enjoyed the hell out of it, in fact. She was, quite simply, the most fun I could ever remember having in my life, and that was saying a lot. Fun had been a close friend of mine for some time.

As far as I was concerned, she and I were a permanent

arrangement that never needed to stop. In fact what I needed was to maintain it. I wanted to keep her around *for good.* This had nothing to do with that.

But I couldn't fuck her? That seemed like a strong stance to take.

A little extreme, I decided.

This was about two different needs altogether, and the one didn't have to have anything to do with the other.

But she was waiting. For love, or some nonsense that didn't matter, because whatever it was, it wasn't me.

But if she *wasn't* a virgin, some evil voice in my head piped in, what would a little consensual sex hurt?

Or hell, something else. A dozen satisfying activities came instantly to mind that would leave her physically intact, more or less. Did she care about what *kind* of a virgin she was?

It was worth asking, I decided.

CHAPTER THIRTEEN

I waited a few hours before I approached her in her office. She was dressed for work now, in possibly the worst outfit I'd ever seen. No one ever would have guessed about her take no prisoners body in that getup. Ignorance is bliss.

She was pulling her OCD act, lining everything up just so on her desk, long boxy skirt showing nothing but her ankles, with horrible tan pantyhose, and horrid flat, orthopedic looking loafers.

I moved behind her quietly.

I ran my nose along her jaw, breathing her in. "We're good, right? You're not upset with me?"

"Are you demented?"

"A little bit, sure. Will you answer me, though?"

"We're fine," she said without looking at me. "I've organized your entire chaotic system," she said in that matter of fact way of hers. "I'm fixing your messes all the time, cleaning up after all of these other assistants you've had, who, as far as I could tell, did nothing but dress sexy and make thirsty TikToks all day."

She wasn't wrong. It was why I'd hired them then, and why I'd hired her, an actual professional, now. But that plan was obviously backfiring on me in a hurry. "Things are fine," she continued, "if you quit trying to fuck it all up, Thorn."

"Oh ho, it's Thorn now, huh?"

She just kept organizing, not looking up.

"I need you to take some notes for me out at the pool," I told her, not bothering to explain the subject change. "Go put on a swimsuit."

She looked up and started shaking her head.

I shook mine back. "I know what you're going to say. Some bullshit about doing other work or wearing that atrocity of an outfit to the pool. Save it. Your job is to accommodate me. Go change into a swimsuit and get your adorable little ass outside."

She looked mad enough to spit as she replied, "All right," blandly.

I rubbed my hands together, smiling and soaking up her delicious reaction.

I loved that, the vagaries of her.

She saw the fiendish light in my eyes, let out an annoyed grunt and stormed from the room.

I got off on riling her.

It was kind of cute.

No, it was flat-out cute.

In fact, it was disgusting. We were halfway to married.

I was out and swimming within five minutes. It took her thirty, and she came out in that infamous black bikini.

She came and sat at the edge of the pool, small laptop in hand.

"Go put that away," I told her.

"You wanted me to take notes."

"I want you to swim a few laps with me first. It's good

exercise."

She glared at me, but she took the laptop inside.

I was there to meet her when she stepped into the pool.

She paused.

I grinned, and she looked at me like I was a shark in the water.

When she was in, the water up to her hips, I moved close and straightened to tower over her. I circled her waist with my hands.

"You're a tiny little thing."

"I'm a normal sized woman," she told me, staring up at me boldly. "You're the one who's huge."

I couldn't help it. I smirked. "I've never had any complaints."

She blushed and looked away.

I was so hard my teeth were aching.

The things knocking around inside of me were too powerful to be compared to anything I could remotely remember. I felt primitive. Ungovernable.

It was an effort to be halfway sane, let alone articulate, but I tried to shoot my shot again.

"I don't blame you for thinking I'm a bad candidate to be your first," I told her softly. "And that's fine. I don't need to fuck you. And yes, you're a virgin, but there are all kinds of virgins." My voice was soft as air and dark as night. "Just turn off that devious brain for a few hours. Let me introduce some mindless pleasure into your life." I was whispering into her ear by the end, and when I finished, I bit her lobe oh so softly.

She snorted.

Snorted!

"Knock it off, Turner," she said lightly. "Your flair for the ridiculous is kicking up again."

I blinked, pulling back. "Aren't you even curious about

it?" I asked.

"About your flair for the ridiculous? Not particularly. Not today. Maybe hit me up tomorrow."

"Not that. I mean, aren't you curious about sex? Kissing. Touching. Getting off. Any of it. I've got a bit of everything," I paused. "Well, a lot of everything actually."

Her face tightened up like I'd offended her, which I supposed I must've. "Just stop," she muttered, turning her face away.

Her body was telling me a different story. Breath panting in and out. Hands on my wrists, keeping them at her waist instead of pushing them away.

"Hear me out," I began in my most cajoling, seductive voice.

"No. Someone's got to tell you no, Turner, and much to my sadness, that task seems to have fallen to me, so here it goes: It's an unfortunate part of life, sometimes, not getting your way. But the answer is no. I'm not going to sleep with you just to satisfy your curiosity."

That took me aback. "I never said anything about me being curious. I'm *ravenous*. I was asking you if *you* were curious."

"Well, I'm not."

"Not even a little? Never mind. My point is, I wasn't saying *I* wanted to do it for curiosity. I want to do it because I'm earnestly attracted to every part of you, and it's become a very . . . substantial effort for me to keep my hands to myself, and I've decided that I'd prefer not to. Emphatically so."

"Well tough, boss. You'll get over it."

I took my hands away from her body and for a moment she held them before letting go. But it was just for a moment.

"Whatever you want," I said softly.

I said it like I hated it.

I said it like I meant it.

CHAPTER FOURTEEN

It was Sunday and Ro was gone. I was bored and I missed her. It was pathetic, but I didn't beat myself up about that.

I found other ways to keep busy. No, not writing. I needed my assistant around to keep me on task for that.

No, this was pure, ornery mischief.

I'd been working on it for a while, so it wasn't solely impulsive. Ill-advised? Check. Terrifically messed up? Check. Out of line? Check.

All those things, but not impulsive.

I'd ordered Ro an entire new and normal wardrobe. Head to toe, everything from hats to stockings. I'd even ordered a collection of floral church dresses, modest but pretty instead of bulky and ugly.

I'd plotted it out better than I did most of my novels. I'd thought of everything, from business casual to her Sunday lazies.

The lingerie was completely out of line, especially the

French maid teddy, but I'd never been known for my restraint, and that part of the prank had been an impulse I hadn't even wanted to curb.

I gathered every hideous piece of clothing she owned and piled them up out back next to my fire pit.

I could have, probably should have, hired help for this, to get it done faster at the very least, so she didn't catch me at it, but it was just too much fun. I relished every bit of the task, from shamelessly going through her things to carefully hanging up and folding every new piece of clothing.

It was a huge closet to fill, but I took a good stab at it.

The cherry on top was the aforementioned French teddy hanging conspicuously on the outside of the closed closet door. It was the first thing she'd see when she walked in her bedroom. It was perverse and inappropriate, and my favorite part.

She came home when I was still tossing her clothes into the fire pit, though I was close to done.

"What's this?" she asked, no expression on her face.

"A bonfire of your lack of vanity," I said smugly. I'd been waiting to get that line out for a while. Weeks.

She didn't react. In fact, she didn't seem to appreciate my clever quip at all.

It was a bit deflating. Her reaction was the sole reason I'd done any of it.

"Get it," I tried again, "because your clothes are so ugly, you have no vanity, and this is a fire."

She just stared at me. "It's hard to laugh at your willful destruction of my property," she said quietly, "all my worldly goods." She pointed at the atrocious polka dot blouse in my hand. "Mrs. Anderson gave that to me right before she died."

I made a face, I couldn't help it. "You're not convincing me to keep these awful things by telling me they belong to dead people." I punctuated my point by tossing the blouse in the fire.

Finally I got a reaction out of her.

She shot me a bland look that promised retribution. "Sentimental value not your thing, huh?" she asked with spectacular detachment.

"Not at all. If you want to keep any of the junk that's left, you're going to have to wrestle me for it."

She did her little smile that wasn't a smile, her eyes flashing.

Now this, this was what I'd wanted. "Something to say?" I asked with an unrepentant smile. "Bring it on, cupcake."

She just shook her head. "Burn it all. It's fine. I'm actually not that sentimental either."

I puzzled over that for a bit, knowing it was a clue about what she was planning as retribution.

I frankly couldn't wait to see what she came up with.

I had an open bottle of wine, a terrific Russian River pinot noir, beside me. I took a swig of it, grimaced, and offered it to her.

She shook her head, biting her lips to keep from smiling.

"Understandable," I said agreeably. "I hate wine, too."

"You've already drunk half the bottle."

"I'm also not a quitter."

There it was, finally, the laugh I'd been waiting for.

It warmed me, head to toe.

Her revenge was effortless, at least the first part of it was.

She just started wearing the clothes I'd bought her. They actually fit her, showed her knockout body off.

Fitted little skirts with slits. Nicely tailored button up shirts. Fitted, ass hugging slacks. Conservative mules and pumps with sensible heels. I'd had to buy some of her shoes from the kids' department; her feet were so itty bitty. She stopped wearing hideous pantyhose because she simply didn't have any and hadn't bothered to get more after I'd torched all of hers. I got to see pieces of her bare flesh constantly.

Sometimes she even wore the skintight bodysuits I'd added with little hope that I'd see them in action. They went perfectly with a pencil skirt and when she paired the two together, I was practically useless for anything except the one thing I was *not* doing lately.

She was turning business casual into a personal kink for me.

Every time she walked in a room, I was reminded of the fact that I'd thought I'd hired her because she wasn't a dime and here she was, the hottest creature I'd ever seen in my life.

It was slightly perturbing and extremely distracting.

I pretended to be focused.

I was particularly and ridiculously distracted by the fact that her clothes were tight enough now that I could see when her nipples were popping.

I set the thermostat a few degrees lower to keep them that way constantly.

She often mistook my preoccupation with *her* as my usual procrastination.

I let her.

"Get off the internet and start writing," she came into my office and told me for the twentieth time that day.

I hadn't even been focused on my computer screen, internet or no. I'd been spaced out and thinking about her. She'd turned me down twice and no meant no, so I didn't need to tell her what had really been plaguing me.

Instead I played along. "This is important," I told her, just to rile her. "It's research."

"You said you'd say that."

"That does sound like something I'd say about me."

She bit her lips, trying not to smile, and I gripped the edge of my desk.

She wasn't done, the pint-sized hellion. "If you don't give me five hundred words in the next hour, you're going to have to run naked along the fence of your entire property.

I stared at her. "You're telling me to go streaking? As a *deterrent*?"

She nodded, eyes glinting. "Chop chop, cupcake."

She walked away, and it took a lot not to go after her.

I met the word count goal, even brought my laptop into her office to rub it in.

She was bent over her desk, ass facing me. She was wearing a skirt, and thanks to me it wasn't a tent that went down to the floor. I even caught a glimpse of the back of her thighs. And the shape of her ass… I could barely look at it, the way the fitted skirt hugged her curves.

She moved, wiggling a bit as she wrote something on a notepad.

My mind went wild, picturing those plump, ripe, fuckable breasts in my hands while I took her from behind.

Well, shit.

I snuck up on her because I wanted to see what was making her wiggle like that.

She was drawing. Already formed was a precise depiction of Mayhem the Unicorn.

I couldn't tell what he was doing so I moved closer and leaned over her to look.

I shifted forward a bit more, my hips straining at her in spite of my brain telling them to stop, but they had a mind of their own. If she'd just back into me so I could feel her, just a little.

The rest of the picture took shape as I moved close. The blue unicorn was back, holding a handful of balloons and floating high in the sky. He looked extremely stressed out, eyes popping out of his head.

Below were the little pink unicorn and Mayhem, pointing and laughing. It was all very expressive and just precious. I loved it.

"You know," I mused into her ear, "it seems like Mayhem does more bullying himself than actually *preventing* it. You have a confused message for your unicorn."

She turned her head to look at me and pursed her mouth, another tell that she was trying not to smile.

Unfortunately, or fortunately, depending on how you wanted to look at it, she also moved her ass just far enough back to brush against my aching cock.

I put my hands on her hips, to push them away, probably, eventually, maybe, but she straightened just then and actually leaned against me, looking back and up, up, up at me.

"The thing you call love," I said. I just couldn't shut up. "What it really is is intimacy combined with sex, and we can have that without making it fiction."

"You know what the most amazing thing about you is?" she asked idly.

I started to preen. Oh how I loved hard-earned compliments. "My abs? My biceps?"

She scoffed. "No. You're not even warm."

"My dreamy, bright blue eyes?"

"It's that you actually believe the ridiculous nonsense that comes out of your mouth."

She did have a point.

"Not *all* of it, but most of it," I corrected.

She turned suddenly and reached up to my face.

I held very still, caught, fascinated, enthralled by the idea of what she'd do next.

She ran her thumb slowly over my bottom lip, once, twice. My eyelids drifted shut, but I forced them open to watch the way she was looking at me.

It was insane, with the amount of hedonistic delights I'd

buried myself in over the years, but I'd swear it was the most sensual thing I'd ever experienced.

I was trembling. I'd never wanted anyone like this. Her thumb on my lips was more intense than full on penetration with another woman. It was bedlam.

I told myself, in some twisted attempt at comfort, that I only felt this newfound level of desperation due to the simple fact that I'd been depriving myself, but even I had a hard time buying it.

Deprivation alone could not account for *this*.

My hand moved, I watched it, though I didn't control it at this point, to caress her breast.

I took a deep breath, then another, my need rising up to the surface until I was choking on it.

"Not to be overdramatic," I told her gruffly, rubbing her nipple through her thin white blouse, "but if I can't get my dick inside of you soon, I think I might die."

She laughed, the sadist.

She moved away, but she was as affected, as unsteady, as I was. She went behind her desk and sat down heavily, like her legs couldn't hold her weight anymore.

I put my hands up in the air, backing toward the door. "I get the hint. But if you ever change your mind, you know where to find me."

She just watched me, her eyes eating me alive, and I wondered how a virgin had perfected a soul-sucking stare like that. It was out of fucking line.

She stopped me when she spoke.

"You're overwhelming, Thorn," she said quietly and with no expression. "Too much of everything."

"Is that a compliment?"

"Not even close."

I squinted at her. "Are you sure?" It was worth a shot. I could spin anything. When she didn't respond, I changed tactics. "You know, you're pretty overwhelming yourself."

When she squinted back like I'd made her curious, it felt like a small but pointed victory. "Is that a compliment?"

I smirked. "Absolutely." I walked away.

I was still receiving my usual texts from women. Somehow I wasn't even a little bit tempted, in fact I'd taken to categorically discouraging them.

For some reason none of them took me seriously.

A name I vaguely recognized sent me a particularly close up, detailed picture of her vagina.

Me: No ty. I'm a vegan now.

Her: Lol. Want me to come over tonight?

**Me: No, I'm out of town indefinitely.
And I meant it about the vegan thing.
Look elsewhere for your fix.**

Another of my old regulars sent me a nude of her using a particularly hardcore toy on herself.

I sent her a gif of a bible whacking someone over the head with blinking text across it that read, 'Begone, Satan.'

That didn't seem to faze her at all going by the fact that she sent me a video immediately following that. I didn't even look at it.

The two girls from the counter incident were sending a steady chain of filth my way, as well. I ignored them for quite a while before finally responding.

Me: I'm taking my priest vows. Repent and stop texting me those. They are the devil's work.

It didn't even slow them down. I stopped so much as opening most of my texts, and I wondered what was wrong with me for multiple reasons: Why had I indulged so many meaningless flings with such vigor? Followed shortly by: Why was I so unmoved, so wholly *un-tempted* by them now?

CHAPTER FIFTEEN

My dad showed up out of the blue, which was never a welcome development. I saw him about once a year for two to three days, and it was always a wonder that I was still speaking to him at the end of it.

Ro answered the door, as she usually did, and led him back to my office. She looked a little shell-shocked and I glared at him, wondering if he'd already managed to say or do something awful in the short trip from the front to the back of the house.

"Hello, Carson," I said to my father, already feeling hostile.

He smiled at Ro and winked at her.

I felt my hands curl into fists.

"Get me a cup of coffee, doll," he told her.

"She's got a great rack under those conservative clothes," were the first words out of his mouth, before she was even out of fucking earshot.

"Don't even think about it," I told him, voice low and

outright mean. "That one is so off-limits, you don't even want to know.

He looked intrigued. "I beg to differ. No one's off-limits."

He was still effortlessly bagging anything with legs and a vagina from the ages of eighteen to twenty-six, and showed no signs of slowing down. My shameless, womanizing genetics were stellar.

For some bizarre reason women rarely turned him down, and that included the one woman I had ever foolishly committed to.

"I'll rearrange your face if you so much as look at her wrong," I said, and I absolutely meant it.

He was in his late fifties, but the bastard just seemed to be getting more handsome and distinguished with age, and he'd *always* liked his face, so it was a good threat.

Still, he just looked even more intrigued. "So *you're* bagging her, and it's serious."

I cut my hand through the air. "Knock it off."

"Where *is* that sexy secretary with my coffee? She's taking her sweet time. Maybe I'll go find her myself."

"Is your wife with you?" I asked him.

That put him in his place a little. He suddenly looked disgusted and annoyed. He waved behind him, and I could not begin to guess what he was indicating. "She's somewhere close by. You know she never lets me get far."

We continued to catch up in our antagonistic way and when a full half-hour had passed, and I realized that Ro had completely ignored his request for coffee I was as tickled by her as I'd ever been.

"Do you ever miss Mom?" I lobbed out idly.

That was me picking a fight. He didn't, but he should. My mom had been a saint.

But he was a sinner, so of course he didn't care.

My dissolute father sighed like I'd just disappointed him.

"For your sake, I do. But for mine, no. I've told you, son. Women are all the same. One's as good as another when you're on top of them.

"Misogynist asshole," I remarked casually.

He continued, unfazed, "She did make great crepes, but you know, so does my chef."

"I can't believe she gave you the time of day. She was so much better than you. You weren't even worthy to kiss her fucking feet."

He shrugged, trying to look unaffected, but I could tell by a new tightness around his mouth that I'd gotten to him. "That's what every boy wants to think about his mother. Tell yourself those lies if you must."

"And you keep telling yours."

It was about that time my father's wife arrived.

She was my age and still a real stunner. Red hair complemented by lovely tan skin, sky high legs, curves for days, lips made for sin, and the kind of strikingly beautiful face that inspired poetry.

If I was brutally honest about her, which I emphatically was, she'd peaked in her mid-twenties. Probably too much time in a tanning bed.

We were both well into our thirties now.

They'd been together for over a decade, which I think we'd all have agreed was a small miracle. Neither of them were cut out for marriage. It was possible that they'd only lasted so long out of pure apathy. Why would you end something that you'd barely ever let affect your lifestyle in the first place?

I smiled unpleasantly at her. "Hello, Ida."

She smiled warmly at me, far happier with our little family reunion than I was. "Turner, aren't you a sight for sore eyes?"

I rolled *my* eyes at that. She was as incapable of charming me as my father was, which was an impressive feat.

I didn't hate her, though I used to. These days I just kind of pitied her and was embarrassed about our past together. I'd never understood her motives, but surely she couldn't have wanted her life to turn out *this* sad.

"*Where* is that secretary?" Carson asked the room at large.

"Get your own fucking coffee," I told him blandly. "You know where the kitchen is."

He waved vaguely toward his wife. "Ida, get me a cup of coffee."

She was unfazed. "Cream and sugar?"

He looked at her like she was a particularly fascinating bug on his windshield. "You don't know how I take my coffee?"

She sent him a sultry stare. "We both know you didn't marry me for my skills in the kitchen."

It was almost impressive how seductive she looked and how unaffected he was by it. Same for me, to be frank.

"Black," he told her. "Fucking blow up doll," he said when she was out of earshot. That was downright polite, for him. He waved between us. "She's useless for anything else. Guess we both look silly for falling for *that* one's little tricks."

"Speak for yourself. I was too young to know better when I met her. What's your excuse?"

"If I divorce her now, she'll take half. I'd rather be miserable with *all* of my money."

I'd heard him tell that joke at least fifty times. I wondered how many times he'd told it in total. It had to be in the thousands.

Ro bustled into the office, setting a stack of papers on my desk. "Sign these at your leisure, and let me know when you're done so I can send them out."

She left promptly and without acknowledging my father.

He was baffled. I was delighted.

"How long are you staying?" I asked. He always stayed for at least two days, and I wasn't looking forward to it.

"However long I feel like. Tu casa es mi casa, son. You certainly have the room."

I let out a heavy sigh.

"Pretty sure you got that saying mixed up," I pointed out.

"Well, you're the fancy writer."

Going by his answer, I figured I'd be kicking them out in about two days. I'd had to do it before. My dad liked to push his luck.

I started reading and signing the contracts Ro had brought in.

"Contracts are signed," I yelled automatically when I was done. I didn't like to text her. It was more fun to shout down the hall and annoy her.

Ro came back and gathered the contracts.

"Too good to make a cup of coffee, eh?" my dad asked her as she passed by.

"For *you*, most definitely," she said without missing a beat, already out the door.

"She's got a mouth," Carson said, looking like he'd tasted something sour. "You put up with that kind of insolence?"

I didn't bother to tell him that I ate it up with a spoon and sprinkles on top.

Instead my eyes narrowed at him. "You must have really pissed her off between the front door and my office. What the fuck did you say to her?"

He rolled his eyes. "For the love of God," he said dramatically, "everyone's *so sensitive* these days."

Was is too early for Scotch? I checked the time.

Way too early.

Also, I didn't want to show or share the good stuff with my dad. Not because I was the least bit cheap or couldn't afford it. Just because he didn't deserve it. And of course I was diametrically opposed to sharing *anything* of value with him.

Eventually and thankfully he left my office to go do God

knows what with my stepmommy dearest.

I instantly went to speak to/harass Ro in her office.

She was sitting at her desk, working on her computer. She looked up when I walked in and shut the door. She raised a brow.

"What did he say to you?" I asked her, trying not to sound as upset about the possibilities as I actually was.

She shrugged, her face stoic. "Nothing important. He's a piece of work."

"That he is. Please stay far away from him while he's here."

"Obviously," she said and I smiled.

"His wife, Ida, seems nice," she remarked.

I scowled. "She's not. Stay away from her, too."

"What, why?"

I thought about it, wondered why I wanted to tell her, if it was for the warning or because I just liked to share things with her in general, which scared me.

In the end I think I did it because she might find out anyway, and I wanted to see her reaction when she did.

"Ida is my ex-wife," I told her.

Her reaction was as gratifying as I could have hoped. I'd truly shocked her. Her mouth just kept opening and closing like a fish.

I wanted to stuff something in it. Stuff it *deep*.

I wanted to know what she had to think more.

"Ex-wife?" she asked finally.

"Ex-wife," I affirmed with a world of self-disgust.

"*You*? You have an ex-wife? And she's your *stepmother*?"

"Correct," I said, eating all of her expressions, just gobbling them up.

"How did I not know this?" she asked.

"Not many people do. I don't like to admit to it. It's embarrassing as hell. She's a nightmare, but somehow I thought it would be a great idea to marry her."

"And then she married your *father*?"

"Correct."

"When? How? What was the timeline for all this?"

"I was very young and stupid and met and married her before I understood what that meant. She and my father met and did something very similar."

"So there was *overlap*?"

I was perversely gratified at how much disgust there was in her tone. "Not by choice on my end," I remarked.

She looked so disgruntled and upset that I wanted to hug her. And hump her leg like a dog.

"That's the most messed up thing I've ever heard."

"Correct," I said, a laugh in my voice. Only Ro could make me find the whole fiasco of my father and ex-wife just this funny. Her uncharacteristic, involuntary reaction put it all into just the right perspective.

"This isn't funny," she scolded me.

Our eyes clashed, both of us sharing a small smile as I said, "Sure it is."

"They're *horrible*," said Ro sometime later. She'd just been staring off into space, absorbing it all.

I smiled fondly. "I'm glad we agree."

I remembered that I came to see her for two reasons aside from looking at her adorably mischievous expressions. I got back to the first one. "What did my degenerate father say to you?"

She didn't answer.

I glared. "Sleep in my room tonight." I wasn't joking, but I said it like that just to see her reaction.

She stared, her eyes doing something fascinating.

I smirked. "Not like that. At least, not unless you insist. I just… I don't trust my dad."

"You think he'd really try something with me? Something

I couldn't handle?"

"I think he'd make you extremely uncomfortable and then I'd kick his ass. I should probably avoid that, so please sleep in my room. I'll put on fresh sheets.

"Where will you sleep?"

"There's a sofa in my room. I'll camp out on that. I just want you to stay close to me while he's here, okay?"

She studied me. "You aren't actually worried I'd be tempted by anything he has to offer, are you?"

I was horrified. The thought hadn't even crossed my mind, but what I said was, "Of course not. If you can resist *me*, you can certainly resist that old reprobate."

She kept studying my face and finally said, "I'll sleep on your sofa."

It took me a beat to realize she was agreeing to sleep in my room and after processing my relief of that I said, "No, I will. Thank you for agreeing."

She shrugged. "You know your loser dad better than I do."

With that I grabbed my laptop and took to working in her office, locking us in.

"Are you *hiding* from them?" she asked archly.

"If only. Listen, will you join us for dinner? The housekeeper is coming over to make Beef Wellington. It will all be especially tedious without you."

"Fine. But only for the food, not to be supportive or anything like that. Perish the thought."

We shared a smile.

"Softie," I told her in a taunt.

"Coward," she taunted back.

TYRANT

CHAPTER SIXTEEN

Dinner was as unpleasant as I knew it would be, though Ro did go above and beyond to make it more entertaining in general and made sure it finished on the perfect note.

My dad started in right away when he felt we'd been waiting too long between the first and second course.

"Only a part-time housekeeper these days? And no dedicated wait staff for dinner? Books not selling like they used to?"

"Did you go too long between meals, sunshine?" Ro asked him. "Did you miss your snack time?" She spoke to him in just the perfect way. Her tone was wry but light. She made him sound like a petulant child and a malcontent, both.

He just glared at her.

As we dug into the main course, which was fantastic (My housekeeper is a wonder.), my dad just had to pipe in with his negative two cents.

"It's a decent Wellington," he said around a mouthful of

food, "but my chef's is far better. That's what you get for having a housekeeper cook instead getting yourself a real professional."

"Hopefully you'll be able to muscle it down," Ro told him blandly. "Tell me, with a better Wellington, would you just have inhaled it outright?"

Half his serving was already gone, and I could tell by the way he glanced down at it that she'd made him feel foolish.

And look foolish, of course. And like he had poor manners, to boot.

"I haven't heard much buzz about your upcoming release. Is it even being promoted? Do you suppose your fifteen minutes are up already?" My father took that dig right after he finished the last bite on his plate. He had cleared it and stopped complaining about the food after Ro's last comment.

"When you reach a certain level you don't need the same promotional blitz for every release. The books sell themselves for an author like Turner." Ro smiled unpleasantly at him. "You haven't learned anything about the industry your son's been so successful in? I wonder why."

The 'I wonder why' was said in such a way that I thought she was accusing him of something, like perhaps that he was jealous of his only son.

I thought it was interesting and perceptive how quickly she'd picked that up.

My dad was on his second bottle of expensive Napa cab when he said, "At least your taste in wine is better than your taste in women. We have that in common."

"You can taste it when you drink it that fast?" Ro asked him. Again with her it was the delivery, the perfectly flat tone that made it such a solid hit, as though it wasn't even worth it to her to get worked up into something so petty as an emotion when dealing with him.

It was his breaking point. He leaned forward, giving her a very nasty look. "You've got a mouth." He sneered. "Someone needs to show you what that smart mouth is really for," he told her softly. "I'm surprised my hot-blooded son hasn't already done that. Disappointed even. Let me know if you need *me* to do it, Turner."

I tossed down my napkin, standing up in a temper, ready to fight, but Ro had this. She fucking had it.

"I can see why you'd want quiet women around with that fragile ego of yours on display," she said in an almost singsong way that made it all the more mocking. "Those of us that like to talk probably only tell you one thing: Your son is much better than you. Richer, stronger, more talented, more compassionate, kinder, funnier, and certainly better-looking than you are or will ever be. That's why you resent him, why you try to take every petty dig you can, try to steal every silly thing from him you're able to manage, but you know better than *anyone* that that doesn't change the reality: You're a washed up old loser, and even before you were old and washed up, you were *never* as good as him."

"I don't have to listen to this," my father exclaimed dramatically, stood up, and stormed from the room.

I looked at Ro. She had her chin raised, and I don't even think she meant to sass me in particular, but she was staring insolently back at me, daring anyone to disagree with her tirade.

I don't know what Ro saw in my eyes then, but it made her squirm in her chair.

I'd never had someone stand up to him for me before. No one had ever assumed I'd needed them to. The fact that she had was almost too much for me. "You complete me, cupcake," I told her fondly as I sat back down, and was a little frightened at how much I meant the words.

"Like lightning and thunder," she said saucily, raising a

brow at me. It may as well have been a red flag. I almost jumped across the table.

"Well, that was awkward," Ida said.

We both looked at her. I'd forgotten she was even there.

"How could you leave Turner for *that*?" Ro asked her, then blushed. If I could read Ro now, which I could, she hadn't been able to keep the question in.

"Yes," I drawled, "do tell us your reasons for such a lapse in judgment, stepmother dearest."

I didn't actually care at this point, but I was enjoying the way this was riling Ro beyond all sense or reason.

"Oh, please," Ida said with an eye roll. "We were falling apart before I ever hooked up with Carson. We weren't going to last. You'd checked out emotionally. Did you think it wasn't obvious?

I thought about it. She wasn't totally wrong. There wasn't a universe where we would have lasted, her and me. I hadn't understood at all what I was getting into when I'd married her. I'd been infatuated with an idea I'd created in my head that had little to do with the woman herself, a fiction I'd weaved on my own.

Nowadays I just wrote novels.

"And I didn't *leave* Turner for *that*," Ida added. "I cheated on him for *that*, he dumped me, and I moved on with *that*."

"That's despicable," Ro said with no expression and absolute conviction.

Ida shrugged.

"Why him?" I asked her. I'd always been genuinely curious. A lot of men had been after her. He should not have been her first pick.

"I *did* love you, but I thought you were too young and immature to go the long haul. I wanted stability. I thought he'd be a more grown up version of you."

We both laughed pretty hard about that one.

"I'm sure it didn't hurt that he was far better off financially than I was at the time," I mused when I caught my breath.

She shrugged, not denying it. That was the thing about Ida—she was utterly incapable of embarrassment. Shameless to an extreme. Under the right context, I'd once found it charming. In the bedroom, mostly. Now it just made her seem a little soulless.

"Now what's for dessert?" she asked with a smile as though we hadn't just been discussing her mile wide character faults.

"Bananas Foster," I answered in just the same way.

"Oh! I should find Carson and bring him back. That's his favorite!"

Ro was studying the other woman like she was a particularly deranged mental patient. I was getting a real kick out of it.

"Don't bring him back," I said pleasantly. "You can deliver some to him in his room when you're done, or hell take both of yours to go."

"No, no, I'll take mine with you two and bring him his later," Ida said cheerfully, "Bananas Foster is always better fresh. He's the one that threw a fit. No reason I should be punished for it."

When she finally left to deliver my father's dessert to him Ro said, "It's amazing how many character flaws that level of beauty lets you get away with." She sounded as riled as I'd ever heard her.

I smiled at her, a very personal, we're the only two people in the world smile, and said, "So true. Now let's go to bed together, cupcake."

"Do not say it like that."

Ro sleeping in my room had been all my idea, but that didn't make it any easier for me specifically to get through.

It was a long night, but in spite of that, a very pleasant one, one I would repeat as much and as often as I could.

She came to my room soon after dinner. She'd already readied herself for sleep, was in her PJs (a loose T-shirt and boxers), and she climbed right into my bed, no hesitation.

Where was her sense of self-preservation?

"I can't wait for you to meet my parents," she told me as she pulled the covers, *my covers*, up to her neck.

I wouldn't be washing my bedding again for quite some time.

"Why?" I asked, instantly distracted by her getting into my bed and saying something so interesting at the same time. She knew how to catch my attention. "Are they crazy too?"

"They're the two cutest people on the planet." Deadpan. "Where do you think I got it?"

I was standing over her in my bed before I even realized what I was doing. She was flat on her back, our eyes locked when I said, "I can't wait. You should invite them to visit soon."

"This place might shock them. You'd have to keep all the crazy sex on counters down to a minimum and hide your fornication room from them."

I was offended and a little angry she even thought she had to say that. "First of all, don't call it that. It's a sex room. Fornication sounds like something you should say as you're thumping a bible on my forehead. Second, I've been on my best behavior for quite a while—because of you. You think I wouldn't do the same for your parents?"

"Okay, I'll tell them they're welcome any time, then. Goodnight, Thorn."

"Goodnight, cupcake." I didn't leave, still staring down at her. "And call me Turner. You know Thorn is my surname, right?"

"It just suits you, and friends call each other by last names all the time."

"Maybe bros that work together."

"We're basically bros that work together."

"No, we're not," I said very, very softly.

There was a brief stare down.

"Tell me you don't want me," I said quietly.

"How is that going to help?" she asked me.

"You don't get it."

"Don't get what?"

"I need you to say it," my voice was low and thick, my blood pounding. "Because I *want* you."

"You want everyone, so what does that even matter?"

"This want is not a little thing. It's not an itch, it's an *ache*, and it's become so pervasive I can't *think* straight. I want *you*, you particularly, and I've never wanted anyone or anything like this before. I need you to tell me you don't want me, because I'm hanging onto my last *thread* of control, and if you tell me you don't want me, it might keep that thread from breaking."

Her eyes were enigmatic when she finally said, "I don't want you," in the softest whisper. Aside from the volume level, it was indistinguishable from her usual sarcasm, but I took it anyway.

"Thank you," I said on an expelled breath and walked away.

"You're not welcome."

"Hellion." I turned off the light, laid down on the couch, and shut my eyes.

"Reprobate."

"Virgin."

"Ho."

"Marry me."

"You don't believe in love, remember?"

"What's that got to do with marriage?"

"Jackass."

"Prude."

"Hedonist."

"Killjoy."

Our voices were quiet but full of amusement as we tossed the words back and forth between the sofa and my wicked, wicked bed.

"Libertine."

"Puritan."

"Rake."

"Are you finished?" I asked her. "Get all that out of your system?"

"I could do this all night."

"I could do a lot of things all night." My voice was velvety smooth and full of all of the sins of the dark. "Would you like me to show you?"

"Degenerate."

"Old maid."

"Slut."

"Tease."

"How am *I* teasing *you*?" The little minx sounded genuinely baffled.

"By existing."

"Brazen tramp."

"Selfish prig."

"Unrepentant lech."

"Frigid bitch."

"Loose asshole."

"Hey now, that one's not even accurate."

"You have loose morals and are an asshole. What did you think I meant?"

"Smartass."

"That one's practically a compliment," she responded.

I didn't have to look, I knew her smile matched my own.

"Cum dumpster," she tried.

I was genuinely shocked. Just scandalized. "First of all, where did you hear that?"

"You," she muttered. "One of your stories to Dair."

"I don't think you even know what that means. Second, inaccurate. Would you like me to demonstrate?"

"Dick."

"Yes, that is how I would demonstrate."

"Shameless hussy."

"Cold-blooded harpy."

And so it went. On and on.

We didn't stop for quite a while. Neither of us could seem to help ourselves.

In spite of the physical torture it put me through to have her so close and *in my bed,* I wanted to do this every night just for the insults alone.

That and the warm feeling in my chest.

CHAPTER SEVENTEEN

I woke up with the worst morning wood of my life. I thought I was going to die.

Ro was already awake and moving around. In my room. Her luscious little body probably still warm from my bed. *Mmm.*

My bed still warm from that luscious little body. *Yum.*

"How out of line would it be if I started jacking off right now?" I asked her, half hopeful, half full of it.

"Good morning to you, too. And that's just rude. You *asked* me to sleep in here, you know."

"And now I'm asking to jack off. Seems perfectly polite to me. Asking you to give me a hand with it, now that might be a bit uncouth."

She snorted and walked out.

I got up, crawled into my own still warm from Ro—*yum*—bed, buried my face in my pillow that smelled like her, and had at it.

I started cursing myself almost the moment I was done. Now I'd have to change my sheets right away, erasing all traces of her.

That's about the time Ro delivered my morning

cappuccino.

I sat up, straightening the covers just so, hiding the evidence, kind of.

She stared at me, then the bed, then me, then handed me the coffee, no expression on her face. "Should I be worried or offended about whatever you're doing here?"

"You should be both. Also, you should have shown up five minutes earlier."

"Change the sheets, cupcake," she told me as she walked to the door.

"You're sadistic," I called back.

"Perish the thought."

I tried to hide from our visitors in Ro's office again, but that didn't last two hours before my dad found me.

I was sharing Ro's desk with her rather than finding a reasonable solution just because it irked her and got her to pay more attention to me in general.

I'd pulled a chair up across from her, plopped my laptop down and did nothing but play footsies with her for at least a half an hour.

She'd resorted to kicking me rather viciously when I said, "Stop that or I'm going down there to nibble on your toes."

"Procrastinating podophile," she muttered, eyes on her computer screen.

I was deeply offended until I realized what she'd actually said. "How do you even know what that is, and what it's called? And no, I don't actually have a foot fetish, though I could make an exception for your tiny little bitty, high-arched, princess feet."

"This is you trying to prove that you *don't* have a foot fetish?" That sassy raised brow. "Waxing poetic about my arches?"

I held her eyes. "To be perfectly honest, at this point what I think I have is a Devereux Laurent fetish."

She blushed and looked away.

My erection tried its best to go for the gold and raise her desk off the floor. It certainly put in an honorable mention. "Say something mean to me," I told her gruffly. "Tell me you don't want me again."

"It's simple: You've built me up into a challenge in your mind because I said no and you're not used to hearing the word. That's all this perverse infatuation you've cultivated for me is."

I respected the effort of her little speech, but she was so far off that it did nothing to help me. "I don't need a challenge. I've never been that guy. I'm enough of a challenge to *myself* that I've never had to seek outside help to meet that particular need. Try again."

"You're not attractive. No one thinks you're pretty."

I laughed. "Now I know you're lying. Try again."

"You're tacky and I hate you." Perfect deadpan delivery.

"Nope. That did the opposite of what I needed. Try another."

"We both know it's not going to work. I think your love language is insults."

"Say something nice then."

"I actually think you're a good person."

I almost came on the spot. There went *that* theory.

I was actually kind of working—only occasionally distracting myself by touching the tip of my finger to her nose when she wasn't looking then snatching my hand back before she could smack it—when my dad interrupted us.

"I need a word, son," he said from the doorway behind me.

He already sounded out of sorts, and I hadn't even insulted him once today. Yet.

"Secretary, go get me a coffee," he had the nerve to say.

Ro didn't even look up.

I swiveled in my chair and looked at him. I opened my mouth to say something, I don't even know what, but it would have been deeply unpleasant.

Ro beat me to it, her tone sublimely unconcerned. "Get your own coffee, sunshine."

My dad stood there and fumed for a beat. "You going to let her talk to me like that?" he asked me.

I smiled pleasantly. "Encourage it, even."

"At least give us some privacy so the men can speak here, doll."

At that she did look up at him, raising a brow. "This is *my* office. Have your privacy somewhere else, *doll*."

I was trying not to smile as I told my dad, "Go wait in *my* office. I'll be there in a minute."

I turned back to her. We studied each other, her gaze curious, mine fond.

"Why do you put up with him?" she asked.

Question of my life, that. "I don't even know. I guess because he's my only family, and I don't know how to cut people off, particularly when they're that persistent. If he visited more than once a year, I suppose I'd be more motivated, but probably not even then. He's an ass, but I'm all he's got."

"Softie," she told me affectionately.

She'd walked right into it. "I have definitive proof to the contrary," I drawled, "if you'd care to see it."

Her eyes smiled more than her mouth did, crinkling at me while she pursed her lips to restrain an outright grin.

I tore myself away from those eyes to go see what my unwelcome, dissolute father wanted.

The second I walked in the door he started in on me, launching a pitch for his latest scheme. I sat down and let him go on for quite a while. He liked to talk.

When a half hour went by and he showed no signs of

letting up, I held up a hand. "Let's cut to the chase," I said with a sigh. "Are you asking me for money again?"

That set him off into a tirade about my lack of business sense and how I had no idea how to sniff out a good investment.

"I'm not the one asking for money here," I slid the words in when he had to pause for air. "How much is it this time?"

"You don't have to say it like that. Like you're doing me some huge favor."

"To be clear, I am. If these so called investments ever pay off for you, I've certainly never seen my fair share of it."

"I thought you were doing well. What do *you* need the money for?"

"That's not remotely related to what I said. You're calling this an investment. I'm taking exception to your wording. If you need money from me, just tell me how much."

"Just fifty k. If you're doing so well, you won't even notice."

I wouldn't notice, not in my bank account anyway. What I did notice was that he couldn't stop being an asshole even in the time it took him to ask for money. I sighed. I *was* a softie. "Fine, but this is your birthday *and* Christmas gift for the year. You aren't getting so much as a card after this."

He was, at least, in a better mood after that. And he did leave me alone, pausing briefly at the door to say, "You-you're a good boy. Thanks, son."

Ro came in almost on the tail of him walking out. She just stared at me, and I could tell she'd heard at least some of our dysfunctional interaction.

Finally she spoke, "You big softie." Each word held its own little universe of delicious affection. I could have soaked in it for hours. Days. Years.

And also, she fucking walked into it again. "*Something* is big on me but, full disclosure, it's not soft."

She left to run errands, and I stayed home to stay on track for the day's word count goals, so I didn't see her again for quite some time.

Unfortunately, I did see Ida and my father, together and separately, quite a few times. They just kept popping into my office and annoying the hell out of me with various complaints and demands.

I took my daily swim and Ida was there in a white thong bikini, perched on the edge of the pool, her feet and calves dipped in, while she called out encouragement for my laps like I was doing something impressive.

Even with how obvious she was being it took me a while to realize she was flirting like she thought we might rekindle some old flame. Yikes.

"Do you need money, too?" I asked her suspiciously at one point when she just wouldn't leave.

She looked surprised but not for the reasons one might think. "Too? Carson asked you for money? He didn't even tell me! I'll make him pay for trying to hide money from me again." With a huff, she left.

Well, that did the trick.

And my dad kept seeking me out to give me 'advice.' He was waffling between trying to get me to fire Ro to speculating about how he might go about seducing her.

He was such an unrepentant piece of shit I could hardly take it sometimes.

And Ro was still gone. I kept texting her complaints about the company I was being forced to keep, but she didn't respond.

By 5 p.m., I started drinking copiously—the good Scotch.

I'd had enough of my dad and Ida for the *year,* but somehow that didn't make them disappear.

I drank until I was fuzzy-headed, decided that was a good development, then drank until I was whistling, then dancing and singing.

That was when Ro found me.

My mood brightened considerably.

I was still hanging out in my office, though I'd stopped being productive quite some time ago.

She took a seat on my sofa and studied me like I was being particularly interesting. "Aren't you the belle of the ball?" she asked sardonically.

She studied me some more.

I just knew she was thinking up new insults for me.

I sat down.

She was such a sassy piece.

"I am," she agreed.

Oops, I'd said that out loud.

"It's far from the worst thing you've said out loud today."

Oops, that too.

"Why were you gone so long? What were you doing?" I asked her. Against my will it came out as a drunken whine.

"Avoiding your father, obviously."

"If he bothers you, I'll rearrange his face," I told her confidently. I'd gotten into several memorable physical altercations with my asshole dad, and I'd been winning them since I was seventeen. The ones before that, well, I figured they didn't count. My dad figured otherwise, because when we got to grandstanding, those were the only victories he could boast about, when it came to me. "And if he touches you, so much as your fucking pinkie, he's going to wake up in a hospital." The words were a drunken slur, but I meant them down to my soul.

"I can handle myself," she said softly, shooting me a look that, even drunk, I could see the affection in.

She changed the subject. "Did you meet your word count goal today?" she asked.

"What will you give me if I did?"

"I'll let you sleep in your bed with me tonight."

I stared and I couldn't tell if what she'd said was making me feel more sober or more drunk. One thing was for sure, it was making me more deranged by the second. "Excuse me?"

"Just sleeping, to be clear. But the bed is huge, and I saw your legs hanging off that sofa last night. I felt bad. Since you won't switch, we'll share."

"I can't tell if you're just messing with me."

"Of course I'm messing with you, but not just. I meant what I said. Did you meet your goal?"

"I did," I said smugly.

"There will be a pillow between us at all times."

"I can work with that."

"You're not supposed to be *working* anything here."

I ignored that. "Wow," I was a bit shell-shocked. "Sharing a bed. Is it going to be too much excitement for your virgin sensibilities?"

She leaned her head against the back of the sofa and started to snore.

I knew it would only encourage her, but I couldn't hold back my laugh.

I tried to sober up after that. I didn't want to miss one minute of this.

I started to make myself a cup of coffee, but Ro shooed me away and took over.

"Where are my dad and Ida?" I asked her. They'd been pleasantly absent from bothering me for longer than the usual stretch.

"I booked them a nice restaurant reservation and a show on the strip to give you a break."

"You complete me."

"Like fire and gasoline."

"That's it. Let's start planning the wedding."

"Marriage isn't a joke."

"Sure it is."

We were looking at each other, identical expressions on our face in spite of the fact that I was less than sober. She handed me a cup of coffee, and I drank it dutifully.

I might have drifted off briefly. I woke with a start, not wanting to miss a thing.

I blinked a few times, and she was suddenly at my side, tugging on my arm.

"C'mon. Up and at 'em. I can't carry you."

"Carry me where?"

"To bed."

My body followed her without needing any permission from my brain.

CHAPTER EIGHTEEN

As soon as we got into my room I threw myself on the bed, reaching my limbs out to take up as much room as possible. "How huge is the bed *now*?"

The sound of her muffled laugh was music to my ears.

She took care of me in much the same way I'd handled her when she was drunk, with patient attention.

I kept my eyes closed and let her tuck me in.

Silence reigned for a time and when she spoke it made my breath catch in my throat.

"You're not him," she said with quiet vehemence. "You're nothing like your father."

I felt a little lost, my mind warring with how what she said made me feel, how deep and fundamental of a cut it was to have her talk to me like that. Like she cared about me. Like she believed in me. "Why are you telling me this?" I asked her.

"Because I think he has you convinced that you're the same, and you're not."

I looked at her and our eyes locked, me lying down, her sitting at my hip, leaning slightly over me, and we shared a moment of almost painful intimacy.

Of course I ruined it. "Is it uncivilized for me to ask you how soon you'd like to be fucked into the mattress?"

She took that better than I'd expected. "Impossible sex fiend," she said lightly and walked away.

She was settling down on the other side of the bed when I asked, "Are you really not the least bit attracted to me?"

"Not even a little bit. You're hideous."

"I don't believe you."

"You wouldn't."

"Prove it."

"Excuse me?"

"Let me kiss you."

"Excuse me?" she sounded genuinely shocked. Me talking about sex didn't faze her but a kiss gave her pause. She understood me too well.

"I will not excuse you. Just one kiss."

"Excuse me?" she repeated.

"Just let me kiss you once, and then tell me you don't want me. Then I can actually believe you and move on from this obsession. You can touch me too, though you don't have to. You call the shots. Let me kiss you once, and you get to decide what comes next."

"No sex," she said, like it was an absolute.

"Whatever," I said dismissively, like I wasn't even perfectly consumed with wanting that. "There's plenty to do before you ever get to sex. Things I'm particularly good at." I came up on an elbow and wagged my eyebrows at her.

"Only one kiss. Nothing else."

"Whoa, whoa, whoa, don't be so hasty. A least let me kiss you before you go making big decisions like that."

"You're drunk. We can't go there when one of us is drunk.

That's one of your rules, right?"

"You're getting that all mixed up. *I* can be drunk."

"Because you're a man?"

"Because I'm me. Because I consented before I was drunk. Because I'm always willing where you're concerned. Everything's on the table for me when it comes to you. Carte blanche."

Like she hadn't heard one word I'd just said, she just reiterated stubbornly, "One kiss. And *I* will do the kissing. You have to lie there and just *take it.*"

I felt a bit unhinged by that, but what I said was, "Whatever you like, cupcake."

I held my breath as she got up from her side of the bed, came to mine, and sat again at my hip.

She put her hands on both of my shoulders and bent down. Her silky dark hair was down, a rare sight, and it trailed onto my chest.

Our eyes were locked when she said softly, "Close your eyes, Thorn."

I obeyed, but not quietly. "Don't call me that," I began, "I'm not your bro—"

Her pillowy soft lips pressed to mine, and I went silent and very, very still.

Her mouth explored mine like the touch of curious fingers. Her tongue darted out to lick like she was memorizing, teasing me relentlessly before pushing inside. I gave instantly and let her in with open arms, our tongues twining together like long lost lovers.

She kissed with tender focus. Like she'd never done it before but had perfected it through sheer talent, unbridled sensuality, and perfect instinct.

Like she'd just discovered kissing and was ravenous for it. Like she'd just discovered everything.

It didn't speak well of me, but it was true nonetheless: I

couldn't remember the last time I'd kissed someone on the mouth, lips to lips. My foreplay tended to consist of my mouth going somewhere else pretty quickly and no one had ever complained about that.

It spoke very well of her that my thoughts veered so far into outer space that I had the distinct thought: *I never want to kiss anyone else after this, not ever again.*

Madness incarnate.

She pulled her tongue away, and I fought her a bit to keep it. She bit my bottom lip, I groaned, and she delved back in, kissing me with perfect passion and rare, innocent artistry.

I was lost.

Without permission from my brain, I found my arms pulling her on top of me, lining our bodies up so she was straddling me, my hands gripping hard, stroking her butt, humping my impossible, unstoppable erection against the addictive heat of her in restless, desperate motions.

I wanted to climb inside of her.

I wanted to consume her whole.

I moved my hand between us, sliding my fingers into her loose shorts to graze her sex.

I felt her, hot and wet, for one brief moment before she pulled back, stood up, and walked away unsteadily. The effort not to trap her close but to let her go made my body tremble, head to toe.

She went into my bathroom for a long time, and I was able to calm my body through sheer force of will.

I didn't want to scare her off. I was scared enough for the both of us.

She came out and turned off all the lights.

"I'm not drunk anymore," I said roughly to her. "Get back here."

"I will not."

"Let me eat you out. It's a kiss, too. Just farther south."

"Down, boy."

"Why won't you marry me again?"

"Because you're too sentimental and romantic, obviously."

She settled on her side of the bed now, a pillow set between us as a barricade.

"Say it," I told her in deadly earnest. "I need you to say the words. Before this gets out of hand."

"I don't want you. Now go to sleep, you horny bastard."

I reached a hand across the barrier between us. She understood and took it.

I held her hand on top of the pillow and she let me. "Will you say that to me again but in your sexy phone voice?"

She actually did it, the diabolical imp, pitching her voice just so, "Go to sleep, you horny bastard."

"The other part, too."

"I don't want you. You're not gorgeous or hunky at all. I'd throw rocks at you if I saw you in the street."

I purred. "Don't stop. Keep going."

"You're lucky I don't kick you out of this bed."

I'd never been so charmed or turned on in my entire life.

CHAPTER NINETEEN

She was already gone when I woke up the next morning.

I didn't even bother to get dressed before I sought her out.

She was in her office, working away like nothing was amiss.

"Morning," said Ro briskly. "Go put on a shirt, and I'll get your cappuccino."

I'd had my mouth open to say something else entirely but that distracted me. "You're making a *shirt* the condition of my morning coffee now?"

"I'm trying to. Is it working?"

"Not at all. You couldn't pay me to put a shirt on now."

"Could I bribe you?"

"It would have to be a better bribe than a cappuccino."

"I'll sleep in your bed again tonight."

I was already heading back to my room when I called out, "Deal!"

I was dressed and working in her office, perfect cappuccino in hand, when I brought it up.

"Should we talk about what happened last night?" I asked tentatively.

She didn't hesitate. "No. We should never talk about, or so much as refer to it, again."

"It won't just go away."

"Sure it will."

I tried to drop it, I really did.

My thoughts were just too all-consuming and intrusive to let me.

"I want to touch you," I told her, voice low and husky.

"Stop that. Don't use that tone on me."

"What tone?" I asked innocently.

"Your seductive tone. I know what you're trying to do. It won't work on me."

"Is my seductive tone as bad as your phone sex voice?"

"How should I know? And I don't have a phone sex voice."

I tried again. "You don't even have to touch me." My voice was low, guttural. "I'll do all the touching, all the pleasuring. I just need to put my hands on you." I paused. "My fingers inside of you. And I want to taste you. I want to feel you come *humming* against my tongue."

"That escalated quickly."

"I'm not talking about sex," I continued, unfazed.

"Really," she said sarcastically.

"Certainly not right away. Just my hands and mouth and your body. You don't have to get me off."

She sent me a glance that was distinctly uncomfortable. "I'm not sure I understand. What would you even get out of that?"

I'd get to touch you, I almost said, but thought better of it.

It was bad enough that I knew how desperate I'd become

for her, I certainly didn't need to share the knowledge.

I just stared at her intensely.

"I don't understand you at all," she remarked.

"Let's get to understand each other better, then. With my tongue on your clit."

"Stop that, you incorrigible ass."

"Then tell me you don't want me. Tell me you don't want my hands on your body. Tell me you don't want my lips all over you. I need to hear it again."

She opened her mouth, and I waited for the words I needed, the obligatory rejection she would deliver just how I required. Instead she said, "Fine."

"Fine? Fine what?"

"Fine, put your hands on me. No sex."

My brain short-circuited. I stared. "Do you mean it?"

"It's debatable."

Exhilaration resonated through me. She meant it. "Let's go to bed," I said thickly. "Right now."

"I'm not going anywhere near your sex room. Not ever."

"Yeah. Fine. Of course. We can use your room, if you want." I thought she might prefer that over my wicked, wicked bed—which was precisely and perversely where I wanted her.

"No. Yours."

Yes, please, I thought. What I said was, "Mine?"

She nodded.

"Fine. Mine. But... why would you prefer my room?" The way she had said it made me curious, like there was a punchline in there somewhere.

The steel rod in my pants was throbbing in time to the beat of her wiseass cracks.

"So I can leave when I'm done with you. That way you won't get all clingy or try to sleep over. I'm not a cuddler, but I'm guessing you *are*."

"Stop that," I told her, feeling absurdly fond. "Stop being so adorable. I'm already hard. Now let's go to bed."

I stood. She didn't. I raised a brow.

She shook her head. "Not right now. Tonight."

I sat heavily and considered having an outright tantrum.

"That was cruel," I told her solemnly. "You're a terrible woman."

She ignored me, focused on her computer like we hadn't just had an earth-shaking conversation.

"At least let me see you naked," I tried. "To tide me over."

"Nope."

"You're no fun."

"*Liar,*" she said softly and like she could see into my very soul. "You have so much fun with me."

"Tease."

"Horndog."

"Ballbuster."

"Wanton."

"Can I just see a nipple?"

That got her eyes off the computer. "Just one?" she asked with heavy amusement.

"I'll take anything."

"Show me your dick."

My brain stopped working for a bit there. "Excuse me?"

"You heard me, cupcake. Take out your cock, and I'll show you a nipple."

"That wasn't part of the plan. We were going to pretend my hard-on doesn't exist while I get *you* off, remember?"

"Are you going to whip it out or not, Thorn?"

"Don't call me that," I said, but I was already moving to lock the door.

I went and stood by her shoulder where she sat at her desk.

She turned slightly, looking up at me. She appeared so

unruffled in that moment that all I wanted to do, the purpose of my whole existence, was to *ruffle* her.

I cupped the back of her head. Her lips were inches and a few layers of fabric away… It was a heady experience.

"Hey, now, that wasn't part of the deal," said Ro.

I chuckled. "I wasn't doing that. I was just…"

"What you *weren't* doing was taking your dick out."

"Is your sole purpose in life just to surprise me with the crazy shit that comes out of your mouth?" I asked her with concentrated, abject affection.

"You're one to talk."

"You really want this?"

"What was your first clue?" she asked wryly. "I've been so subtle."

"Why?"

"Why have I been so subtle?"

"Why do you want me to take it out? Do you have any plans… after it's out?"

"Nope. Not one. I'm just curious. Is that all right with you?"

"Anything you want is all right with me. If you asked me bury my face in your ass while you read my Wikipedia page out loud, I would do it."

"Very specific. How about we stick to the basics?"

"I can do that. Do you want to take it out yourself, or should I do it?"

"You do it," she said it like it was a dare.

I took her hair down.

"No one said my hair was on the table," she told me.

I pulled my shirt off.

"No one told you to take off your shirt," said Ro.

I grinned. She loved it. Her eyes were eating my abs in adoring little bites.

I didn't draw it out for another second, pulling the loose

waistband of my athletic shorts and boxer briefs out and down and showing her what she wanted.

She stared. It was gratifying when her breath started to pant in and out of her in short bursts.

My breath was just as unsteady.

She didn't ask, but I stroked it for her.

"You're big," she said blankly.

"How do you know? How many dicks have you seen, virgin?"

"And so thick," she added, ignoring my questions.

She leaned forward just a fraction and came around to answering, "And if ten inches isn't big, we're living in an alternate universe. That's how I know. Math."

"Nine and a half. And if you breathe on it, I'm going to come. This is fair warning. You have me so primed it won't take much."

She leaned forward just far enough and *breathed*.

I shut my eyes, fighting for control. "Okay, maybe it's ten now. Just for you. You really do have a mean streak. You wicked, little harridan."

"Come, then. I want to see it."

"Where?" My voice was unsteady. "Where do you want me to come?"

"Where would you suggest?"

"I'm not picky. This is ladies' choice right here. Tell me what would freak you out the least. I don't want to scare you off."

"I guess it will be a mess?"

"Yes," I said succinctly. I was really feeling out of control, just beastly. "Where would you like the mess?"

"I don't know," she said like she'd honestly never considered it before. "I guess I just want you to look at me while you do it and come wherever you want to."

"God, *don't say that*. You're not ready to say a thing like that to me."

"What came to mind?" She licked her lips. "What did you think of just now, when you said that? I want to know. Where do you want to come the most?"

"You're about to make me come just from talking. I'm not exaggerating here."

"Do it, then." The dare was back in her voice. "But first tell me where you want to come the most."

Right as she said it she breathed on me again.

That was it. I cupped the back of her head, angled my tip and pressed it against her soft as flower petals lips. Miracle of miracles, they opened. I pushed in the barest amount, not wanting to overwhelm her on the first try, and her eyes widened as she stared up at me. I bit my lip, our eyes meeting.

"Lick it," I told her thickly.

Her tongue caressed the underside of my head, and I came like it was my first fucking time letting a woman touch my dick.

I stroked her silky hair as she swallowed my cum. Our eyes were locked the whole time as she took it, got it all down in hard, struggling gulps.

It was glorious.

I didn't linger at it long, a little ashamed I'd gotten off before she did. It wasn't to my credit, that lack of control. I was better than that, but I'd clearly been at my limit.

I put my dick away but stayed poised above her, still stroking her hair with one hand, the other against her jaw, rubbing my thumb over her luscious lips.

"You even swallow," I said reverently.

"Was that not what I was supposed to do? Why else would you put it in my mouth?"

"What a sensible woman. A real keeper. And yes, that is *exactly* what you're supposed to do. Marry me. And it's your cunt."

Now it was me catching her off guard. *Yum.* "Excuse me?" she asked.

She was very, very ruffled. It was intoxicating. "I'm answering your question. I want to come in your cunt the most. A little old-fashioned, I know. Balls deep, to be precise. I want my tip mashed up against your womb as my cum fills you to the brim. Now show me that nipple."

It didn't work out quite like that.

Eventually I maneuvered her into letting me sit on her chair. I had her straddle me as I fondled her big, soft tits.

Getting my hands on her, any part of her, had been something I'd thought about too much not to have specific plans, and for her breasts the plans were pretty exhaustive. I kissed her, hot drugging pulls while my palms memorized her glorious chest over her blouse and bra.

By the time I had her top off, I don't even think she noticed, her focus on our lips mating together addictively.

She pulled back when I unstrapped the back of her bra.

I was looking at it. It was black and lacy.

I shifted my hips. I was hard again, and I let her feel it right where it wanted to be.

I slid her bra off and stared. "Maybe I do believe in love. I think I'm in love with your tits."

"My prince charming."

I cupped her in both palms, she was more than a handful, and rubbed her nipples softly.

They were already hard nubs and beautifully, terrifically responsive.

Her reaction was one of shivering, delightful acquiescence.

I'd always assumed that seducing her would be largely cerebral. That enticing her with words was the way to her heart and between her legs, just going by how clever she was.

I'd pegged her all wrong, and I couldn't have been more

delighted.

She was a closet sensualist. She was putty under my hands.

I felt high on the power of it.

And then I put my mouth to her, licking and sucking at her nipples, and out came that gorgeous phone sex voice of hers.

"Oh God," she said. "That feels so good. Don't stop. More. More."

God damn, she was a talker. I never would have guessed.

And nothing could have driven me madder.

I was moving my hips as I sucked, dry humping as I nuzzled, rubbing, kneading, fondling her soft flesh, wallowing in it.

I pulled back and stared. Her light pink nipples were darker now and wet from being sucked on. I tugged lightly at them in tandem, then harder. I pushed them together and started sucking again, paying carefully equal attention to both.

"You're my favorite," I murmured to the left one, then, "You're *really* my favorite, don't tell your sister," to the right one.

"You're such a weirdo."

"What does that make you?"

"Dement—"

We both went still and quiet as someone tried the doorknob, found it locked, and started knocking impatiently.

"Turner?" my father's voice called, loud and impatient. "Are you in there? Secretary, where is Turner?"

We stared at each other. I'd never wanted to strangle my father more, and that was *really* saying something.

"Go wait in my office!" I shouted at him. "I'll be there in a minute."

Ro and I just stared at each other. I started fondling her again, tilting my head back, inviting her to kiss me.

She shook her head at me. "I need to get back to work, and you need to deal with your father."

I scowled. "I don't want to," I said petulantly.

"Let me get back to work, and I might let you see a nipple again tonight."

I nodded at her breasts, still weighing them lovingly with my hands, "Put the heavy hitters away and I might."

"You put them away. You're the one that got them out."

"You could turn anything into a challenge. And I'm not sure I have the heart to cover them up. I just got them. It's too soon."

"One more kiss," she told me softly, "And then you have to put them away."

She pressed her lips to mine, and I forgot everything in the world until she was finished with me.

"Turner," she told me, trying not to laugh. "You need to let them go. They're not your toys."

"You're perfect," I murmured to one big, perky breast as I put it away. "Don't mind her," I told the other. "She's just jealous."

"Stop that! I can't even tell if you're pitting them against each other or turning them both against *me*," said my Ro, giggling. *Giggling*.

I was in heaven. This was going to be *so* much fun.

CHAPTER TWENTY

My father didn't even have anything much to say, he was just back on his usual complaints about Ida and Ro and all females in general.

I was in no mood to indulge him after what he'd interrupted. In fact, I was still working through the urge to bash him over the head with my laptop.

"I need to get back to work," I told him firmly. "I assume you guys are taking off today."

"Tomorrow maybe," my dad said like he hadn't made up his mind yet, like he might stay even longer.

The only reason I didn't tell him outright that he had to leave now was that I wasn't sure I could talk Ro into sleeping in my bed once he was gone. I really could see her leaving my bed to sleep in her own after a hookup.

Ro walked into my office with a smile and I could tell she was up to something. "I booked you and Ida a couple's massage at a very nice spa," she told Carson cheerfully, "but you need to leave fast to make it on time."

He glared at her but asked, "Where *is* it? I like the spa at Aria."

"I sent Ida all the information. She's already heading to the car. She's says she's leaving you behind if you don't hurry."

And just like that she got rid of both of my headaches for the day.

"That was beautiful," I said. "Please tell me there's no appointment and you were just pranking them both.

"I thought about that, but then they'd just come back faster. As it stands they'll be gone at least five hours just with the treatments I booked. Longer if they use the rest of the facilities."

"Trying to get me alone?"

"You wish. Trying to have a productive workday, more like."

"Are you really going to make me countdown the hours? You realize this is torture?"

She was merciless. "Get over it. I'm leaving to run some errands."

She left, and I followed her. "What errands?" I asked, nearly touching her, I was walking so close on her heels, looming over her.

"Your publisher is throwing you a party on your release day. I'm going to check out a few of the venues they're considering to tell them if you'll approve."

"Isn't this something *I* need to go with you for?"

"Not really. I'll know what you'd prefer the second I see it, trust me."

"There's no way that's true, and even if it was, I want to see for myself. And I'm driving."

"Control freak."

"Cock-teasing diva."

"You'll still need to reach your word count for the day or I won't sleep with you."

"Do you even hear yourself?"

"I do. You've had a decidedly corrupting influence on me. Are you happy?"

I was. I really was. In fact, I couldn't remember ever being happier.

All of the venues were in casinos on the strip, and I couldn't resist slowing down dramatically in front of something completely unrelated that we were passing by.

She saw where I was going and made sure I saw her roll her eyes.

I pushed it even farther, turning, pulling up to and parking at the little white chapel.

We stared at each other. I grinned. "Marry me, and I'll give you a raise."

"You sure would. Getting half in the divorce would certainly be a raise.

"That's cynical." I paused for effect. "Wives usually take more than half. And divorce isn't a joke, you know."

"Sure it is."

She was right as usual, about the venues. She didn't even have to ask me after we got a tour of the space we were shown in the Cavendish casino.

"This one," she said, and she was right.

It was a lovely modern space that was basically a large multi-level suite with floor to ceiling windows and views of the strip. None of the other venues had even come close to comparing.

She was so smug about it that I wanted to bite her. In fact, I did.

I backed her slowly to the wall right there, boxing her in with my arms.

She looked unfazed. "We don't have time for whatever *this* is," she said, unruffled.

I bit her lower lip, licked it, and started kissing her.

We weren't even alone. The person showing us the room was getting quite the show. I couldn't make myself care.

The only thing that made me stop was Ro herself pushing me away.

"Move it along, nympho," she told me and walked away.

As an insult, it lacked heat. And she was very, very ruffled.

"Any other errands we need to run?" I told her as we walked back to the valet.

"That was it for today."

We were passing by Frankie's famous tattoo parlor, and I pointed at it. "What would I have to do to get you to have my name tattooed on your ass?"

"Are you reciprocating?"

"Of course. I'm not an animal."

"You'd have to get my full name. Just getting Ro is a copout."

I could tell she was messing with me, just being outrageous to see who broke first. She'd come to the right place, or the wrong one depending how you wanted to look at it. "Devereux spelled out on my ass. Deal. And you have to get Turner, written in letters with thorns all over them."

"Deal," she said instantly, with relish. "You get yours first."

"You're evil. Truly."

"You think I'd *trick* you?" she asked, pointing at herself and making a mock innocent face.

"I should do it just so you'll feel guilty about it later. I'm not above a pity fuck."

"Call Frankie," she said casually. Like she was positive it was all one big joke, and I'd never follow through. "Make the appointment. She's booked out for years, but I bet she'll fit you in for an ass tattoo in one hot minute."

"It would be a funny episode for the show," I mused. I stopped, took out my phone, and called her.

That was when Ro started to look at me like she wasn't quite sure if I was joking anymore. A bit ruffled.

I would have kept going just for that.

Frankie answered, and I told her the plan.

She was beyond excited.

"Have you been drinking?" she asked suspiciously.

"I'm dead sober. Can you fit me in right this second?"

"Are you serious? The camera crew is here. It's not convenient, but your name recognition and what you're asking for will be impossible for my producers to turn down, so I'll make it work if you're serious, which I'm pretty sure you're not." She paused. "You're just messing with Ro, aren't you?"

"Well, yes. But I'm still going to do it."

A small hand took the phone away from me. "He's just messing with me," Ro said into the phone tonelessly. "Sorry, he's got issues. Yeah. See you later."

She hung up and gave me a look that made me feel genuinely bad although I wasn't even sure what I was supposed to be feeling bad for, exactly. "You were going to do it." It was an accusation.

"Well, yeah. I said I was."

"You don't even have that many tattoos, and you were going to put my name on your ass permanently."

I smirked. When she put it that way it was even funnier. "So?"

"So, how are you okay with that? Why is there nothing *on this earth* that you take seriously? How can you not mind wearing around a permanent reminder of a joke you pushed too far?

"I don't really know. I just didn't. I didn't mind at all. I like jokes and reminders of jokes. I thought it was hilarious and kind of a cute idea.

She was genuinely upset. "Let's go home," she said shortly.

She started walking and I followed her.

"How are you not *covered* in tattoos?" she muttered.

"I don't like many people enough to mark my ass with their name. No one but you, if I'm honest."

"Just stop." She was very upset. I hadn't seen her like this before, wasn't sure what to do with it. "There has to be a *limit* to *all* bullshit, even yours."

"I can't decide if you're over or underestimating me there, but I meant what I said."

She didn't say another word for the entire trip home.

It was a herculean effort on my part, but I kept silent as well. Everything that came out of my mouth just seemed to be pissing her off since the tattoo idea, and I didn't want to completely blow all of my chances for the night ahead.

I parked my car in front of my house and looked at her until she returned my stare. "Are we good? Are you still mad at me?"

It took her a long time to answer, and when she did it was like she'd been holding in a floodgate. "You need to be able to take something seriously, to hold *something* sacred, to care about *something*. Don't you see you've got to care about something? Otherwise how can anyone ever trust or believe in you?"

I was undeniably dense about things like this, but even I was starting to see that this was about more than the tattoo.

Still, I wanted to make a crack. For once, I didn't. I was too wary of her in this mood.

She wasn't done. "You would have gotten the tattoo on a lark. Tell me, would you carry the marry me bit that far? Is even that *utterly meaningless* to you?"

I knew I was in trouble because I chose my words carefully. And I wasn't completely honest. "What, are you offended on behalf of the institution of marriage?" I tried, saw her face, then tried again. "It was just a joke. Marriage is not meaningless to me. I won't joke about it anymore if it makes you uncomfortable."

"That's not the point. You can joke about anything with me, but sometimes you need to see where the joke ends. Does that make sense to you?"

I studied her, wondering if I should tell the truth.

"Tell me that makes sense to you," she said, this time making it an order.

I obliged now that she'd made it clear what she wanted from me. Lip service I could do. "That makes sense to me."

Thank God she dropped it after that.

I got my word count in that day. Of course I did. I'd never been so motivated in my life.

And even so, she didn't even try to make it easy on me, the pint-sized despot.

I was in my own office, being responsible, staying on task, when she brought me an afternoon shot of espresso.

"You're an angel," I told her, taking it. "A saint."

But she wasn't done. Without a word, she moved behind my desk, behind *me*.

She bit my earlobe very softly.

I rocked back, letting my broad shoulders brush into her, getting nice full contact with her pillowy tits against my back. I made a noise that sounded suspiciously like a purr. It was the briefest contact, but it felt impossibly illicit.

The barest foreplay with Ro was more satisfying than completion with anyone else.

But she was in an ornery mood, and I suffered for it.

"I've changed my mind," she spoke with her phone sex voice into my ear.

My heart plummeted. "You can't do that. That's mean."

"I'm talking about your word count, you big baby. It's doubled for the day if you want me in your bed tonight."

"You're mad with power. Tripping on it like a petty tyrant." A thought struck. "Hey! *You're* the tyrant! How can you live with yourself?"

She laughed and moved away.

"I hate you," I said to her retreating back.

"Liar," she said, sublimely unconcerned. "I'm all that's keeping you going at this point. You can't live without me."

I hoped that she was joking, that she didn't know that was becoming painfully close to the truth.

CHAPTER TWENTY-ONE

It was a long day, for obvious reasons. And for all of the torture it was still quite fun. Ro in a nutshell.

It was nearing dinnertime before I realized that my dad and Ida weren't back yet.

I was still writing, doubling my word count had me on the ropes, when Ro walked past my office and I called her in. "Any idea where my dad and Ida are? Are they *still* at the spa?"

She smiled conspiratorially at me, and I knew whatever she was about to say was designed to make me smile. In fact, I was already smiling before she said it. "I made them more reservations on the strip to keep them out of your hair tonight."

I stared at her with that absurd fondness that was starting to feel alarming as it moved my face into the now familiar lines. "Are you absolutely positive," I said softly, "that I can't tattoo your name on my ass?"

As she was walking away cursing me, I called out after her,

"Too soon?"

We had dinner together in the breakfast nook attached to my kitchen. This had become a habit. We took almost all our meals together. She sat on the bench seat near the window and I sat in a chair facing her. I wanted to be closer, but I loved watching every one of her expressions the most.

We were having roast chicken and vegetables that my housekeeper had left in a crockpot for us after she was done cleaning. Ro had made friends with her, and now she left us dinner at least four times a week. The Ro effect. Everything just fell in line around her. Including me, apparently. I had met the impossible word count she'd assigned me for the day.

"Word count for sexual favors," I mused. "Not what I was expecting from you, but apparently it works."

"Eat your food," she told me blandly.

"If I clean my plate and finish before you, can I eat *you* out under the table?"

"Stop it."

"That's not a no."

"You're impossible."

"*Me*? In the impossible Olympics, you'd get the gold, cupcake."

I stood, came around the table, and slid next to her on the bench seat.

"What are—" she began before I kissed her.

She let me, softening almost instantly under my lips, giving way to me like we'd done it a thousand times instead of a handful. She was a natural.

While she was distracted, I inched her skirt up and started playing with her through her panties, rubbing my fingers over he clit with a light touch.

She shivered head to toe. It was delightful.

I pulled back from the kiss to speak, my lips still pressed to hers, "You're so responsive. That's just what I love. We're so compatible. I want to play your body like a musical instrument. I want it to dance to my tune. I didn't *only* learn to play the violin. I also became proficient at working this little bundle of nerves right here." As I spoke I was showing her just what I meant, pushing my hand inside her panties and pinching over the swollen nub very, very softly and then rubbing it between two fingers, stroking her off with the most delicate touch.

It was utterly gratifying to watch what that did to her. I made her fall apart with breathtaking speed.

Considering her inexperience, I was rather impressed with us both.

"See?" I asked her between desperate kisses. "I know exactly what you need. And this is just my hand. I'm even better with my tongue."

"I don't believe you," she was panting, kissing me, losing her mind, "nothing could be better than that."

I pulled back to preen at her. "I told you you'd like it." I palmed her, pushing a finger carefully inside. "You're *sopping* wet," I moaned.

Her eyes were scrunched closed in the most adorable way, her face pained as she said in a miserable voice, "That's embarrassing."

"It shouldn't be. I love it. Nothing your body does under my care should embarrass you. Do you have any idea, could you even have a clue, how much I've fantasized, plotted, worked to get you like that?"

I took my finger out, sucked it clean, *the taste of her, finally,* and smoothed her skirt back into place. "Now, *for the love of God,* can we go to bed?"

"Drama queen," she muttered as she got up and started walking.

I was so obsessed with the fact that I was following her to my bed, to *at last* do wicked things to her there that I didn't even have a response for that bit of sass.

She noticed. "No comeback, cupcake?"

"I think lust has fried my brain. And it's your fault. Way to go, you vixen. At least we're even now."

"Even?" she asked, confused. "How so?"

"For a minute there I'd gotten off and you hadn't."

"Do you always keep score like that?"

"Yes, of course."

"Why?"

"It's only fair. Even bad sex is kind of good for men. Women are different. A more finely tuned device. An exquisitely made mechanism. A man needs to know what he's doing to make it good for her, and not many do. Or at the *very* least he has to want to and try his best. Nature is sexist, I know, but I'm trying my best to enthusiastically make up for the disparity."

"No wonder you have to kick them out of bed."

I wasn't touching that with a ten foot pole. I didn't want to talk about other women with Ro, didn't want to think about them, and I certainly, emphatically, did not want her thinking about me with them.

She was all brash confidence until we walked into the bedroom. There she became adorably shy.

I had just the thing.

I distracted her with soft, drugging kisses as I backed her to the bed. I pushed her down and climbed over her, still kissing. I took her hair down, burying my hands in it.

It was a joyous challenge to slowly strip her while I kept her too occupied to be self-conscious that I was getting her naked in my bed.

I got her topless first and paid proper tribute to her spectacular chest, sucking and pulling at her nipples, burying my face between them and pushing the soft globes to hug my head. I couldn't help it, I motor-boated her until she giggled delightfully.

I put an ear to her left breast. "What's that? You want me to fuck you and your sister? Well, if you insist."

"Stop that." More delicious giggles. "Don't talk to them, you weirdo."

"Do you want to know what I've named them?"

"I certainly don't."

"Mischief and Mayhem."

"You're not allowed to commandeer my unicorn name and pervert it."

"As we've established—I can pervert anything. And it's already done. Resign yourself to it. Mischief and Mayhem like their names. No takebacks."

"Which one is which?"

"If you can't figure that out I'm not telling you. It's between me and the girls."

She wasn't a bit nervous now, and I sucked hard on Mayhem while I stripped off her skirt and panties with expert speed.

She only realized she was completely naked when I was spreading her legs, fitting myself between them.

"Oh," she said, her hand touching the top of my head like she wasn't sure how it had gotten there.

I opened her gently with my hands, leaning down to her sex. She was shaking and gripping my hair as I parted her soft flesh and lightly touched her with my tongue. Her hips bucked under me, and I started to suck at her most sensitive flesh.

She screamed.

"God, your clit is sensitive," I murmured into her. "Let me try this."

I blew air on it.

Her response was gratifying. She was cursing and praying and thrashing about. I pinned her by the hips to the bed and worked her over with my mouth; my tongue, my lips, and just the lightest brush of teeth.

I didn't climb up her body until I'd made her come—loudly—three times.

I kissed her lips deeply, loving the taste of her, letting her taste herself with me.

I was lost in her, fingers working her now while I kissed her like the world was ending.

Her hand did not pass go, it went straight for my dick and squeezed.

I was fully dressed, this was about her, not me, but I let her stroke me over my clothes for a few beats before I pulled her hand away.

"Leave my cock out of this," I told her gruffly. "It's still your turn."

"Well, if it's my turn, I want to touch you. I want to see your body, to feel your skin. You've made me look at it often enough, *teased* me with it. Now let me *touch*." That whole speech was in her phone sex voice, and I no more could have turned her down then I could make my cock soft with her naked underneath me.

She didn't have to tell me twice. I stood up, stripped, then covered her, rubbing the fronts of our bodies together deliciously. I purred, and she got loud and bossy.

I ate it up like it was her responsive, virgin cunt.

She pushed me to my back and I complied. I wanted to see what she'd do more than *anything*.

I put my arms above my head and stared her down.

My hard-on was trying to leave my body and fight its way violently to her. "Do your worst, cupcake."

She sat up, moved to sit at my hip, and started tracing a finger over my abdomen.

I smirked, a pained one, but a smirk nonetheless. "I knew you were obsessed with my six-pack."

"Not as obsessed as *you*," she said, and now she was stroking both hands along my stomach and chest, rubbing me down like a happy dog that'd shown her its belly. "And it's an eight pack. I bet you do a thousand crunches a day just like Patrick Bateman, you psycho," she added.

"Insults and caresses at the same time. *Yum*. You get me."

"You contrary creature," she said affectionately, playing with my nipples now.

"Mmm. Insults are my love language, remember? You're the one that said that, and you're never wrong, if I recall."

"You're really going to talk the whole time, aren't you?" she asked me archly, moving up to her knees to kneel at my side.

I wasn't talking then, my eyes swallowing her in big, luscious bites.

She leaned over me with one hand on my shoulder and stroked my hair back, her substantial breasts dangling over me, so close but so far away from biting distance.

"Will you get on birth control?" I asked her. I honestly hadn't known that was going to come out of my mouth, and it almost ruined the mood.

She froze, staring at me.

One hand reached to grab her hip, to keep her from running away, probably. The other hand palming her tit was just reflex.

"Pretty please with as many orgasms as you can handle on top," I literally begged. "I haven't been with anyone in months, I just got a checkup and another clean bill of health and I'd give my left nut to be inside of you bare."

"I have not agreed to have sex with you." She even said it with a straight face.

"Does it feel silly to say that when we're naked in bed together, or does it just *sound* silly?"

"I reiterate, you're really going to talk the whole time,

huh?" She bent down and kissed me, her mind-boggling tits smooshing deliciously against my chest, her hips still held apart.

"You can touch me however you want," I breathed into her mouth. I reached a hand to rub her sex, pushing a finger inside. She was tight enough that her walls gripped even that, and my eyes nearly rolled back in my head.

One of her hands was busy clutching at my shoulder, holding herself up, but the other clever little hand began to move, to wander, feeling at my neck, my chest, my stomach, my hip—I sucked in a breath—then back up to knead at my chest again.

"Anywhere you want," I prompted her.

She snaked a hand back down my body and started rubbing again at my hip. If she was trying to drive me insane, it was brilliant.

She licked her lips, and with a groan, I licked them with her.

"You mean, mmmm," she almost hummed, "you want me to, mmmm… " She lost her train of thought as my finger began to move inside of her, thrusting shallowly in and out.

"Yes," I said, sucking her lower lip into my mouth then letting it go reluctantly, "whatever, however, whichever way you want. Explore me."

Her curiosity overcame her reservations—finally—and one hand slid down, at last getting to the point.

We both gasped as she finally filled her hand with me.

She pulled back and moved to kneel over my lap now.

I groaned. I watched her watching herself stroke me.

"It's, um," she began.

"It's what?" I prompted when she didn't finish. It was hard to even get that much out. I was fighting for control. I wanted to mount her on the spot and force her head down to suck my cock, both at the same time.

I found her with my hand again and pushed a finger back inside of her and moved it in a shallow, smooth imitation of the main course.

"It's nice," she finally said, her voice breaking on the words as I started finger fucking her in earnest.

"Nice?" I asked. Her hand had stopped moving, but her head was curved down far enough that I could feel her breathing on me.

As she came, squeezing my finger like it was a cock, I just about lost it.

Fuck it. I pulled my finger out and touched the back of her head, gripped her silky hair, and pushed her down. "Put me in your mouth," I said, not knowing if it was an order or a plea. Both probably.

"Velvety smooth but so hard it could break things," she finally got out.

"Were you searching for the right description this whole time?" I asked her affectionately even as sweat broke out over my entire body. "You're such a writer at heart."

I pushed her and arched my hips up, aiming until I was pressed against her lips.

She let me in, thank God. I got a little overzealous right off the bat, pushing deep enough to gag her in one go.

"Fuck, sorry," I said, sitting up and pulling her away by the hair. I liked the way that felt and pulled again just for fun then used it to bring her lips to mine. I kissed her as I dragged us both to the headboard.

I leaned back, still sitting up, and put her hand back on my dick, never letting her mouth leave mine the entire time.

When I finally let her up for air she asked, "Didn't you want me to… ?"

"Suck my dick? Always. But let's show you the ropes properly. A hand job first, I think. Go ahead, keep stroking."

"Is this right?" she asked, applying herself to the task with both hands.

"It is. You're such an overachiever," I told her admiringly. "I've never appreciated that quite so much as I do right this second. Right there, stroke the head."

"Am I squeezing too hard?"

"No. Just don't stop. Fuck. Don't fucking stop."

I paused. "Wait, stop."

"Contrary as ever," she pointed out.

"I changed my mind," I said, "You learned enough about hand jobs for the moment." I pushed her head down into my lap. I gripped her hair in both hands and showed her what to do.

She was no deep throater, but I thought she could come close with time. "You're a natural," I praised her, "With a little more practice you're going to excel, you ace student, you."

She tried to talk with my dick in her throat, the perfect little minx, and I almost laughed and came at the same time.

"Use your hands around my base. That's right. Stroke and suck. I know you swallow, but just a warning, I'm coming fast. *Yes*. You're so fucking good. God, you don't do anything half-assed, do you? Ah, fuck, marry me."

I came against the back of her throat, and she fucking took it. When she unlatched that flawless mouth from my cock after she'd swallowed, a few more drops of cum followed her and she bent down to lick it clean.

I gasped.

"I don't like a mess," she spoke against my tip.

"Jesus fucking Christ, where have you been all my life?"

I pulled her back by the hair to kiss me again and really let her have it. I had her straddling me naked without even realizing it. I was touching her everywhere. I couldn't get enough. I palmed her breasts. "Unless you have an objection, I'm going to fuck these next."

"I thought that was a joke. You're really going to do that? How?"

"Yes, and it's called a titty fuck, and I'll show you the how, obviously. It's messy and not something we'll do all that often, but I'm going to fuck you in absolutely any way you'll let me until you tell me to stop." I was saying all of this between passionate kisses and she answered the same way.

"You really aren't capable of shutting up, are you?" she asked.

"Look who's talking?"

I pushed her on her back and spread her legs wide. I sat back for a moment to take her in like that. Her body could have been invented by my own mind, it was so well suited to my exact specifications. And right now it was more sublime than ever in its thorough satiation.

She was so soft and sweet like this, so relaxed and quiet.

Well, quiet for about one second. "You're hard again," she said, sounding surprised.

"Getting there in a hurry, cupcake. How else did you think I was going to fuck your tits? With my personality?"

"It's big enough," she muttered.

"Was that a compliment or an insult? Your words and your tone were telling different stories."

"Does it matter?"

She didn't say anything after that because I was kissing her again. I held myself up on my elbows and had her mouth until she was mindless again. I moved down her body and showed her once more what else my unstoppably busy mouth was good for. I added fingers and tipped her over the edge again.

By then I was near mindless myself. I climbed up her body, stopped when my dick was at her cunt to rub against her sopping wetness. It took all I had not to push inside. Instead I lubricated myself, watching my dick rub against her cunt, slack-jawed, and kept moving up.

I straddled her ribcage, grabbing handfuls of her magnificent tits and pushing my randy cock between them.

"Don't talk to them while you do this," she warned.

It may as well have been a dare.

She was trying her best to crane her head down to watch what I was doing, and it was adorable. Not so adorable that I didn't try to push into her mouth at the end of every stroke. She'd just situated herself so perfectly for a double feature.

I gave a stirring pep talk to Mayhem and Mischief as I humped her chest, praised them both as I pumped harder and faster.

I called out their names, not hers, when I came.

She was cursing me. I was trying not to laugh.

"It's so messy," she said, staring down at her sticky breasts. She sounded more fascinated than concerned.

"No, it's not," I said, waited for her to look up at me with a question in her eyes, then started to rub the cum all over her, coating her with it. "Now, *that's* messy."

She was giggling helplessly as I dragged her into the shower.

I washed her, pushing her palms against the wall as I soaped her up and touched her everywhere. The water ran cold before I was done.

I dried her off, picked her up, and put her back in my bed. She was fairly limp at this point, but I wasn't done.

"This is your fault," I told her. I was between her legs, sucking on her nipples and fingering her while she writhed helplessly. "I've never waited so long for anything in my life as I did to get my hands on you. Now I'm going to *wallow*."

It wasn't fair—fair was never an option—but I teased her sex with my tip, pushing in just the barest amount. "It'll be good. I'll make it so good for you."

I wanted to come inside of her, right this instant, wanted it so bad my teeth ached, but I pulled away and put her hand on my revived dick instead.

"How many times can you… ?" she asked.

"Less than you but more than this. How about we find out? You count, I'll do the rest."

CHAPTER TWENTY-TWO

The next morning we couldn't stop smiling at each other. Conspiratorial smiles like only we were in on the joke. Like we were naughty children that had just teamed up to get away with something impressive and disruptive.

Even my father and Ida couldn't ruin my good mood.

In fact I saw them off cheerfully, so much so they were shooting me suspicious looks as they drove away.

"Fucking finally," I said as the car left my drive.

"If I reach my word count early can we spend the rest of the day in bed?" I asked sometime later. I was working at my desk and Ro had come in to hand me an espresso.

"If you add an extra 1k to it we have a deal."

"Power mad authoritarian!" I called to her back as she left my office.

"Lackadaisical hedonist," she called back.

But sure enough I met the word count by four p.m. It was a little scary how well she knew how to both work me and make me work.

I used her next Sunday absence to move a bunch of her stuff into my room. I didn't let myself think too much about it, didn't let myself see it as a big step, let alone a necessary one. I just focused on the convenience of it and the way it would rile her and how that would amuse me.

Her reaction wasn't what I was expecting, but as usual with Ro, it was better.

First of all, she didn't notice right away. When she did, it was late at night and she couldn't find her toothbrush.

It took a few trips through the house for her to figure it out and then she confronted me with a simple, "Why are you so obsessed with me?"

"Because you're perfect," I told her solemnly.

She wasn't buying it. "Shut up. Whatever. I was already sleeping in here so I guess it doesn't matter. Just don't get used it. When I'm done with your body, I'll go back to my own room and you won't complain about it."

"Yes, ma'am." I saluted her.

"Smartass."

"Cute ass."

"That's not even an insult. It's actually a compliment."

"Cute pain in my ass."

"That's better."

I grabbed her and dragged her into bed.

And days went by like that. Weeks. I wouldn't have described them as blissful, not out loud at least, but I thought it more than once.

I was on the phone, arguing with an old college friend of mine when Ro walked into my office.

"Let me ask my boss what she thinks," I told him.

"This is my friend Jason," I told her, pointing at the phone. "I'm trying to tell him he needs to quit his job. He works for Vice, and I think they're trying to kill him. Ask me why I think that."

She played along. "Why do you think that?"

"He's on location in the Congo right now. This man can't wash his hands without applying lotion immediately after, and they make him live without indoor plumbing. This man couldn't fight his way out of an internet café, and they send him to the worst bush wars in the world. Tell me that doesn't sound like they're trying to kill him."

"When you put it that way, it does sound a bit suspicious," she agreed.

"Your boss?" Jason was asking me, and I could tell everything going on on my end was cracking him up.

"Yeah, she was supposed to be my assistant, but now she's running my life, so that seems like a more appropriate title, don't you think?"

Ro was still standing in front of my desk, and I realized she was waiting for me.

"What do you need, cupcake?" I asked her, ignoring whatever Jason was saying now on the other end.

"I'm taking off for a few hours."

I studied her, head to toe. She was wearing a pretty floral dress—that I had picked out for her, of course. Her hair was different, braided back from her face, but with a few teasing tendrils framing her face.

Uh uh. Not good.

She was even wearing a bit of makeup. Mascara and lip gloss, maybe a touch of blush, I thought.

I got a sick feeling in my gut.

"Why?" I asked sharply. "Where? It's a Tuesday, you know."

"I'm more aware of days of the week in general than you are, so yes I knew that. And it's after five, and I'm allowed to come and go as I please, I think we'll both agree. I'm not an actual hostage, and I'm allowed to have a social life."

Everything she said was true, of course, but I really didn't like the way she was saying it. That she was saying it at all.

"I've got to go," I told my friend, "I'll talk to you later. Please quit your job."

"Catch you later, man. Invite me to the wedding."

I paused. "I would, but she refuses to marry me," I said and hung up. Boy, was that going to run around the rumor mill and come back to bite me in a hurry. I just didn't care. In fact, it kind of tickled me.

I gave her my undivided attention. "Now, where are you going?"

She sighed, crossed her arms and looked like an adorable, bratty child as she did it. "I have a church… social thing."

"What kind of social thing?"

"It's like a dance, but we mostly stand around and talk. It's a nice way to meet new people in the area."

"A dance?" I asked her, voice cold.

She rolled her eyes. "Anyway, don't wait up."

"What the fuck is that supposed to mean?"

"Absolutely nothing. I'll be home before nine. Bye."

And then she just left. She didn't even look back.

I was beside myself.

I spent an hour in my gym with a punching bag before I was willing to acknowledge what I was feeling.

If she was going to a dance, there would be men there. It was a church function, not an all girls club, so it was literally impossible that there wouldn't be.

I was jealous. Jealous at even the thought of her talking to other men. Would they think she was single? Did *she* think she was single?

Was she single?

We didn't talk about stuff like that, but I just figured she knew we were exclusive. I wouldn't put my hands on her and then touch someone else, and I just assumed that she knew that's how it was with us.

I should have gone with her. It would have been worth the risk of me catching on fire as soon as I walked in the door of a church to avoid the way I was feeling right now, which was helpless and shut out.

I started texting her at the two hour mark.

Me: Tell Mayhem and
Mischief I miss them.
When will you be home?

I waited and waited, and she didn't respond. My mind was on how much more she'd have in common with men she met at church, how much more of what she was looking for that they'd have to offer. In my mind, I was not coming out ahead.

Making her come and making her laugh didn't seem like enough of an edge to compete with say, sharing her belief system.

What if she met someone? What would I do?

Jealousy was a new emotion for me, and I decided on the spot that I hated it with the passion and heat of a thousand angry suns. I also decided to fight it with both fists—to go down swinging.

Me: Answer me or
I'm going to start sending
you some pics that would
make Jesus blush.

Still no response, but she was back before nine.

I was shirtless in the driveway waiting for her. She stepped out of her car, and I was on her, pinning her to the door and ravishing her mouth like we'd been separated for years instead of hours.

Eventually I pulled back. "Did you miss me?" I panted.

"You're ridiculous," was her response.

"I missed you. If you met any men tonight, I'm going kick their asses. If anyone touched you, I'm going to pull them apart with my bare hands."

"What do you think goes on at these things?" she asked, her eyes squinting at me like I'd lost my mind. "I didn't even dance with anyone. There are five times as many women as men so you don't have to worry about anyone looking at *me* twice."

"What does that mean? You sound salty about it. Were *you* looking? Were you *hoping* someone would look at you twice?"

"Oh, shut up, you crazy bastard," she said and pulled my lips back to hers.

I was inching her skirt up when I heard it. A high pitched sort of piercing noise. Quite an unpleasant racket, really. I pulled back and stared at her. "What *is* that?"

She smiled and I knew instantly from the smile that she'd done something impossibly ornery. "I got you a surprise."

My eyes narrowed. "A good surprise or a bad surprise?"

"The best surprise. It's going to change your life."

"You're finally going to let me put it in? *Thank God.*"

"No. Shut up. Go look in my passenger seat."

I obeyed her, shooting her suspicious looks the whole time. She just looked too smug for it to be anything but a joke. A joke on me—not with me—going by the unholy light in her eyes.

I opened the car door to find a tiny black ball of fluff staring at me. It yapped once, then again. "What," I asked through my teeth, "is that?"

"That is Machiavelli. We'll call her Mac for short. She's a teacup poodle."

"What," I asked, still through my teeth, "is it doing in your car?"

"Arriving at its new home. It's our pet."

I almost dropped the issue right then just for the fact that she'd said 'our' and it fascinated me. Still, it was just too much, even from her.

I stayed on task. "Did it not occur to you," I gritted out, "that I don't have any pets in my house because I don't *want* any. I don't pretend to know the meaning of life, but I'm positive I'm not here to pick up some other animal's shit."

She was impressively unaffected by my speech. "You'll change your mind within the week. You're going to fall in love with her."

"What do you want to bet?"

"I'll give her back if you don't, we'll keep her if you do."

"Kind of straightforward stakes. How about we throw your virginity on the table, as well?"

I saw her face.

"Fine. Fine. I guess it works. Deal."

"Now pick her up," Ro told me.

I glared at her, but I did it. It was like holding fluffy air. She weighed literally nothing and stared up at me like I was her entire reason for existing. What a strange creature.

"Machiavelli is not a proper pet name," I told Ro, still staring at the stupid little dog. "Let alone a girl one. Why would you even… ?"

She shrugged. "I thought it was funny. She's not even two pounds and she's not likely to top out at more than four. I wanted to give her an impactful name. Tiny body, mighty spirit."

"And Machiavelli was the first thing that came to mind?"

"It made me think of you and it was funny. Quit making everything so complicated, cupcake."

"Machiavelli reminds you of *me*?" I was more than a touch

insulted by that. "And you know, *I* came up with cupcake for *you*. It's a little offensive that you can't even be bothered to come up with a unique endearment in return."

"Really? That... offends you? You want... a unique endearment?" Her voice was rich with fascination.

I handed her the ball of fluff and folded my arms. "I don't think that's too much to ask."

"Okay, tall boy."

"No. No. *No.*" I pointed at her. "Stop that. An affectionate one, not something filthy."

"You have a problem with filth now? Are you feeling okay?"

"Well, no, I love filth. But it's filth that you heard some other women name me. It's... belittling to us. I want something from *you*."

She was studying me like I'd said something particularly interesting. What she said though was, "How about muffin? It's like cupcake without the frosting. Like you and me."

"First of all," I began, "a muffin is not at all a cupcake without frosting. It's an entirely different thing. Second, if one of us has the frosting, it is *me*."

"Well you already took cupcake, muffin."

Ro tried to hand Mac back to me, and I refused, making her carry it inside herself.

I was following her through the front door when I asked, "You know you're outrageously out of control at this point, don't you? Out of control *and* out of line."

"What are you going to do about it, muffin?"

CHAPTER TWENTY-THREE

I followed her through the house and when I realized where she was going I said, "It's bedtime. What are you doing in your office?"

"It's not bedtime. It's not even nine p.m."

"Let me rephrase. It's take you to bed to mess around until we're tired enough to sleep time."

"I need to do a few things. You go on ahead without me."

"Without you? What would be the point of that? You want me to jack off?"

"That's your business."

I was downright surly now. This night had not gone my way even a little bit. "If you're working, I'm working. Let me know when you're done, Miss Workaholic."

I went and sat at my desk and did nothing productive. I was sending her funny memes when something small and wet touched my bare foot.

I pushed my chair back and looked under my desk.

The tiny dog was sitting there and staring at me. "You look ridiculous," I told it. "Like a stuffed animal with a personality." It just continued to give me adoring eyes.

Ro walked in then. "Oh, there she went. She must like you."

I glared at her. "Where… How… *Why* did you even get this thing?"

"A sweet little granny at church was selling them and I jumped on the chance. Poodles are a great breed. My parents have two. They're smart and sweet and easy to train. Pets are good for you, you know. They make you happier."

"It thinks it's a dog," I noted. Its poof of a tail was wagging, its whole body moving with the motion. "It does little dog things but it's smaller than a rodent, and not a large rodent. I don't want a dog, but if I did it wouldn't be something utterly useless like this thing."

Ro was unfazed. "We'll see. This is only day one."

"You're not as cute as you think you are," I told it. The cursed thing was still giving me that soul sucking stare. "What does it want from me?" I asked with disgust.

"Love."

My brows shot up and I sent Ro an arch look. "It's come to the wrong place for that. I thought you said it was smart."

"The more shit you talk about this dog, the more silly you're going to look when she steals your heart. I'm not above rubbing it in."

That reminded me. I leered at her. "Me neither. Come here."

"Nope, sorry. I'm only attracted to men that love dogs. We're obviously not compatible."

"Come closer and say that to my face. Better yet, come sit on my lap and tell me all about it."

She got the puppy, staying carefully out of arm's reach the entire time, and walked out of the room.

"Quit trying to normalize my life!" I yelled after her.

"Never," she returned.

About twenty minutes later, I went looking for her. I peeked into her office, and she was bending over her desk, her hand busy drawing. The little Muppet was sleeping in a corner on what looked like a nest of blankets she'd put together.

I approached her quietly, pressing myself against her back and taking a look at what she was drawing.

It was another adorably savage unicorn drawing. Mayhem was smiling like an angel and holding a black little ball of fluff with sweet eyes.

They were watching while the pink unicorn used a gas can and her cigarette to set the blue one on fire as it screamed in agony.

"That's sexual harassment," she noted wryly.

"Oh, yeah? Get a load of this." I pushed my erection against her backside. "That picture is a bit bloodthirsty, even for you." I rubbed against her as I spoke, humping my hardness into her softness.

She'd dropped the pencil and was bracing herself against the desk now. Perfect. I took out my dick, lifted her skirt, and kicked her feet smartly together. I reached between her legs and was gratified when I found her wet. With one finger, I traced a path along her cleft, dragging her panties to the side.

I'd grown from hard and primed to heavily aroused and ready to mount.

"Squeeze your thighs together," I told her. I shoved my cock between her legs, thrusting without going in, her wet cunt making the slide smooth.

I reached around her and dragged her dress and bra down so I could grip her breasts as I continued to pump. I leaned down and bit her earlobe very softly as I said, "You think I'm good with my hands and my tongue, but this is where I'm best of all. This is just a pale imitation of what my cock can do to your pussy. I'd ride you so good. Squeeze harder."

I snaked one hand down and found her clit. I rubbed as I humped faster and faster between her legs and along her sex. "Nothing's more satisfying than going balls deep into cunt. For you, for me." I pinched her nipple and clit at the same time, and she came.

I gripped her hips and started rubbing harder, letting loose. When I started to come, I reached for her panties, shoving my tip inside to soak the lacy cloth. I rubbed the material against us both. "So close," I rasped into her ear. "My cum is all over your sex. Get on birth control, cupcake."

For once she didn't say anything. I felt her forehead. "Why are you so quiet? Are you feeling okay?"

When she caught her breath, she said, "I couldn't get a word in. You were talking enough for both of us."

We showered together. She delighted me by sitting on the bench seat under the spray and worked on her deep throating skills. She was outdoing herself every day.

Still, I pushed it even further. I just couldn't help myself.

I pulled her mouth off just short of coming and pinned her hard and chest first into the wall of the shower.

I got her off with my hands. She was dripping wet and I dragged the moisture from her sex to her back entrance.

I got down on my knees and tongued her ass enthusiastically while my fingers got her off again, one working her clit, the other fucking her with purpose.

It was a few steps past straight intercourse as far as these things went but I was going to put it absolutely anywhere she let me and there wasn't any way I wouldn't at least shoot my shot here.

Literally.

I stood up, pushed a finger in and met resistance. "Take a

deep breath," I whispered into her ear.

She did it, and I buried my finger in her ass.

I started stroking in and out, my other hand busy on her clit.

She was trembling and panting but strangely quiet.

"I'm going to fuck your ass unless you tell me to stop," I rasped into her ear roughly. "Tell me to stop," I added for good measure.

She didn't say one word and I dragged the head of my cock against her sex, getting lubed up on her pleasure.

I timed it just right, she was coming from my fingers rubbing off her clit as I pulled my finger out and pushed the head of my cock into her back entrance and she took it easier that way.

Easier but not easy. I was big and even a handful of orgasms can only get you so relaxed.

I was halfway in when I stopped. "Tell me this is okay," I told her, voice pained. "Tell me you want this."

She'd just been so quiet. I had to hear her voice.

"I want it," her answer was quiet and breathless, but she didn't fucking stutter.

I rammed home and lost my mind, owning her ass with a purpose, finesse gone, brain off, every thought out the window as I gripped her hips and fucked her how I *needed* it. Hard and fast and perfect.

It was so fucking good that I proposed to her at least twice before I came balls deep.

I was kissing and touching her everywhere when I finished. I pulled out slowly and washed us both, hands reverent, lips on every piece of flesh I could touch.

"Was that okay?" I asked her. I was well aware I'd crossed a line, done something we'd never even discussed before. I was drunk with the headiness of it, but not so out of it that I didn't need to know her thoughts on the matter.

"It was," she said, her voice steadier than mine.

I was reassured. I kissed her deeply and got her off again.

We got ready for bed, and it was only as I was lying down to sleep that I realized what she was doing.

She was making a little nest for the puppy beside the bed.

"Put it somewhere else," I told her. "It will bother us if it sleeps in here."

"I'm going to get the stuff to crate train her tomorrow, but for tonight I'd like to keep her close in case she needs anything. I don't want her wandering off before the house is puppy proofed. Also, it's her first night away from her mama, and I don't want her to be scared."

I glared at her. "Stop that. Being adorable won't get you your way every *single* time. Letting it sleep in my room is going too far."

She'd been pulling back the covers on her side to get into bed but at that she straightened. "It's fine. I'll sleep in my own bed tonight so we don't bother you."

I didn't like that. I hadn't slept alone since we'd started messing around, and I found I didn't want to. Not at all. One of my favorite developments of late was waking up with her in my arms and making her come before she'd even opened her eyes.

Who knew I cuddled in my sleep? I couldn't remember ever doing that with Ida, and I'd never stayed to sleep with any of my random hookups. Like a lot of things, it was probably more about Ro than my previous patterns.

Whatever it was, I didn't want to miss it for even one morning. "Don't do that. Come back to bed. I can ignore it for one night."

"Are you sure? We wouldn't want to bother you. I do kind of miss sleeping in my own bed… "

"Get your cute little ass in here."

When she was in bed, I snatched her against me, her back to my front. I spoke into her ear, "You're not even a little spoon, you know. Not even a tablespoon. You're a tiny little teaspoon."

She giggled and I ate it up. "Why are you so obsessed with me?" she asked cheekily.

"Because you're perfect."

The next morning I was face deep in her pussy when a few little yaps had her tensing underneath me.

"I need to get her—" Ro started to say.

I covered her mouth and continued sucking on her clit, fingers pumping until she fell apart.

She was very cooperative after that. It didn't hurt that the puppy had gone back to sleep on its own. She had my tip in her mouth when I stopped her.

"Put a pin in that. I want you to go down on me while I'm at my desk. Like I'm your boss and you're my naughty secretary. I'm going to pull your hair and tell you what to do, and you're going to call me Mr. Thorn."

"Hmm, okay. So you're into office kink now?"

"First of all, it's your fault. And second, probably. Third, *we* are into office kink."

The puppy was sleeping, and Ro was on her knees between me and my desk, my legs open to let her in close. "Take my dick out," I told her. My hand was massaging the back of her neck.

She started to do it. "Say yes, Mr. Thorn."

She shot me a look. It wasn't quite a smirk, but it was close enough for me to know she was amused. "Yes, Mr. Thorn." She even used her sex voice.

She took my heavy length out and gripped it in both hands.

I took her hair down, burying both hands in the silky mass, and pushed her down. She had me halfway down her throat when I said, "Wait. Take your tits out. Mayhem and Mischief don't want to miss this."

She almost gagged as she laughed and pulled her mouth off my cock at the same time.

But she did it, unbuttoning her shirt and opening her bra to show me her glorious breasts.

"Good morning," I told them fondly.

"You already said good morning to them. It was right before you ate me out for half an hour. Did you forget?"

"See how she tries to come between us?" I asked her chest, my fingers pinching both nipples. "I could never forget. Now get back to sucking, cupcake."

She didn't take offense. She never did when it came to anything sexual. It was possibly my favorite thing about her, and that was saying a lot.

"Yes, Mr. Thorn," she tried to say around a mouthful of cock.

Or at least I thought that's what it was. I was reading between the lines there.

She was getting so good at blowjobs that it was almost embarrassing how fast she could make me come. Record breaking stuff, for me.

She twisted her hands around my base as her head bobbed with my hands pushing and pulling her head up and down by the hair. I came and she took it, raining soft little kisses all over my dick before putting it away.

It was magnificent. She was.

We smiled warmly at each other. I motioned with fingers to lips. "Chef's kiss, cupcake."

I pulled her up onto my lap and started kissing her passionately.

"I'm going to run some errands," she told me from the doorway of my office sometime later. "Taking Mac with me."

She was walking away before I could respond.

I caught up to her easily with my much longer stride. "Where are you going? Why would you take Mac? You don't think I can be responsible for a tiny Muppet for a few hours?"

"That's debatable, but I'm taking her because I'm going to a pet supply store to get her all the things she needs." She paused. "I didn't figure you'd want to come along."

"I'm coming along," I said almost at the same time.

"Witch," I muttered.

"Clown."

"I'm driving."

And so we found ourselves going up and down every aisle in PetSmart.

I held Mac while we walked. Only because Ro was pushing the cart and Mac seemed too tiny to set down in it.

I wasn't losing the bet, but we still went overboard with pet supplies. I just kept finding dog toys and Ro seemed to think our little beanie baby should wear clothes for some reason. And then there were leashes, collars, treats, food and water dishes. A small crate and pet carrier. We had to go through everything quite thoroughly just to be sure we didn't miss any essentials.

We were waiting for a machine to let out a personalized tag when Ro said, "I've figured out your punishment if you don't make word count today."

"Why does it have to be punishments? What do you have against bribes?"

"You get everything you want all the time. There's nothing to bribe you with."

I could have argued with that rather obviously, but I let it go. "What's the punishment?"

"You have to listen to only John Denver music for an entire day."

"What the fuck kind of a punishment is that?"

"A funny one."

I didn't realize she'd sabotaged me until about six p.m. The puppy just kept coming into my office, and I brought some toys in there, even set up a little bed. I sprawled out on the floor and started throwing a mini tennis ball I'd gotten, and she stumbled over her feet getting it back to me.

When I realized I was teaching her to fetch and she was picking it up quite easily, I was delighted.

"Ro! Come here!"

She appeared in my doorway like she'd been waiting to be called.

"Watch this," I told her and threw the ball.

The itty bitty thing couldn't even get her mouth around the minuscule tennis ball, but she grabbed a bit of the fuzz on the outside and carried it with valiant effort back to me. "She *is* clever," I said unconsciously.

I realized what was happening and glared at Ro. "I see what's happening. You're trying to win the bet *and* sabotage my word count."

"Not at all. Even I didn't know you'd be this obsessed with her. Want me to keep her out of here? I'll be happy too."

"Oh, you'd love that, hogging her all to yourself."

She bit her lips to keep from laughing as she turned away. "Whatever you want, boss. Just let me know."

I picked up the puppy and looked into her adoring eyes. "See how she says the word boss so sarcastically? Yeah, you picked up on that too, didn't you? She's so sassy she doesn't even know how to put it away, and that's why *I'm* your favorite."

I didn't altogether appreciate the loud laughter that Ro left behind as she walked away.

The week went by in a blink. I couldn't remember ever having a quicker passage of days, in fact.

I knew the second Ro realized that I was keeping the Muppet. I was working at my desk and she walked in, looking around.

"Have you seen Mac?" she asked.

I met her eyes, no expression in mine. "No," I lied.

Just then a little bark erupted from my lap.

Ro raised a judgmental brow. "You know, I talked to the person that sold her to me. It will be no trouble to bring her back. There's already another home lined up if you don't want her. Just say the word. I concede. You can win our bet right now."

I was rubbing an ecstatic Mac's belly as I told her, "You are *so* evil, but I think you know that. You don't have to gloat, you know."

"Me? Gloat?"

"Yes. You're laying it on a bit thick. You are not convincingly guileless, so that's a dead giveaway."

"Oh no, you misunderstood. I'm full of guile. Is that better?"

"You're too much. I should take you over my knee."

"Then you'd have to move your precious baby."

I tried to glare at her, but it was hard to be convincing when she delighted me so. "Stop that," I tried. "There has to be a limit to your sass."

"You think so? By the way, I know someone with a cat that just had a new litter of kittens."

"Don't you dare."

CHAPTER TWENTY-FOUR

I started to fantasize constantly about being inside of her, even of taking her virginity. The way it would feel to be buried deep, skin on skin, the drugging tightness of her walling me in, taking me inch by inch, the delicious difficulty of it. The struggle of stretching something that had never before been breached.

How much I'd have to prime, work, and tenderize her to get my whole big self in.

The way it would feel when I broke the barrier inside of her. The finality of it. I decided that was just deliciously perverse enough to do it for me.

It was the strangest thing, nothing I'd ever even been interested in before, but now I was consumed by the idea.

I'd always liked experienced girls with little to no inhibitions. What had changed? Why were all of my instincts so off when it came to this little termagant?

"How fun is it even to be a thirty-year-old virgin?" I asked her out of the blue as she brought me an afternoon espresso.

"I'm twenty-three, you ass!"

I bit back a smile. I was well aware of how too young she was. "Whatever. Thirty will be here before you know it. What are you even holding onto? How innocent can you possibly remain when you've learned to suck my cock like a fucking artist?"

"Your point?"

That made me smile outright as I continued, "Nothing's more real than that. And let's be honest here, I've probably gotten you off more in the last two weeks than you have your whole life."

She made a face.

"Tell me I'm wrong. You with your brutal honesty. Tell me."

She sighed, looking sour. "You're not wrong."

"I'll tell you what. I want you to talk to all of your girlfriends, ask them if they were in love their first time, see if it was a pleasant experience for any of them. You do that and come back to me. I'm not one to make promises, but I promise you that if you let me be your first, I'll make it incredible for you."

She was wearing her stoic face, the one that drove me crazy, because I *still* couldn't read it.

"Come here," I told her.

She came, albeit unhappily.

I pulled her onto my lap, straddling me. 'You realize that it's just the barest excuse of a technicality at this point, right?" I was rubbing her butt and starting to get carried away with it. I wanted her. I *always* wanted her. "For the love of God, I've fucked you in the ass."

I closed my eyes, letting my own words distract me into delicious sensory memories for a moment.

"I know that," she said quietly. "I'm not an idiot. Listen,

you can stop making your arguments about it. I already made up my mind a while ago."

I didn't like the sound of that. "Oh?" I asked casually.

"I went on birth control," she told me quietly. "An IUD."

I felt my eyelids grow heavy, my breath pant out. I felt a surge of lust so great in that moment it made me rock back in my chair as though I had to give it room to breathe.

Which was perhaps apt as my hard-on right then tried to spring her to the ceiling. "For me?" I asked like it was a long wished for birthday gift.

She sighed. "For you, you shameless, irresistible hussy."

"Can I fuck you *now*? Let's take the day off and do it right."

"Let's not get into any bad habits. You'd try to take every day off to stay in bed if I let you. Tonight. We'll call it quits early. Don't get all weird about it. I can tell by the gleeful look on your face you're going to overreact to this. We are not throwing a party for you taking my V-card. Don't overhype it."

"Can I wear my Birthday Bitch sash?"

"Stop it right now."

"Can we at least wear party hats?"

"Don't make me change my mind."

I was full of nervous energy for the rest of the day. That and piercing lust, and an all-consuming, undiluted craving.

She was putting the puppy to bed in his kennel for the night, and when she took longer than I thought she should I went looking for her.

She was coming down the hallway. She was wearing the French maid teddy. "That's overkill," I told her, but my tone said something else.

She arched a brow. "You picked it out, but if you don't like it you can take it off yourself."

As soon as she was in arm's reach, I snatched her off her feet and kissed her. I cupped her butt, lifting her to me. I deepened the kiss, rubbing my dick into her warmth.

She moaned softly into my mouth, and it was too much.

Anticipation raced through me. Exhilaration.

I had her on her back on the bed without even meaning to, when the last thing I wanted to do was rush this. But I didn't stop, didn't know if I could.

I covered her, bringing our bodies flush, punch drunk with the idea that there were no breaks tonight, nothing to hold me back. I kept kissing her and it was wonderful, and the way she responded under me, the way her arms wrapped around me, her body humming with a tension that answered my own, let me know she felt wonder as well.

Eventually I stood up beside the bed so I could just look at her. I was shaking a bit, the tips of my fingers trembling. Nerves. I was having nerves about sex, jittery like it was my first time instead of hers. It wasn't normal.

I usually took my time. Because why not?

Apparently that sexual leisure was something I'd taken for granted, and I found that out at the worst possible time.

I wanted to fuck us both raw this second, and I wasn't sure how to resist the urge.

I stripped her teddy off, making a note to savor it more another time. Right now I needed us both bare.

I sat at her hip and touched her, palming her cunt. She was already wet, thank God, but so small, it was daunting.

My fingers had her memorized at this point, but now having them inside of her, experiencing her softness and warmth around them, and fixating on what else would get to memorize the feel and compression of her tight walls now had me forgetting myself.

I was so hard it bordered on pain. I pushed three fingers in with the intention of stretching her.

My eyes shut in agonized pleasure as I reached her barrier. I'd been very careful with this in the past, it had fascinated me as only a true novelty could, but I'd behaved myself.

Now I tested it, pushing until she was squirming under my hands.

There were so many things I wanted to do in the proper order, tonight in particular. I wanted to make her come a dozen times first, but I was witless with a powerful lust beyond anything I could remember.

I wanted to come inside of her this instant. Deep and deeper, to the very end of her, until I was touching her womb. Needed it.

For the first time I could ever remember, I lost it.

My control. My mind.

All sense of space of and time.

I'd wanted so badly to make it good for her.

I'd been so sure that would be an easy task for me.

Instead I snapped and became a wild man, all parts of my better nature deserting me to the overwhelming urge to own her body in totality, *to rut.*

I was on her, pushing her knees to her chest, my tip kissing her entrance, before I even had the thought. My body was driving faster than my brain.

I pushed in almost against my own will. I simply could not stop. I pushed until I butted up against her barrier.

I moaned and shuddered.

She squirmed a bit under me in discomfort and I couldn't stop. I pushed her silky thighs wide part, pinned her hips prone, and drove in, rending her hymen in one strong push.

I felt something great and strong move within me, and it struck me powerfully and profoundly.

It did not, however, stop my progress, or so much as slow it.

Barely pausing, I pushed deeper still, not gauging her reaction, only able to focus on my own task, my own pleasure.

I didn't ride her easy for a first time, the taste of her bare and squeezing me making me snap in a way I didn't even know I could.

I was mindless, lunging in until I was touching her womb and it was mind-blowing and wonderful, and I'm not sure all of my brain cells survived it.

She made a noise underneath me, and I didn't have the mental capacity to understand what it meant, let alone to stop. I didn't even pause for it, driving into her then pulling out again with no allowance for her tiny, vulnerable self.

It was so fast and out of my usually stellar control that I felt I might've blacked out.

I came balls deep, back arched, jarring into the end of her mercilessly.

My heart was pounding in my ears, I was panting like I'd run a marathon instead of rubbing out one quick orgasm.

But what an orgasm.

I felt like I'd been stomped into the ground by my own lust, and every second of the stomping had been wondrous, beyond anything, surpassing absolutely anyone.

I was twitching inside of her and grinding my hips, fucking every last tremor of that exquisite madness out of me when I came a little back into myself.

She was completely still beneath me.

I was horrified. I pulled back to study her.

Her eyes were closed, her face scrunched up tight.

"Oh my God," I said, realizing that I hadn't made it good for her. I had in fact, hurt her. "Oh Ro, I'm so sorry. I don't know what came over me. I just lost it."

She opened her big Bambi eyes and reached a hand up to pat me on the cheek. My heart turned over in my chest. It was the sweetest thing I'd ever experienced, her comforting me after I'd fucked up—literally—at her expense.

I held her hand there, watching her face tenderly.

"Shhh," she said and I realized I'd just been apologizing, over and over. "Shh. It's okay," she said in a slightly hoarse voice. "It's okay," she repeated. "It hurt a bit, and I didn't come, but… I kind of liked watching you lose it like that."

I was still inside of her. I'd been pulling out slowly, reluctantly, but I felt myself swelling up again at her words and I eased deeper into her warm flesh. "Tell me to stop if you want me to stop," I told her roughly. "I can't do it on my own. Does it still hurt?"

"Not badly. There's mostly a soreness there, and a *lot* of stretching, but that's normal, right?"

"I didn't want it to be normal for you, I wanted to make it good."

Neither of us had to say it, but that ship had sailed. I'd have to make it up to her. I planned to, exhaustively. Later.

I was moving, little involuntary thrusts as I continued to grow deep inside of her. Unconsciously I pushed forward and high into her, breaching her deeply. "Oh God," I breathed out. And snapped. Again. I drove in deep and just kept going. I couldn't even give her a smooth ride. She was too small, and I was too big, too overcome, too defeated by my own ruthless need, driving in and out like a madman, ramming in jarringly and forcefully and pulling out in a heavy, brutal drag.

I came like I was falling apart. It was unstoppable, cataclysmic. And I came back into myself as slowly as the last time, my weight pushing her into the mattress, my dick still twitching inside of her.

I lifted up to check her face. "Did I hurt you that time?" I asked with trepidation.

She grimaced. "A bit. I'll live."

Such a fucking trooper.

I wanted to fuck us both unconscious. I wanted to die doing this.

It was a drawn out process as I pulled slowly out of her. I groaned a protest as I tugged myself free, watching my progress with rapt adoration. I already wanted back in.

"Bareback is new for me. It's going take an adjustment period." I said it like I was tasting the words. Very few things about sex were a novelty to me.

Ro seemed to have the monopoly on that.

"Don't you like it?" she asked, sounding a touch vulnerable.

That did crazy things to me, that vulnerability, the fact that, after all I'd just put her though, she was worried about *my* pleasure. "I enjoyed that more than I have ever enjoyed anything in my entire my life. And that's not the right question at all," I said, trying not to lose it and mount her again.

She gave me a small, game smile. "What's the right question?"

"How will I ever go back? And can I come inside of you again, this instant?"

I glanced down and saw the mess, then parted her legs and studied it. Cum and blood and her own moisture were mingled on her soft, pale thighs, seeping out of her sex.

I pushed her legs wide and used a delicate touch to open her sex and study. "You're not too raw. I was overzealous, but it's not as bad as I thought."

"You missed your calling. You should have been a gynecologist."

"Not the first time I've heard that." I paused. "But stop distracting me."

I pushed a finger into her, watching her face.

She gasped, and I just about lost it again. "Feel okay?" I

asked, adding another finger and pumping them smoothly in and out. She was adjusting well and wetter than ever thanks to all of my cum leaking out of her.

She nodded. I watched my hand work her over, my dick somehow growing hard again in record time.

"I need you again," I moaned, looking up at her face. "Is it too much?" I was rubbing her clit as I spoke.

At least I got her off once before I flipped her over and mounted her from behind. I rutted to my wicked little heart's content, hands holding her breasts as I, at last, found a smooth rhythm that lasted more than thirty fucking seconds.

I still lost it at the end even then, the orgasm surprising me again, my cock jerking out cum while I was mid-stroke. I bottomed out and emptied deep, pushing her face flat to the bed as I rubbed every bit of my seed into her overflowing pussy, humping her into the mattress until I realized what I was doing, (which took quite a while) pulled out and flipped her to make sure she had enough air.

She seemed a bit dazed but otherwise unharmed.

I held her for a very long time afterward, staring at the ceiling while she dozed peacefully, and my mind was full of lovely chaos.

Sex was supposed to be fun and uncomplicated.

A pleasurable, mindless pastime.

Whatever happened back there had been too intense for fun.

It held too many ingredients to be uncomplicated.

Affection, reverence, lust, obsession, compulsion, need, longing, addiction, compatibility.

Intimacy. Devotion.

I knew all of these were worrisome developments for my lifestyle and peace of mind in general, but at that moment I was just too delectably sated, too entirely content to care.

CHAPTER TWENTY-FIVE

I'd always had a healthy sex drive, but after that night it sped into a higher fucking gear than even I knew existed. I'd never been so insatiable, and more exceptional, the object for that need only had one target.

I'd never wanted anyone or anything the way I wanted her and having more of her only seemed to make that symptom more acute.

I tried not to think about it, which was actually pretty easy being that my brain was addled with lust nearly every waking hour.

She was toasty warm and naked in my arms when I roused the next morning. I had her cradled against me, my chest to her back as though even in sleep I'd kept her close.

I eased my hips back. My poker hard dick had been trying find its way inside wherever it could without my active permission.

She was dead asleep, deeper than I'd ever seen her. I'd used her to exhaustion, past all good sense or reason, and I wasn't done.

We were both covered in a sheet and I pulled it off, easing her onto her back. The way her soft, opulent body rolled over bonelessly was a perverse drug for me. I sat up, parted her thighs and just looked at her.

She was so lovely, pink and swollen, and all mine.

I moved down the bed, between her legs, bent her knees up and parted her flesh, easing her open with my fingers. Yep, something about this *exact* cunt had captured me fast, and I couldn't even make myself want to fight its hold.

I leaned very close to her sex and blew my warm breath over her flesh, eyes aimed up at her.

She shivered and shifted, rousing a bit at last. I lightly touched my tongue to her clit, watched her breasts quiver, then went to work.

I brought her out of sleep by eating her out, an act of both rapt atonement and repentant fixation.

When I came up for air I said, "I've made you come and had my cock inside you for most of the night. Now we just need to sync those two things up and we'll be gold."

She shook her head but said, "Okay," she blew out a breath, "why don't you show me what you got, tall boy?"

I could tell it was all bravado, she was sore, I'd worked her over good, but I had to go and look again anyway, opening her folds and studying her carefully. "I need to be inside of you again, but I seem to lose my mind every time I get in there. I need to figure out what's going wrong before I really do fuck you raw."

"On a plus side, that's the only time I've ever seen you stop talking when you weren't dead asleep."

"When my dick was in you? Before I've come? Well that's easy to explain. Your cunt took me to another dimension where I lost the ability to speak English."

"I forgot you were a poet, too."

I licked my lips. "Did you forget I was silver-tongued as well?"

Her answer was my name, cried out as my tongue played her clit like it was a perfectly tuned violin.

She was still a bit senseless when I mounted her. She was relaxed and very wet, but I still pushed into her with difficulty. She hadn't gotten less small over the night and I hadn't gotten less large.

Stretching her was a delicious experience for me, but even as I wallowed in it I watched her face, worried I was hurting her again. Still, I couldn't find the voice to ask her. She was right. I couldn't talk with my dick inside of her.

I rubbed her clit with one hand, the other pushing her leg high as I rooted for a more generous angle.

She moaned and shifted, just the slightest amount, but it sent me back into that mad place, and I rammed home and without pause started fucking her in earnest. It was pure muscle memory that kept my fingers working her clit, the other hand flying to grip a ripe tit lovingly, pinning her one sky high leg up by hooking it over my shoulder.

I actually got her off that time before I jarred deep and shot my load. "I'm never going back," I panted into her ear. "Condoms are bullshit."

I regretted saying it. We both knew it was her and not the lack of condoms I was obsessed with, but she played it off well.

"I wouldn't know," she said lightly, "I've only been ridden bareback, neener neener."

I laughed and kissed her until she had to push me away, both off and out of her. I swear I would have spent the day there.

"I have a good long-term bet lined up for you," she told me sometime later as she walked into my office.

Mac was on my lap and gave a happy yap when she heard

Ro's voice. I held her up so she could look at her mama.

"A punishment, you mean," I corrected her just to be contrary. "I actually like John Denver music now, you impudent minx."

"I knew you would," she said smugly, smirked, and took Mac from me.

I stared at her, processed that bit of impertinence, opened my mouth, closed it.

Ignored what she said altogether.

Her smugness grew, the little brat, as soon as she saw I had no response. "Yes, a punishment," she forged on, clearly feeling victorious. "This one will be for if you don't make all of your goals for the upcoming fall season."

"I'm listening," I told her archly.

"You're going to watch Christmas Hallmark movies with me in December."

"Oh, God, no."

"I know. It's a real Greek fucking tragedy."

"You're not serious?"

"I'm dead serious."

"You're outlandish! Why would I agree to that?"

"I'll bribe you."

"With what?"

"I don't know. Think of something you want, I'll bribe you, you'll take the bet, and become my Hallmark watching buddy for the Christmas season." She handed back the puppy so she could rub her hands together like a cartoon villain.

I settled the puppy in my lap, leaned back, folding my arms and reveling in my power. She really wanted me to watch Hallmark movies with her, I could tell. I'd have done it for free, but I couldn't pass up this chance. I knew just what I wanted.

"It would have to be something really good," I warned her.

"The bribe, I mean."

She made a bring it on gesture at me with both hands. "Whatcha got, tall boy?"

"No, no, no. Don't call me that. You got away with it in bed, but it is not going to become a habit. Something sweet, remember?"

"Whatcha got, muffin?"

I smiled smugly at her. "You have to wear that French maid teddy for me for an entire working day."

She leveled a flat stare at me. "Do you even notice how many people come through your property on any given day? Today alone there's the gardener, the pool guy, your housekeeper, a small construction crew for the work you're having done on that guest house, and I have to deal with all of them. Do you even know what goes on around here?"

I hadn't thought that deeply into it. I hadn't thought beyond fucking her in that getup on every flat surface in both of our offices and the kitchen, probably.

Also lately I'd been so wrapped up in her that I barely peeked out for anything important, let alone to notice what was going on about the house. "Only vaguely," I replied. "Why would I? I have you." I paused. "You may wear a robe when dealing with others. Problem solved."

Her brows shot up. "You know that teddy is crotchless, right?"

I was almost panting. I put the puppy on the floor and motioned her to come to me by holding my arms out like she was a child. "I forgot," I told her, letting my arms fall when she ignored them. "Go put it on and show me."

Much to my delight, the unpredictable little gem did it.

She rolled her eyes and called me a sex fiend, but she fucking did it.

I didn't realize that's what was happening until sometime later when she appeared in my doorway in the mesmerizing getup. She was even wearing heels, real ones, the spiky kind.

I studied her more. Her hair was down and tousled, bedroom style. She even had on a hint of makeup, mascara making her gorgeous doe eyes even deeper to drown in, her lips shiny and pink.

I didn't say anything for a good five minutes, and she just stood in the doorway, shoulder leaned against the doorframe, hand perched on her hip sassily, and let me.

It was a treat. I saved the contested part of the teddy for my final perusal, studying the missing crotch of the garment. It was hard to see the finer details from across the room.

I crooked a finger at her. She tried to strut to me, but it was clunky, a bit clumsy, in the heels. That was so adorable to me that I could barely sit still and let her come all the way to my chair. I wanted to *pounce*.

When she got closer I started to reach for her, but she wagged a finger me.

"No touching before lunch. There have to be some rules in this circus of an office."

I was looking at her cute little sex, exposed by the lack of material. "Define lunch," I said succinctly, looked up at her, and ran my tongue over my teeth.

She walked away. "Something that happens at noon," were her retreating words.

It took me fifteen seconds to follow her into her office.

She was already sitting down in that getup and looked to be working like normal.

I studied her desk, moved to it. She had a few things situated in the space underneath it that blocked my view. I moved them, went to the sofa I'd bought for her (so I could comfortably harass her more often), and checked the angle. After a beat, I dragged the low couch to within a few feet of the desk.

She caught what I was doing and started laughing. "As

long as you get your word count, I guess."

I smiled at her fondly and left to get my laptop.

I worked there for a few hours with a perfect view, only occasionally having to ask her to open her legs a bit when she slipped up and shifted them closed.

"You've turned sexual harassment into an art form," she mused.

I pretended that was a compliment. "Why, thank you. You're too kind."

"How's your productivity level?"

"Hmm?" I asked, just staring at her. I licked my lips. "Open up a bit, cupcake."

She parted her legs for me.

"You're so surprisingly cooperative sometimes," I told her with great affection. "It's really a treat. Will you touch yourself?"

"After lunch, perhaps. For now you just get to look."

"I'd just be looking if it was *you* touching yourself," I pointed out. "But fine. Open wider and drape your leg over the arm of your chair."

She did it, and I broke out in a hard sweat.

I pulled off my shirt and took out my dick. I was in a state.

"Put away the live ammo there, muffin," she remarked like we were having tea.

I put my errant cock away, but it wasn't easy.

It didn't look all that comfortable, but she managed to keep her leg draped like that while she worked. I deeply appreciated the effort.

I wanted to say something nice to her. "Thank you for last night. You were… you felt… *better than anything.* I sincerely enjoy being with you." I thought it was a good effort. Feelings and expressing them weren't my best thing when my dick wasn't directly, literally involved.

She aimed soft, tender eyes my way but what she said was,

"You're not going to change my mind about waiting for lunch, you horny heathen."

I threw my head back and laughed.

At noon sharp, I found her in the kitchen. She was wearing a robe, chatting with our lovely, wonderful housekeeper, Penny, who I suddenly wanted to kick out on the spot.

Penny was a delight, and today was no exception. No, it was not at all her fault that I wanted to gnash my teeth and howl.

She was making us ham and cheese croissants and even baking cookies. They were peanut butter with chocolate chips. Ro's favorite, of course. Penny was nearly as smitten with her as I was, and that was saying a lot.

As though she read my mind, Penny beamed at me and said, "Well, I've got to run. Just pull everything out of the oven when the timer goes off."

I almost hugged her, instead restraining myself by smiling at her and wishing her a good day.

I stared at Ro when we were alone. "It's past noon," I told her. "Robe off."

She dropped it on the floor like it was on fire.

I laughed.

Her random acts of obedience never stopped entertaining me.

I nodded at the counter. "Park your perfect little butt up there and open your legs."

She obeyed again, watching me all the while. Her eyes were calm. She was not as desperate as I was, but she would be.

I moved between her legs and parted the two bits of teasing fabric between her legs. I sank two fingers in and moaned.

"Take your tits out of your top," I ordered gruffly. She did it. I was using both hands to finger fuck her, one stroking off her clit, the other fucking in earnest. I licked and sucked on her nipples until they were wet and deep red.

I knew she was close, and I pulled both hands away abruptly.

"What the hell? Don't stop!"

I sent her a pointed look, dropping to my knees. "Not so fun being teased, is it?"

She just snorted and pushed my face into her pussy, the spoiled brat.

I set about spoiling her even more.

I swirled her clit with my tongue, finger fucking her with purpose, one hand kneading at Mayhem.

She was adequately tenderized by the time I rose, slipping my dick out of my athletic shorts, hooking the waistband under my scrotum.

I didn't kiss her, instead I watched my tip play with her, rubbing around her, mashing against her clit until she moaned.

We both had our heads aimed down, staring as each thick inch of me disappeared inside of her.

I was enthralled by the sight, captivated like this act was something new to me, something novel.

I was about halfway in when that fevered, frenetic energy got hold of me again, and I started fucking with hell-bent purpose.

I moved our bare chests flush together deliciously, our eyes locked, and grabbed her hips, pinning them as I hammered into her.

My big hands positioned her tiny self just so, her hips canted forward so that every inch of the top of my cock dragged hard against her as I pulled out at an angle. It was abrasive even to my cock, so I didn't imagine it went easy on her tender flesh and still I couldn't stop, couldn't get enough.

Our eyes were locked though and she was panting, eyes free of pain.

I wanted to say something.

I wanted to kiss her forever.

Instead I threw my head back, spine arching, bottomed out, and came like an avalanche.

"I'm still adjusting," I told her when I was coherent again. It was an apology. "You feel too good. It's messing with me."

She just looked at me with her soul devouring eyes and squirmed a bit. "Can… you?" she asked.

She was near incoherent, but I got the gist of it.

I pulled out, kissed her, and got her off with my fingers.

CHAPTER TWENTY-SIX

I cleaned us both up but didn't let her change.

She owed me a full workday.

I even made her keep her tits out while we ate lunch in the breakfast nook.

We were both ravenous.

She shifted in her seat. "I'm very full of…"

I put my chin on my hand, gazing at her with besotted delight. "My cum?" I finished with relish.

"Yes, that. Can we shower after lunch or is me being sticky part of the deal? I'm leaking onto this seat."

My eyes rolled back into my head, and I held up a finger for her to give me a minute. "You may, but you must put the teddy back on even when you're clean. And I get to wash you."

I washed her squeaky clean and got her off in the shower but restrained myself from taking pleasure.

She kept trying to stroke me, but I batted her hands away. "Why aren't you. . . ?" she began but couldn't finish as my fingers jammed in and out.

"I'm saving it all for office kink on our French teddy day. Do me a favor: mark today in our calendar. Let's make this an annual tradition."

She didn't answer. She wasn't coherent yet. I didn't mind.

I put her back into the teddy myself, pulling the top down so her delectable breasts were still on display.

We returned to work in her office.

She sat at her desk.

I lounged back on the sofa and just basked in the view for a while. "Open," I told her blandly every time she unconsciously started to close her legs.

"I'm going to bend you backward over the arm of this couch," I drawled sometime late into the afternoon, "and stuff you like a turkey."

"That's quite the picture you're painting."

It felt like a challenge. I continued to recite my special brand of poetry at her. "First I'll prop your plush little ass on that desk and eat your peach."

"Another fine portrait."

"I live for the arts."

We shared an eye crinkling smile.

So this was that elusive thing called intimacy. You had to experience it to know how much it had been lacking before. Feel its fullness before you understood its absence. It was so much more than just a word.

It made making love into more than an action. More than sensation. More than want. More than lust.

Our bodies joining was more than a mating.

It was a place we had built together.

It was somewhere remote, separate from every other plane of existence where nothing else mattered. It was only the two of us. No one else existed.

It was where need collided with essentiality.

It felt necessary. It felt right.

It felt safe.

And that was terrifying. But so addictive I didn't let that part bother me.

I was good at putting things off until later.

Deadlines.

Feelings.

I did everything I'd listed at her. I sat in her chair and buried my face in her pussy long enough to make her relaxed to the point of limp.

I carried her to the sofa, laying her back carefully over the arm, her hips propped at the highest point, legs dangling.

It was perhaps an advanced position but she'd always been a student that liked to excel.

I gripped her hips in my hands and teased her with my heavy cock, grinding my shaft against her, close to her entrance but not penetrating at first.

She was writhing under my hands when I finally sank my tip in, advancing forward more slowly than my body wanted to. Her body took me in, devouring, sucking, clutching at my girth deliciously. I made it a little more than halfway before my hips took over, and I rammed my cock the rest of the way forcefully into her.

The madness took over again, but I had enough brain function at least to make it good for her, finally.

I drove into her repeatedly, strong, measured thrusts, as she silently gasped, my finger relentless on her clit.

I pushed down on her hips, arching her back, so that every pull in or out was grinding against the rawest part of her.

Luckily it was hitting a good nerve going by the filth coming out of her mouth.

I fucked her into a limp puddle.

"Is it always like this?" Ro asked me sometime later. I was sprawled out limp on the couch, her limp self draped across me, her head facing up in my lap. "I think I get why you have a sex addiction."

"One, no it's never, ever like this. Only *we* are like this. Our chemistry is out of this world. And two, I do not have a sex addiction. I just really, really like having a lot of it."

"Every day. Several times."

"You say the sweetest things," I told her. "Just give me a few more minutes and I'll do my best." Our affectionate eyes met. "It's the damnedest thing," I began softly.

"What's that?"

We were both speaking softly, our tones almost romantic.

"I think I could fuck us both to death. Certainly I'm willing to give it an honest shot. Literally everything else is a worse way to die."

"My poet is back." She clutched her hands to her chest like a Disney princess.

I stroked her hair, our gazes locked and said, "I could drown in your eyes," and meant it.

She had no snarky comeback for that one.

"I'm not inside of you, but a part me never left you," I continued relentlessly, addicted to the way my words were mesmerizing her. "I can feel you in every one of my cells, a permanent connection."

No witty retort for that one either.

"You're my best friend," I added.

Her soul devouring eyes were taking no prisoners, but still not a word.

"Sometimes when I look at you, my chest aches a bit," I told her. "It's not altogether pleasant, but it feels *necessary*."

No smooth rejoinder there.

I tried to make my voice wary, a little sarcastic. I had to ruin this moment or it would own me forever. "See? I'm a writer. I can do a bit of poetry on command."

That snapped us both out of it, thank God.

CHAPTER TWENTY-SEVEN

I mentioned in our routine morning briefing that I wanted to invite Dair, Iris, and the gang over for a pool party. She looked a bit surprised.

"One of your random hookup parties?"

I was startled by her assumption and frankly a bit horrified. What did she think this was? That I'd casually be looking for other women to hook up with? "Not at all. No single women allowed, in fact. A party for close friends. For Dair's family, and I suppose Heath and Lourdes, and maybe Frankie and Estella.

"Okay, make a guest list, let me know if you have any specific ideas for it, and I'll put it all together."

"Okay, I'll do that."

Uncannily though, Dair called me that afternoon and invited me over to their house for a BBQ that weekend.

"Be sure to bring Ro," he told me.

"Obviously," I replied absently, looking around. "Listen, whose idea was the barbecue?"

"Iris brought it up this morning. Why?"

"We were just talking about doing the same thing this morning. Does your Russian doll wife have my house bugged?"

Dair laughed like that was the funniest thing ever, but it was a fact that Iris had done crazier things.

It was quite the gathering.

Frankie and Estella couldn't make it. They were shooting an episode of their tattoo reality show in Bora Bora for no reason I could fathom other than the fact that Frankie loved Bora Bora and wanted her producers to pay for the trip.

Even without Frankie present, though, her ability to bring people together was.

Iris was good at making friends and their circle had naturally expanded to include some of Frankie's close friends. And Frankie, being somewhat famous, had a few famous friends, as well, some that Ro even recognized.

I'd met them all a few times, but I didn't know most of them well. I'd just never had that much room for blissfully happy married couples in my life. Dair, being my idol, was the exception, and Heath by extension.

It was a fun group, though, and it was fun to show and then introduce them all to a somewhat star struck Ro. Anything that could ruffle her tickled me as a rule.

"Is that Tristan Vega?" she asked me quietly.

Everyone was outside except for us. We'd just arrived and were scoping them out through the floor to ceiling back windows of Dair's extravagant mansion.

"It is. That's Tristan Vega, his exquisite wife Danika, and their gaggle of children are scattered all over the yard. I've lost count of how many there are. Frankie and Estella's daughter is in the mix somewhere. She's staying with their family while her parents are in Bora Bora. Hey, if Tristan and Heath got into a fight, who do you think would win?" I was a big guy, but both of them were NFL linebacker massive.

She ignored me, still looking. I saw when her eyes landed on a tall, beautiful man with dark blond hair. "Is that *that* billionaire?"

I smirked. I liked that she didn't know his name. He was a little too pretty boy eye-catching for my peace of mind. I didn't particularly want Ro's eye caught by anyone but me. "James Cavendish. He stars in one of the best sex tapes of all time, but I wouldn't mention that to his face. He's since reformed, and I've heard the whole thing is a bit of a sore subject. Oh, and he's married to that lovely blond woman he's got handfuls of that looks like a Swedish bikini model. Her name is Bianca. They have some kids running around out there too. Three of the blond ones are theirs. See over there, there, and there." I pointed. "The ones that look just like them."

I remembered a story she'd enjoy. "Iris was once caught counting cards at James's casino. They're friends now and they laugh about it, but she's still monitored every time she goes onto the property."

She looked at me, jaw dropping. "Are you serious?"

"Oh yeah."

She laughed. "I don't know why I'm surprised. That's *so* Iris."

"Right? I *knew* you knew she was *devious*."

She continued to scan the stacked pool party.

"Is that that famous actress?" Ro asked me quietly, awe in her voice. "Wow, she's even more stunning in person."

I sent a cursory glance toward the bombshell in the tiny white bikini. She was standing very close to her very obviously possessive husband and chatting with Iris.

I went back to watching Ro's face, where the true entertainment was for me. "Yeah, that's Scarlett Durant," I confirmed, "and yes, she is even more stunning in person," I agreed.

All these gorgeous women with doting husbands were making love and marriage seem downright palatable. I shook off the silly thought.

"I'll introduce you to everyone when we go outside, but for reference that big blond man hugging the smaller, pretty, dark-haired man next to James Cavendish is Bianca's best friend Stephan and *his* husband Javier. And the two guys with wavy black hair talking to Heath are Lourdes' older sons, Gustave and Raf. I think that about covers the people you haven't met before. Any questions?"

"I can't think of any, but that was a bit of information overload."

"It's going to be an interesting party."

"Hey, guys," a deep voice said from behind us.

I turned and eyed my very good friend like he was the enemy, just in case he was.

"Carter!" Ro exclaimed.

Oh she remembered him, huh. I was hoping she'd been too drunk at the time for him to make an impression. I gritted my teeth.

He approached and hugged her like they were close friends. She was wearing a bikini and a cover up, and I had to watch her luscious tits smoosh up against his six pack. "Lovely to see you again, Ro."

I glared at him, but he was oblivious, just smiling as he pulled back from embracing *my* woman.

"You meet your deadline?" I asked him.

"I did. Hey, can we brainstorm this week?"

I glanced at Ro, who was smiling up at my hunky friend. "At *your* house, sure," I drawled. No way was I letting Ro near him again if I had a say about it.

She glanced at me, saw something on my face that amused her, and the smile grew. "Hoyden," I said quietly.

"Sybarite," she returned.

Carter looked back and forth between us, grinning.

I wondered how I could warn him off from her without having to spell it out. It was a unique problem to me, one I'd be stewing through what to do about for quite some time.

Just then a tiny blond whirlwind ran into the house, spotted me, and screamed, "Tunner!" and launched herself at me.

I picked her up, put her on my hip, and beamed at her.

She beamed back and smacked her lips at me. I lifted her slightly and angled my head to let her give me the slobbery cheek kiss she was asking for. "Hello, Violet," I said to her.

She was a gorgeous toddler, a perfect mini Iris, and she adored me.

I didn't like to let it get out, but I was actually good with kids. I liked them. They were fun and funny, and natural troublemakers to a one. What wasn't to like?

"Have you been staying out of trouble?"

She grinned and it was so mischievous I thought she must have been practicing it. "Never!"

I shook my head and sighed. "It's too late. You're already just like your diabolical mother. Nothing to be done but watch you live out your evil genius origin story and stay on your good side."

She wasn't even three, but she giggled like she actually understood the joke. She might have. Who knew? There was a good chance she was another Masters genius.

I glanced up and caught Carter and Ro just staring at me. Carter was smirking like he was making a note to tease me about this later, but Ro... Ro was doing something much more interesting.

A hundred emotions crossed her face, a world of possibilities, a thousand things shut down in an instant, but I'd seen something there, something I'd be dissecting later, some wistful yearning that made my pulse start to race.

I carried a happy Violet as we headed outside, and I made the rounds introducing Ro to everyone.

Violet only wanted down when Heath started throwing kids around in the pool and she wanted to join.

I set her down and she scampered off.

"I was not expecting that," Ro told me quietly.

I met her eyes and smiled. "I'm even more charming than you thought. Impressive, I know."

She just shook her head as though I'd ruined the moment.

"Didn't think I'd be good with kids, did you?"

"I didn't think you'd like kids, to be frank. You didn't even like puppies until Machiavelli made you fall in love with her."

"That was your fault as much as hers. Don't sell yourself short."

"I rarely do."

It was sometime later when I'd followed Ro and Carter into the pool. I had the strange and unpleasant feeling that they'd forgotten I was even there.

He was telling her some details about teaching high school English in one of the worst public schools in the city, his way of giving back.

She looked very impressed.

Barf. I made sure Carter saw me gagging behind Ro's back.

He looked very entertained and not at all bothered, the bastard, just continued to talk to Ro like they were old buddies, or worse.

Did he assume she was single?

Did *she* assume that?

He was talking about coaching football and how it wasn't just about the sport, but a good way for under privileged kids to get scholarships that change their lives.

I rolled my eyes and thought about throwing something at him. I was holding a cup of good Scotch, and I debated whether I wanted to drink it or nail him with it.

I was crowding Ro from behind as she faced him and listened like he was the most interesting guy in the world. She didn't even seem to be aware that I was there.

If they started talking about church, I was going to shank him and let him bleed out in the water.

I was already looking around for something sharp.

My back was to the side of the pool, and I felt a light tap on my shoulder.

I turned and smiled with delight at my two favorite little hooligans.

They were staring intently at me like they shared a brain, and I just knew they were about to do or say something hilarious and delightful.

The two little boy cousins didn't look much alike. Dair's boy, Cameron, was the spitting image of him, dark hair, serious eyes that were way too intelligent for someone so young or anyone in general.

Heath's boy, Gerard, was, in contrast, the spitting image of him: a stocky blond pit bull of a child. He looked like he could have been the other boy's bodyguard, or a child assassin.

No, they couldn't have passed for twins, but they operated like they had shared a womb.

The little boy prodigy was staring at me intently, studying me like I was some sort of specimen. The little pit bull had his arms folded like he was acting as backup.

"My mom says you're a wastrel," Cameron told me, "I wanted to see what she meant."

I aimed my glare across the yard at the gloating blond bombshell who was his mother. She tipped a glass at me, smiling. It was probably water since she was pregnant and just starting to show in her bikini, still absolutely stunning with it.

I tipped mine back.

I looked at the kid and pointed at Iris. "Did your mother put you up to this? Did she tell you to say that?"

The prodigy giggled and ran off. The pit bull stared me down a bit then followed suit.

"You're a menace!" I called out to Iris.

She giggled, the same joyful light in her eyes as her son had.

Adorable but a bonafide menace.

Dair was moving by us in the pool now, dragging a squealing Violet around on a float.

"Give it to me straight," I told him. "How deeply is your meddling wife plotting against me?"

He just laughed and shook his head.

Without meaning to I hooked an arm around Ro's waist and pulled her back into my chest.

I felt her stiffen and I let her go instantly. We'd had a very practical, reasonable conversation on the way here where we'd agreed not to tell anyone our business, about keeping it to ourselves and keeping our distance from each other around everyone else. I'd just forgotten for a second.

I looked around to see who had noticed. Iris was smiling at me rather smugly, but no one else seemed to have taken note, when I'd have preferred for literally anyone else to have seen it.

Cameron and Gerard were crowded around her, when she bent down and whispered into both of their ears.

They ran up to me grinning. They both had her infectious smile. "Mom says you're being reprogrammed. What does that mean?" Cameron asked.

"What does comeuppance mean?" Gerard asked at the same time.

"I knew I wasn't just paranoid!" I shouted at her.

She shrugged, unfazed. "I was never hiding it. I warned you. I'm doing God's work."

"Dair," I called out to my friend, who was pretending to ignore me. "Tell your calamitous wife to stop plotting against me!"

Dair ignored me but Iris responded, "I'm plotting *for* you." She called out, "Don't worry your pretty little head about it."

CHAPTER TWENTY-EIGHT

Shortly after that my latest book released and I went on a book tour. Of course I made Ro come with me. I barely let her leave my sight these days.

I got a real kick out of the readers, particularly the real fans, the ones that knew my books better than I did, but I always got a strange but powerful case of nerves right before a signing.

Having Ro on hand was helpful with that.

Our first stop was a bookstore signing in New York.

We checked into the hotel and the second the bellhop left our room, I was on her. It had been a long flight of teasing touches, and I'd had plenty of time to think of just how I needed to get my fix.

I stripped us both down, had her grip the back of a chair, and admired the picture her nubile young self made in that position, arching for me so prettily.

I pressed my chest against her back, my throbbing erecting prodding against the meat of her butt.

I made her spread her legs farther, and bent my knees,

pushing my cock between her legs, rubbing my swollen head up and down her slick entrance, finding her cleft and breeching. When my tip was in, I shoved, propelling myself deep.

I held her in place with my open palms, mouth moving over her shoulders, hands stroking down the graceful arch of her spine.

I palmed one bouncy tit, the other hand getting to her clit with a purpose. I was in a rush. I got her off fast before really unleashing on her perfect, tiny body.

I had both her wrists in my hands as I pumped into her from behind, pounding in and out with hard, jarring thrusts.

It was so good. So. Fucking. Good. As I drew closer I got rougher, lost myself a bit, though Ro never seemed to mind. I plowed deep and came with a shout and held myself there, grinding her on the base of my cock, my tip jarring into her cervix. I kissed all over her back and shoulders as we caught our breath, my hands on her breasts, handling them with ownership and possession. I sucked at the side of her neck and said, "I missed this."

She choked out a breathless laugh. "We had sex last night."

"That was many hours ago, cupcake. We didn't even get a morning round in, that damned flight was so early."

We got a chance to sightsee a bit around the city, though not as much as I would have liked since Ro had never been to Manhattan before. We'd have to come back so I could give her the full tour.

We were exploring around Rockefeller Center when Ro stopped in her tracks.

I followed her rather obvious stare to watch a cute old couple embracing, cheek to cheek, their faces full of peaceful adoration. They were doing some sort of old people shuffle that probably used to be dancing.

"That's what I want," she said quietly, her face full of earnest yearning. "All I want is to have someone kiss me like that. Hold me like that. Touch me like that."

After that little speech, I studied the old couple like they were my direct competition. "They're *fine*, I guess. Not *that* adorable. We're cuter than them, to be honest."

"I'm not talking about us; I'm talking about what I want for the long haul. What I expect when I find the one. I want that cute couple cuddling in public at eighty love. That's not you."

That more than stung, even if it was true. Especially then. "Who says?" I asked. Just to be contrary, I told myself. "Don't put me in a box. It's provoking."

"Please," she said with an eye roll, "you don't subscribe to romantic love even existing, let alone a lifetime of it."

"Fair point. I can kiss and hold and touch you any way and anywhere you want, though, which was your original point."

"You don't get it. It's not the actions themselves, it's the feeling behind it, and the longevity of those feelings."

I was beginning to understand that very thing, so much so it was beginning to frighten me.

What I said though, was, "I'll show you some longevity as soon as we get back to the room, cupcake. As much as you can handle, and I promise you will feel it. Every single inch."

I gave her a wolfish grin and she smiled gamely, letting me ruin the serious moment, as usual.

She assisted me at the signing, always knowing what I needed before I did. Absolutely everything was better with her around. I knew before five minutes into the event that I'd never do another signing without her.

About halfway through she snuck me a glass of Scotch in a coffee cup that said, *This might be wine.*

When I realized what was in the cup, I sought her out with

my eyes and raised my brows.

She moved close behind me to whisper in my ear. "You have this certain look you get. I call it your Scotch face. You were wearing it so I scrounged up some Scotch. Not the good stuff, but you'll survive, muffin."

"You complete me," I told her solemnly, not looking back at her, not needing to, instead signing yet another book.

"That's obvious."

We flew to Philadelphia the next day and went through a similar routine.

We traveled well together. I was seasoned at it, and Ro, though she hadn't traveled much, was no complainer and every delay and setback was taken in stride.

Every day Dair sent us pictures of Machiavelli being hugged by his adorable kids.

Me: No matter what happens,
you don't get to keep our puppy.

Dair: That's true but after
playing with this puppy for a week
I'm pretty sure we're going to
have to get the kids another one.

Me: Be sure to do
yourself a favor and get
an actual dog and not a
Beanie Baby like we did.

Ro saw that text when I was showing her the latest pictures of Mac and smacked me on the arm.

"Are you offended on behalf of our Beanie Baby?" I asked her, amused.

"I am. You're her daddy, have some loyalty."

It was evening and we were in a hotel room, lounging on the bed. I grabbed her and pinned her underneath me. My words were a rasp into her ear. "Call me Daddy again, but this time in your phone voice."

She giggled, and my switch was flipped.

I dragged her clothes off, talking all the while, telling her what I wanted her to say to me in her phone sex voice.

She just got quiet, shaking her head, not saying a word.

She didn't speak to me until I was inside of her. Didn't make a peep until I plugged her up tight.

I didn't move once I was buried in her, just burrowed my root in hard and held myself there, feeling her, basking in my own little piece of paradise.

Her sex voice drifted to me in a soft, taunting drawl, "Get a move on, Daddy."

The delirium took over, and I started moving with a purpose and didn't stop until we were both a limp puddle of satiation.

Afterward, still inside her, I flipped us until she was settled on top of me, the weight of her heavy, bare breasts against my chest, rubbing her nipples against the overheated skin of my chest.

"I think we found a new kink for you," Ro mused, tracing lazy circles around my nipple with her index finger.

"Not new. You could read the phone book to me in that voice and I'd come."

In Seattle, I showed her the space needle. And tried to fuck us both into a stupor.

I was sitting at our hotel room's lone desk doing a phone interview when I caught sight of her coming out of the bathroom in a towel.

I covered the speaker and ordered, "Come and ride me, cupcake."

In another one of her random acts of obedience she did it, dropping her towel on the way.

I took my dick out, phone still to my ear.

I helped her straddle me with one hand.

It was the first time she'd ridden me like this, and she did it with the focus only an unrepentant perfectionist could.

She wiggled and positioned herself just right, sinking down onto my cock with singular focus.

"Is this right?" she asked when she'd seated herself properly.

It was more than right, but I couldn't manage to get a word out, as usual.

Instead I crushed her soft chest against mine, my arm a secure band around her waist and bucked her into an intense, rough ride.

I could last long enough inside of her to get her off these days, but it was pure, adoring effort. The second I knew she was coming, oblivion took me and when I resurfaced, I'd hung up on the interview. Oops.

She was boneless on top of me, her head on my shoulder, her breathing steady. I thought there was a good chance she might actually be asleep.

"It's okay. Just take a nap on my dick like this," I said wryly. "When it's ready to go again it will wake you up, I have no doubt."

She mumbled something, her lips against my skin, that sounded like, "Promises, promises."

In L.A., Ro talked me into a day at Disneyland after the signing. I balked, made her bribe me for it, and had a great time.

We were holding hands in public now and not saying a thing about it. Not saying a thing about any of the affectionate little gestures that were becoming a habit for us.

It wasn't that I didn't think we needed to talk about the dreaded R word—relationship—it was just that we had all the time in the world, and I wanted *her* to bring it up.

I wanted her to come to me with the idea so I could surprise the hell out of her by agreeing without a qualm. Ruffled Ro was my happy place.

I made her stand in line for every photo op we passed. We didn't have nearly enough pictures together.

She made me wait in line for the tiny kid rides that barely jostled you.

I *dragged* her onto the very lightweight rollercoasters in the park. She tried to resist, but it was too ridiculous that she basically wanted to just come here and walk around.

It didn't hurt that when she got scared, she buried her face against me like I was the last piece of land she was holding onto at the edge of the world. I honestly couldn't get enough of her like that.

After Splash Mountain she clung to me, arms wrapped around my waist after we got off the ride and wouldn't let go. I pulled her to an alcove out of the way of the overwhelming rush of amusement park foot traffic. I held her for a good thirty minutes, her face buried in the center of her chest.

I rubbed her back and kissed the top of her head, over and over. "You poor thing," I said sympathetically when she finally pulled back to look up at me. "You itty bitty wuss."

"That's the last rollercoaster," she told me sternly.

I laughed. "Oh no, cupcake, we're doing them all. Cuddle as much as you want to, but brace yourself for it."

"Sadist," she said, face back in my chest.

"Baby," I taunted, stroking her hair tenderly.

In the room that night, I managed to finally get out a word when my dick was busy inside of her.

"Mine," I grunted out as I came.

When she caught her breath, she said, "Hey! You got a word out during intercourse. Way to go, Thorn!"

"Don't you dare talk to me like I'm your bro about a subject like that."

In her phone sex voice she said, "Roger that, tall boy."

I was on her back and just for that I pulled back, bent down, grabbed a handful of luscious ass cheek, and bit it hard enough her make her yelp.

CHAPTER TWENTY-NINE

It all went to hell in a few short minutes. I only pieced together how it had happened later and so reacted poorly.

I came to regret that in a way that I couldn't remember feeling regret ever before.

I reconstructed it after as though I could have somehow changed the outcome of it if I had handled it better. It was the sort thing I'd go over in my head again and again, finding better things I could have said.

We were in my office. I was at my desk looking at my computer, and she was on my phone posting something on social media for me. She used my phone all the time. She was my assistant, so that was unavoidable. She was fastidious usually about using it only for the professional things she needed and never snooping. But sometimes timing just sucked.

I was receiving considerably less filth from women by that point. Ignoring them fixed that almost across the board. A few persistent ones however, just kept going. Those I had taken to treating with a few acerbic comments that were meant to discourage them, which apparently I wasn't that good at.

She was looking at my phone, me at my laptop screen when I received a picture that shocked even me a bit. I was very, very regretful that Ro had to see it.

And I was even more regretful about what happened after she did.

We looked at each other. "I'm deeply sorry you had to see that," I told her instantly and solemnly.

She just blinked, her gaze sort of blank and distant. She didn't say a word, just went back to work.

At first I thought that was a good sign, that she wasn't upset.

It was not a good sign.

Turns out a deeply upset Ro was too much for me just like every iteration of Ro had ever been.

It was maybe a full hour later that I started to see the damage that had been done.

We were working in her office now, me lounging on the couch. She was at her desk and didn't even look at me as she said quietly, "I think this has run its course."

I had no notion what she could mean at first. Denial and all that.

"Those media posts?" I asked, trying to remember what she was working on, exactly.

"Us," she said blandly, still not looking up, her hands not so much as slowing on her keyboard.

I took it as a joke.

Joking was what we did. "Oh yes, we're totally finished with each other, obviously." I said it like it was the most ridiculous notion in the world. To me, it was. "I get Machiavelli in the divorce. And exclusive rights to eating your pussy."

"I'm not quitting, Turner, but the… sex, all of that, whatever it was, I think it's for the best if we call it quits now."

My heart felt like it did a full, excruciating turn in my chest. It fucking hurt. "I don't understand," I said slowly. What was even happening? And why did it feel like a slow motion nightmare? "You're joking." My voice was so weak, I wanted to snatch the words back and say it with new purpose, as though that would make the statement more real, but it wasn't like that.

It was already well beyond that.

"I'm not joking, for once. I can't sleep with you anymore. Let's put all of that behind us; keep this strictly professional.

"You don't mean it," I told her reasonably. "You're upset. I'm sorry I didn't realize you were upset. What can I do to make it right?"

"It's not like that. Let's not do this. It's over. No need to make it a thing. It's just over. We'll move on."

It was not even a proper break up scene. She was relentless and stone-faced. Even in this she couldn't do things predictably. She wasn't heartbroken or hysterical.

Her eyes were dryer than my dick right then.

It was startling and demoralizing how quickly she had me willing to beg. "Please don't do this. We can fix this. There's no reason on earth to end it. Please," I repeated, soft and heartfelt.

She studied me for a while and it felt merciless, no softening in her eyes for me at all. "One question. That's all we need to settle this for good. Has any of this meant *anything* to you?"

I blinked at her, all of the steam leaving my body.

"Yes," I said.

"Okay, so what has it meant?"

She was smarter than me. It was a problem.

I tried to level with her, because I knew where she was leading the conversation. It could only end one way.

Of course, she knew that too.

I answered her, and it wasn't clean and neat, nowhere near wrapped up in the perfect package that it needed to be. "I don't want to stop," I said, as sincere as I'd ever been. "I want this to keep going—*us*—a permanent arrangement."

"Why?"

"Excuse me?" I honestly didn't understand the question.

"Why do you want it to keep going? Because the sex is good?"

I started to answer with an obvious *yes,* but I was smarter than that.

Yes was obviously a trap. "First of all, that's an understatement. The sex is *phenomenal,*" I began—

"Exactly!" she said it like it was an *aha* moment, and I knew I'd still stepped into that damned trap even though I'd seen it from a mile away. "I'm embarrassed to admit that I was trying to turn this into something more than it ever was," she said. "It was foolish of me, but that doesn't change the facts."

I was stunned. Blindsided by her words. She was so stoic that she'd left me more than half in the dark. Was she saying now that she had feelings for me? And if so, what exactly were those feelings? And were they already gone, before she'd even given me a goddamn heads up?

I'd have really liked to know.

A part of me, some strange little, itchy twinge in my chest *needed* to know.

"Listen," I said, rallying again for control of the situation. "You're blowing this out of proportion. Clearly we need to have a talk about our expectations… and our *feelings.*" Boy, that word was a doozy to get out of my mouth, but it felt necessary. "And that text you saw, I didn't even open it on purpose. And my response was clearly a joke. It didn't mean anything—"

"This is my point. None of this means *anything*, and that is not the type of person I want to be. I want to mean something. I want my actions to mean something, and that something shouldn't be that I can't control my own hormones. This is done, Turner, and if you're true to your word, I can keep working here as though this never happened. Business as usual, lives back to normal."

My fists were clenched, and the itchy twinge in my chest had worked itself deeper, turning into a bitter ache.

An ache I'd never felt before, and didn't know what to do with, and was profoundly unequipped for.

"My word is solid," I said dully, a little in shock at how quickly this had gotten out of hand and escalated to this conclusion. "So fine, if this is what you want, what you insist on—"

"I do," she interrupted. "I insist."

"Okay, then we'll just go on, back to business as usual."

She left the room, as though that settled it.

It should have, I supposed, but for some strange reason, I sat there and reeled, nothing feeling settled, no part of me accepting the sudden change.

I went back to my texts, examining the stupid thing that had ended it all.

Me: What, only 2 of you this time?

They'd taken it as a challenge, which honestly hadn't been my point. Sometimes I just couldn't keep the sarcastic, intrusive thoughts to myself, and I'd honestly taken the crack without thinking. I was thinking hard about it now.

I approached her in the kitchen. She was making herself a latte and me a double espresso.

Ever the pro.

I wanted to shake her.

I wanted to beg her on my knees.

"That comment I made, in the text," I began earnestly, "I can see how that might come across badly, but it wasn't how it looked. I was just making an ironic statement, and those chicks took it seriously."

She held up a hand, not even looking at me. "You don't have to do this. I don't have hard feelings. I knew who you were the whole time, and frankly, I think I needed this little reminder."

"It wasn't—"

"Don't, Turner. I'm not changing my mind, and I'm not sure why you'd want me to. You have naked pictures of my cousin in your phone. She's got pictures of your cock in hers. Yes, I saw all of that too. I apologize, it was out of line, but after I saw that text… I looked. I knew you hooked up with her, knew who and what you were from day one. Like I said, I just needed this reminder, and now it is time to move on."

She didn't sound even close to approaching mad, but I was getting there.

I supposed this cold reaction was better than tears or a tantrum, but somehow it felt more fundamentally damaging.

For her. For me.

"Those pictures were from months ago," I told her fake calmly. It was an honest effort not to raise my voice. "Before I even *met you.*"

"She sent you a picture of her . . . privates," she blushed bright red as she spoke, "last week."

"And I didn't respond!" Now I was raising my voice. "You saw that, right? I didn't even open it. I can't control what's being sent to me!"

"Of course you can't." Finally, some spark behind her eyes that spoke of feelings. "Which is my point. I *can* control things like that. How you live is not how I want to live. Who you are is not who I want to be." God, that hurt. And she just kept going. "I need to get back to being the kind of person I can respect." Fucking ouch.

She was so set against me that her rejection felt like a third person in the room between us, and it was fucking brutal.

I just stared at her. How could it be over? It felt to me like it should never be over. How could she think it was over? How could she *want* it to be over? And what on earth could I even do about it?

The answer was demoralizing. I could do nothing. I had no right to do anything at all, in fact the opposite. I had to respect her wishes, and I was supposed to do it with grace.

"I'll keep working here," she told me after a while. I'd been staring at her for quite some time, like if I didn't move from this spot, this moment, I could somehow fix it. "Cleaning up your messes," she continued, not unkindly, "and you and I will quickly forget that *this* mess ever happened."

But I didn't forget. Couldn't.

Couldn't even muster up the will to *try* to forget or move on.

How sad was that?

I caught her quietly moving her things out of my room that afternoon and almost lost it. I sat on my bed and watched her go in and out of my closet and bathroom, not lifting a finger to help.

I wasn't going to help her put me behind her, was incapable of it.

I went into the bathroom to splash cold water on my face as she took yet another armload of clothes out of my room, her expression sublimely unaffected by it all.

I was drying my face when I saw it. Her French teddy was in my little bathroom wastebasket. She'd thrown it away.

Thrown me away.

I grabbed it and stashed it in a drawer before she came back.

I slept with it that night like it was a beloved blankie. Sadly, it did help a bit.

Also, I grabbed Mac and brought her to bed with me for cuddle comfort. That helped a bit too.

The fact that Ro had to come into my room first thing in the morning to find the dog and take her out didn't hurt either.

She was well put together for the day already, in one of her professional little outfits, glasses on squarely, hair pulled back into a flawless bun. It was like none of this was affecting her at all when I wanted to beat my chest and scream and bawl my eyes out like a baby.

She took the tiny dog out of my arms, careful to not so much as touch me. That hurt.

"You can't do that," Ro chided me softly, not looking at me or my almost naked, barely sheet covered body. I don't know if she didn't see or just didn't acknowledge that I was clutching her discarded teddy. "If we're going to crate train her effectively, she needs to learn to sleep in there, to look at it as her comfort zone."

"But where's my comfort zone?" I asked her retreating back.

She didn't bother to answer.

CHAPTER THIRTY

I didn't feel well at all. Something worse than a bad flu. I couldn't get out of bed, didn't want to. My head hurt, and I was lethargic and listless.

It took me a few days to realize I wasn't sick, just deeply depressed.

Ro had been caring for me like I was ill but in a very impersonal, professional way, and I hated it.

Sheer determination got me back into a productive routine again, but the depression wouldn't shake.

I couldn't sleep hardly at all, found myself wandering the house at all hours.

I blamed sleep deprivation on what came next.

It was completely out of line. Even sleep deprived, I knew it.

I went to see her in the middle of the night.

In her bed.

While she was sleeping.

I justified it by telling myself that I just wanted to lay down with her, to hold her.

I was lonely.

It was a sad day indeed when I admitted things like that to myself.

I wore boxers at least. It was something.

She was wearing a thin nightshirt that probably went to her knees. It wasn't there now, as she'd slept it'd ridden up around her hips. I could make out that much in the dark, though not much else.

I slid in behind her. She was on her side, and I spooned her, smelling her hair as I hugged her.

I honestly was just cuddling, though even that was laughably out of line.

She moved her back against me, moaning softly in her sleep.

I blamed that little artless moan for everything that happened after.

My roaming hand cupped a breast, and I shifted, letting my hard dick rub against her backside lightly.

I have no excuse for myself.

Madness took me over then.

And I let it.

Flashes of the night burned themselves with permanent intent into the frontal lobe of my brain.

Me over her, hot skin touching, sliding on top of her, against her, inside of her.

My bothered breath in her ear, panting out one word, over and over.

"Mine."

When I was done, I sat back on my heels, hands on her hips, pulling her to me. I held her on my dick. She tried to wiggle away, but I held her tight. "Just let me feel you like this for one more night, at least. You left me without warning. I need one more night."

She stilled. I took that as agreement that I could do whatever I wanted to her until morning.

And I did. It was a marathon night. I didn't let either of us sleep. I touched her everywhere, kissed her everywhere, worshipped her body like I'd never have her again.

Neither of us said another word though. The night was silent except for the sounds of pleasure and sin. Dawn was creeping in her window before I finally broke the spell.

I was leaning over her, sucking on her nipple as I dragged my trailing cum up her thighs and shoved it back into her.

That's when I said the unquestionably demented thing that made her kick me out of bed. Even I thought her reaction was justified and correct.

"We should have a kid," I said against her skin, "I think we'd make good co-parents. Let me knock you up."

"Get out," she said.

The next morning was another bad scene, and though I deserved it, I could hardly stand it.

She was doing me the kindness of acting like the night before had never happened, like I had never crossed so many boundaries with her. Boundaries she'd been so clear about that I was lucky she would ever so much as speak to me again.

And still I had to push it. Was incapable of keeping my mouth shut.

She'd just handed me some paperbacks to sign at my desk and was on her way back out when I stopped her.

"Wait. Please. You implied, when you broke up with me, that you were trying to turn what we had into something more, but you only said it as you were ending things. Can we talk about that? About the something more?"

"We can't, Turner." She didn't even turn around. "Why do you insist on making this so much harder than it needs to be? Do you know how unfair that is?" I watched her back as her whole body moved with a deep breath, as though calming herself.

She continued, "We both know someone was gonna get hurt here, someone was *always* going to get hurt. And I think we both know that person is me. The least you can do is stop twisting the knife. At least cut me loose before it's even worse."

I stared at her wondering which of us was crazy that we saw it this differently.

"How *exactly* do we know that?" I asked her, trying my best to sound composed when I wanted to throw something. "Why? You're the one that broke up with me. You think that didn't hurt?"

"It wasn't a break up. We were never together."

That one *really* hurt. Because she was right. I'd had my chance, and I hadn't so much as brought up the fact that I wanted a relationship with her, not in any serious way.

Regardless, I had to rally. I wasn't just giving up because I'd been an ass. I was *still* an ass, and I intended to make that work for me. "What did you think was happening here?" I asked, each word enunciated slowly. "I was clearly the one that cared more. I pursued *you*, Miss Apathetic. What did you think that meant?"

She faced me then. Her eyes would have taken out my legs if I wasn't already sitting down. Her words were worse. "It meant *nothing*," she slashed her hand in the air and I flinched. "Nothing more than intimacy combined with sex, remember?"

I sat perfectly still while she shredded my heart with a few matter of fact words.

Words that I had taught her. Words that I had once believed.

Oh the sweet justice of it. Brought low by own cynical ideals.

She wasn't done. "You pursuing a woman is like a lion chasing his next meal. It was simply nature. I ran, you gave chase."

I disagreed with everything she'd said for so many reasons that I didn't know where to start dismantling it.

What I said though, was, "Okay, first of all, your analogy makes no sense. Female lions are the ones that do the hunting." I shook off the intrusive thoughts and got back to the point. Kind of. "Second, male lions are lazy. They don't chase anything, they let the food come to them. That was me before you. I did not chase. I ate what was brought to me. I've only ever chased *you*."

"The only point you're making right now is that you can talk in circles. I'm sorry I used a lion analogy without doing proper research, but my point still stands."

I stood up then and pointed at her. "It doesn't," I said stiffly, restraining myself from flipping my desk. "It doesn't fucking stand, that's what I'm telling you. I wanted to be with you, when I haven't so much as considered that option for longer than I can remember. I *still* want to be with you and you're the one rejecting me, and I want you to quit acting like it wasn't *your* idea to end us."

You hurt me. You're still hurting me, was what I wanted to say, but it was just too pathetic.

"Your flair for melodrama is getting out of hand," she said almost fondly, clearly trying to defuse the situation. "Have you never had anyone else end things with you before? Do you just not know how to react to that?"

Her teasing tone told me she was trying to make light of things, but it wasn't working. Things were fucking heavy, and she was only adding to the weight. "You're being cruel," I told her with as much dignity as I could and walked out of my own office to get away from her.

The next time I saw her I was working sullenly at the

kitchen table and she approached me waving a literal white flag. I squinted at it. "Where did you get that?"

"I cut up one of your shirts. Truce? Can we be friends?"

I sighed and gazed at her with tender gravity. "I'll always be your friend, Ro. You're my very *best* friend. I just wish we could understand each other better. I wish I knew how to get through to you."

"We're so much alike and so different," said Ro. "Sometimes it feels like I can read your mind, and other times I find you to be the most unpredictable person on the planet. It's been an interesting combination."

I looked at the flag again, smirking. "You don't find it ironic that you had to destroy my property to make a symbol for peace?"

We shared a smiled. "That was my favorite part of the gesture."

CHAPTER THIRTY-ONE

Things didn't go back to normal after that but there was a tentative sort of peace. Above all things, I needed Ro to stay in my life as close as I could have her. So of course I tried to respect her mile high boundaries and took what I could get.

A few weeks post breakup, I noticed that she was looking a little different and a touch wan. I studied her more intently even than usual and by the end of the day I could put my finger on what it was.

"You've lost weight," I pointed out blandly as she delivered an espresso to my desk.

She just looked up, blinked at me a few times, and began to walk away. "Maybe. I don't know. Who cares?"

"I care. Why are you losing weight? Are you dieting, or are you stressed out?"

She paused at the door to say, "Being stressed out makes me gain weight, so it can't be that. And no, I'm not on a diet. I don't know what's up. I guess I've been so busy I keep forgetting to eat lunch."

"Well, stop it. Take better care of yourself. Take a proper lunch break every day."

That at least gave me the excuse to start making her eat with me at more meals again. It was something.

For a time things were almost bearable. Not all the way there, but almost.

And then it became so much worse.

She met him at church.

Barf.

I knew something was up when Iris, Lourdes, and Estella came to the house and started huddling around Ro near the end of our workday, talking in hushed voices.

Ro hadn't even bothered to tell me they were coming over.

They all disappeared into her wing of the house. For hours.

And then suddenly they were all downstairs again, heading for the front door, all except for Ro.

I'd been lounging in the sitting room at the front of the house with a sleeping Mac on my lap, not even trying to hide the fact that I was just waiting for them.

I set Mac carefully down and stood when they appeared, and all three women froze at the sight of me, and then made polite greetings as though they weren't acting suspicious as hell.

Everyone was quite pleasant to me.

Lourdes shot me a few sympathetic looks like she might have a clue what I was going through but didn't say anything.

Estella gave me a big hug and patted me on the back, a consoling gesture. I took it. I needed it.

Iris just studied me like she was wondering what was wrong with me. She waited while the other two women filed out of the front door to say to me chidingly, "How could you let her go, Turner? You guys were perfect for each other."

I just shook my head. I didn't have a good answer, and the way she said it felt like a knife to the gut, like she was sure I had blown it beyond all possibility of repair.

When they were gone, I started pacing the house, Mac at my heels. I was passing Ro's office for maybe the dozenth time when I realized she was actually in it.

I backtracked, then stared at her.

And stared.

"What did you do?" I asked her with narrow-eyed suspicion.

"Are you referring to my hair?" she asked back.

That was part of it. It was down and curled. And she was wearing a short floral dress that showed off her figure in a very distracting way. She even had on cute little heels.

Also she had a full face of makeup on, which I'd never seen before. She didn't need it. Her skin was perfect without.

"I prefer it the other way," I told her gruffly.

She glared at me. It was adorable.

"What are you all dressed up for?"

"I'm going out," she said, tone idle.

"Where?" I asked, sick dread hollowing out my stomach.

"Dinner," said Ro, annoyance starting to creep into her answers.

"By yourself?" I asked. My fingertips were shaking. I thought I might throw up.

"With a friend." Her tone was flat, fully annoyed now.

"Just one friend?" I asked grimly.

"Does it matter? What's with the third degree?"

I felt possibly more harassed than I ever had in my entire life.

"Stop prevaricating and answer the question," I said with fake calm.

"I'm not trying to hide anything," she said in the most defensive tone I'd ever heard out of her. "I'm not doing anything wrong. I'm going on a date."

It hurt. Deep in my bones. Pain.

"With who?" I asked, not pulling off the fake calm anymore.

"No one you know. I met him at church."

I stared, and it was not friendly. "At a church dance?"

She flushed.

"I knew it! I knew that was some kind of meat market."

"Stop. I met him after… we were *totally* done."

I had to bite my lips not to say what I wanted to, which was that we'd *never* be done, let alone totally.

She was still talking, still stomping on my heart with her cute little feet. "He's new to town. I'm showing him around."

"What's his name?"

"Aaron."

I hated his name. It sounded so clean cut and normal. "What does he do?" I asked. I was willing to bet he didn't make more money than me, the punk.

"He's an accountant."

Oh I hated his guts. Cast aside for a fucking number cruncher. "Where's he taking you?"

She blushed and I wanted to howl at the moon. "We have a reservation at that new hot restaurant in the Cavendish casino. James was nice enough—"

"Oh, it's James, is it?"

"Well, James through Bianca. She was nice enough to get us in, after I met her at that party and started going to that girls' night thing."

"Fuck anonymous? That thing is sexist, you know. No men allowed? Not very progressive."

She ignored that completely. "I'm meeting him there.

Don't be rude about it. I'm nervous enough as it is. I can't remember the last time I've been on a date."

I had to sit down, mind reeling. My heart felt like it had stopped in my chest.

I'd never even taken her on a proper date.

I was staring at her, eyes stinging.

She saw something on my face that had her feeling my forehead. I closed my eyes, leaning into her touch.

"I think you might be coming down with something," she mused.

"I might," I agreed. "I'm sorry I never took you on a date," I said, voice low and *agonized*. "I have no excuse."

Her tone was completely innocent when she said, "Oh, stop. I never expected that from you. I knew what I was getting into.

I felt a stream of self-loathing pour into me that was *unprecedented*.

"I'm sorry I didn't make you expect more from me," I said quietly.

And then. "Please don't go out with him." I couldn't hold it in anymore.

"Don't do this. No games. We're still close friends, Turner, let's not mess that up, okay?"

I just stared at her, feeling adrift, lost in pain.

She left soon after and I picked up Mac and followed her to the front door, watched her open it, followed her out and watched her get into her car.

Watched her drive away. I might've stood there until she returned if the puppy hadn't snapped me out of it by barking.

I patted her head and went inside. "She'll be back, Mac. She'll always come back."

I wished I believed that.

I was waiting for her when she got home around midnight. Right by the front door with the puppy in my lap.

"Tell me about this guy," I asked the second she walked in the door. "You really like him?"

"I don't know yet. He seems really nice." She paused. "He makes me laugh."

He made her laugh.

He made her laugh.

It was possibly the most hurtful thing she could have said to me.

My mind went wild, finding the most painful ways to take that, pictured her marrying this new guy, moving out, quitting and having his babies.

I have a very active imagination and it did me no favors then.

Was he the one?

I wished I was still the one.

Had I even been the one? Was I capable of being anyone's one?

I could barely choke out a goodnight before I handed off Mac to her and fled.

She went out with him that Sunday as well. I was waiting for her when she came home from that, and I was not keeping it together well.

I was not keeping it together at all.

"Have you slept with him?" I bombarded while she was getting out of her car.

I didn't ask because I wanted to know.

I asked because I *needed* to know.

She stared at me like I was deranged, and I was only relieved by that. "Yeah," she said with dripping sarcasm, "We went to an orgy after Sunday school," she continued, deadpan, "I'm surprised we didn't see you there."

I grinned, feeling lighthearted for the first time in days. "You must have been at that other orgy. Pity."

I wanted to see this guy she wasn't undressing for.

I made sure I was in the driveway the next time he picked her up.

I was wearing flannel PJ bottoms and a wife beater, glass of Scotch in hand.

He was perfectly normal looking. Not too tall, not too big, not too handsome, not too much of anything.

Maybe that's what she liked. The opposite of my overwhelming self.

Ro opened the front door and Machiavelli rushed out, barking so hard her whole body bounced with each one.

He stepped out of the car. They moved toward each other and hugged for just a moment before pulling back.

Ro introduced him to me.

I had to unclench my fist to shake his hand.

Mac was right at his feet, still barking at him like he hadn't passed the dog test. I loved her, the stupid Muppet. I picked her up with my free hand and she quieted instantly, her adoring eyes on my face.

I smiled at Aaron and it felt deeply unpleasant, but still I pressed on, "Why don't you come on in for a drink, Aaron?" I asked.

He smiled in a very boy next door, aw shucks way, and I wanted to punch his teeth out.

"I don't drink," he said like he was apologizing for it.

Of course he fucking didn't. I knocked back the rest of my glass of Scotch.

He just blinked at me with wide eyes.

I tried again. "Why don't you come in for a cup of coffee then?"

They were standing together, shoulders nearly touching.

He wasn't tall, but everyone was taller than Ro, so I supposed that worked out.

"Raincheck on that," he told me in the most affable way, "we have a reservation, so we kind of have to go."

I was looking at them and no matter what she'd said, how she'd dumped me, it wouldn't stop the feelings, the sense of ownership.

Mine, my gut called out, even as I watched that skinny little fucker drive away with her.

I was waiting again when she came home several hours later.

She was barely in the door when I started in on her.

"I don't like him," I told her shamelessly. "There's something off about him. He's not the one for you. I feel like he's a liar."

"Really?" she asked, sounding concerned.

Holy shit. She was going to value my twisted, biased opinion. I wasn't a good enough of a guy not to use that to my advantage. "He's too slick."

"Really?" she asked. "That's a bummer. I wasn't getting that read at all on him, but I do trust your instincts."

She did? It was news to me. Very welcome news.

"I find him to be profoundly exceptionable," I added.

I knew I'd laid it on a bit too thick by the way her eyes narrowed me.

"Stop that," she said, not unkindly. "No games, remember?"

I'd never once agreed to that. That was her thing. I would have played every game in the book if only I thought one of them would work.

CHAPTER THIRTY-TWO

I was brainstorming with Dair, at his house. We hadn't done this in a while, not since I'd been in mourning about being dumped.

Well, we weren't so much brainstorming as I was venting at him about Ro and her new man.

He was gratifyingly sympathetic about it.

Up until he said, "That's one of the toughest things about love. Your heart is in another person, and you really have no control over what they might do."

"Love?" I stared. "Oh please. She's my best friend, if that's what you mean. I suppose I feel that kind of love. I want her, and I value her, I do. She does make me feel things I've never felt before. But romantic love, as in the falling kind? What a bunch of nonsense. That's just a concept invented for marketing purposes. Stop looking at me like that. Just because you've lost your head over a woman doesn't mean it could happen to someone like me. Please. I'm too pragmatic to give into such a notion. Stop smiling like that, as if you know something I don't. You might be older than me, but I'm far more experienced with women. Oh shut up."

"I didn't say a thing," Dair retorted, still with that blasted smile on his face.

I glared at him and we dropped it.

It was only as I was driving home that it hit me.

Holy shit.

I'd thought this way for so long, that unthinking it had never even occurred to me.

Iris was right, goddamn her. I'd needed to be reprogrammed.

Of course. It was so obvious, even to oblivious, self-loathing me.

Just because I'd declared something wasn't real didn't make it so.

I loved Ro. Of course I did.

I loved her so much.

Fuck.

I was in love with her.

As soon as I realized it was real I also recognized that it fucking sucked.

No one ever mentions how much it *hurts* to be in love. How all the numb parts of you are brought to life in an agony of feeling with every pump of your newly made heart. How every careless thing you've ever said suddenly has too much weight, and everything in your past has the sudden potential to end you.

I was in love. I just kept thinking, my mind reeling with the ramifications.

Now what the hell was I supposed to do?

CHAPTER THIRTY-THREE

I changed. My priorities. My credo. My cynical heart. My phone number.

It was necessary.

And I had a plan. A ruthless one. I might be dipping my toes into being romantic, but that didn't mean I was going to be nice or gentle about it.

I planned to be an absolute nightmare, in fact, until I got my way.

Step one: Church.

I was wearing a perfectly tailored gray Armani suit as I waited by the front door. I'd already put Machiavelli away in her kennel.

I was ready early just to be sure she didn't leave without me.

When she saw me, she stopped in her tracks.

The way she studied me was gratifying, the way she couldn't completely hide her reaction was the best thing I'd felt since she'd ended us.

"You look nice," she said evenly. "What are you all dressed up for?"

I opened the front door for her, waving her out.

I was in the passenger seat of her car before she caught on.

She started shaking her head. "No. You don't believe in church. You don't believe in anything."

"That's an exaggeration. And I'd like to go. I'm curious, and I promise to behave."

Finally she just started driving if only because I wouldn't get out of her car.

Church was fine. I wasn't sure what I was expecting, but everyone seemed sort of normal. In fact, everyone was very nice and welcoming.

Except for Ro. She was furious a few short minutes in.

We were in the lobby mingling before the service, Ro introducing me to her friends, because what else could she do?

"God bless," I tried on a few of them. It seemed to float so I kept doing it.

She literally pulled me outside to chew me out. "They may not know you're making fun of them," she said, sounding livid, "but I do. And I don't appreciate it."

I raised my hands, and told her the truth, "I'm actually not. I'm trying to fit in. I heard a few of them say it, and I thought it was what I was supposed to say. I've never been inside of a church before, you know." I paused. "You've met my father. How religious do you imagine my upbringing has been? But I've gotten off track. The point is, I'm being sincere, not snarky. You're my friend and I'm trying to embrace the things that you find important. Isn't that what friends do?"

She wasn't charmed by my very charming speech. "That is not friendship stuff," she said quietly. "That is boyfriend stuff and wholly inappropriate for us."

"Why?" I asked her.

"Don't start with your flair for the ridiculous again. I'm not a prize just because I left first."

"No. You're a prize because you're perfect."

"Knock it the hell off."

I did. Sort of. "So I'm not welcome here, because I'm a skeptic? Is that how your church works?"

She sighed and I knew I'd won a small victory.

"Of course not," she said with resignation. "It's about community. You don't have to believe. You just have to try. Try to listen, try to get something out of it, whatever it is you may be looking for, hopefully something that makes you a better person. That's what church is to me. But if you're going to be here, please just be respectful.

"I am. Truly. I like anything that helped make you who you are. I certainly respect that."

We went back inside right as they were seating everyone in the room where the service would take place, the lobby swiftly clearing out.

We walked to the doorway, and as we looked for seats, Aaron saw us and waved.

He'd saved a seat for Ro, but only one. I shamelessly maneuvered my way into taking *his* seat, the sucker. Now that I was done wallowing in my broken heart, was in fact back in fighting shape, and had a plan, he was *toast*.

I had my arm around the back of Ro's seat for the entire service, and she didn't make a fuss about it, probably loath to make a scene. I decided then that I liked church, and that I would continue to go.

I didn't get much out of the sermon, no profound revelations.

I didn't have a great frame of reference for any of it, but I did what Ro said, tried to listen, and I figured if I kept going it might begin to make more sense. And if not, it was worth it to go just to escort her.

Worst case scenario, I'd spend an hour every week being her arm candy. It sure as hell beat staying at home without her.

After the service, I tried to charm as many people she spoke to as I could. Ro seemed to be friends with everyone, particularly every lady over seventy, and I caught on quick.

I invited several sweet old ladies over for dinner, flirting with and flattering them shamelessly. Not a one of them said no.

If the way to Ro's heart was through adorable senior citizens, I'd adopt a football team's worth of them. More.

Ro was sending me exasperated looks the whole drive home.

"What?" I asked, all cheeky innocence. "I'm charming, I can't help it. What should we make for Ethel, Agnes, Ella, Prudence, and Rose when they come to the house for dinner this week?" I gave her a grin that showed all of my teeth. "See, I even remembered their names."

"You're impossible," she told me, and there was affection in it.

I soaked it up.

"Look who's talking," I told her. "And are you saying you *don't* want to have dinner with those sweet old ladies?"

"No, I'm saying *you* don't really want to. This is some sort of a plot, isn't it?"

"Just you watch, cupcake."

CHAPTER THIRTY-FOUR

Step Two: Sincerity

Another week passed.

We had the delightful old ladies over for dinner, and I charmed them all into a mess Ro had to scrape off the floor.

I went to a church dance with her and turned every lady over sixty around the room twice.

I buttered her up shamelessly before I finally cornered her in her office to have it out.

"I'd like you to consider a reconciliation between us," I began, my tone almost professional. "I haven't been with anyone else since the second day after I met you. And I don't miss it. Well, I do miss sex. Of course I do. But I don't miss the other women. I only miss you. Doesn't that count for something?

"It counts for something. I'm just not sure it's enough for what you're asking of me.

What do you think I'm asking of you?"

"To get wrapped up in you again. When I'm wrapped up in you, you're all I can think about."

I was smiling without realizing it at first. I really liked the sound of that. "What's wrong with that?" I asked, an honest question.

"It's not the sort of thing someone should go through alone. That's no good."

"Who says you're alone? That you ever were with me? You want me to tell you I'm wrapped up too? I'm fucking wrapped. What else do you need from me? I've got more than that."

As a start to my profession of love, it was lacking, but in my defense, she wasn't being at all cooperative.

"Give me something, then," she told me stiffly, like she thought I wouldn't have a real response, like she thought that one sentence was checkmate.

I'd show her checkmate. I had so many responses to that I didn't even know where to start.

What I said, though, was, "Like what? You want some jewelry? . . . how about a ring?"

She rolled her eyes, the termagant.

"I mean it. I'm not joking. I'll really do it. I would like to get married. To you."

She stared, finally, at last, realizing that I was being sincere.

I was painfully formal and as serious as I'd ever been as I began my practiced speech, "I take full responsibility for not communicating correctly, for not telling you how I felt, and what I thought we were, in a timely or appropriate manner.

"We both know I have commitment issues, but what I don't think you seem to realize is that you have some issues yourself. I'd have loved to know how you felt, but you weren't telling me. Not even close.

"You've put me through the fucking ringer because I didn't tell you how I felt when it was time, when it was right, but you know you didn't either. And that's not fair. You can't tell me you developed feelings only after you got over them."

She was breaking her record on staying quiet, but her soul sucking eyes were telling me plenty.

I continued, "You should have told me your feelings," I spoke to her, more gently now. "I would have been… more sensitive. We could have… committed and all that stuff." For my part, I'd almost broken my own record of putting my foot in my mouth, so it'd only been a matter of time before I fumbled my words.

She was there to pounce the moment I did, of course. "Committed and all that stuff?" She looked at me like I was absolutely hopeless. "Because of my feelings?

"Of course," I said, not at first understanding what she was getting at and trying, above all, to reassure her. "Your feelings are very important to me. I'd never hurt you."

"You're so twisted. I don't want you to commit because of *my* feelings. For this to have been something other than what it turned out being, *your* feelings had to be involved too."

"Why aren't you hearing me? They were. They *are*. I care about you. I *really* care about you. And it's not fair that you only ever hinted at how you felt as you were telling me it was too late. Perhaps, if you cared, you should have said something, as well."

She still wasn't talking, and I wasn't finished.

"And you," I paused and collected myself, "I'm sorry, but *you* need to take some responsibility too. You were just as much of a coward as I was. More." I paused. "Coward." I tasted the word. "*You* are the real coward here."

"This… love stuff is complicated for me," I continued. The look on her face was gratifying. She'd gone from pissed to shocked in under a second. Her eyes were wide, mouth slack, and I thought I should probably make her sit down before she fell over.

I guided her into a seat and continued, just unloading on her. I needed her to understand. More than anything, even my pride, I needed that.

"It's not that I've never given my heart to anyone before," I explained to her. "As a child, I gave it away to everyone. Anyone that I could have hoped would accept it after my mother died. By everyone I mean my father and a revolving door of girlfriends. I counted it up, and he averaged one every two months in a ten year period. He always brought them around and told me to call them mom. I did." I swallowed hard. "When I was fourteen, one of them slipped into bed with me. That's why I lost my virginity so young. It wasn't all that fun. I was terrified, and it made me sick afterward, to do that to my dad."

I took a deep breath, appreciating her ability to let me get all this out without stopping me. "You're the first person I've ever told that to," I stated quietly. "But back to my point, that's around the time I stopped believing in love. Quit giving me that look. I'm not telling you this so you'll feel sorry for me. I'm explaining because I had my reasons, and I wanted you to know them, to understand why it took me so long to realize my feelings on love had changed, that *you* had changed them."

And then I did it, the thing I was most incapable of. I cracked my chest open wide and handed her my heart.

"I believe in love again. I believe in you." I smiled. "Now marry me."

She was still speechless. It wasn't the worst response she could have had, I supposed.

"I know this was a lot to take in," I told her gently. "That *I'm* a lot to take in. I'll give you some time to think about it."

CHAPTER THIRTY-FIVE

I sniffed, grimaced, then sniffed again. I was working in my office, and the most awful smell was drifting my way from God knew where.

I went to Ro's office to ask her about it. We hadn't spoken since I'd spilled my guts to her a few hours earlier.

"Do you smell that?" I asked her, nose wrinkled.

She was sitting at her desk, but she didn't appear to be working.

She had a peculiar look on her face, like she was embarrassed but defiant at the same time.

"Smell what?" she asked, fake innocent.

"That was a real piece of bad acting. What's going on with you? And why are you in denial about that smell? God, what is it? And why is it smoky in here?"

I moved to investigate but she stopped me. "There was a small fire in the house, but I've contained it. The smoke is just lingering, but I've opened several doors to help clear it out. It should be better in a few hours."

"A small fire?" I asked her, going to stand right in front of her desk. "Where? How?"

"Where? Your sex bed. How? It was a match."

I couldn't quite believe it. "What did you just say?"

"Your sex bed caught on fire. It's under control now, but the bed didn't make it. It was unsalvageable. Actually, that entire room's a goner. Nothing survived. Oops."

I was just staring at her like she was a crazy woman.

"Care to explain?" I asked carefully.

"I never liked that room. Not at all. So I set it on fire."

I started to get it then, feeling a sense of wonder and joy overtake me. It was a struggle not to smile at her.

"You love me," I told her.

It was like she hadn't heard me. "I was just getting you back," she continued, rallying, grasping at straws in an effort to justify herself. "It was revenge. It's a fair exchange for when you burned my clothes."

I was silent.

She wasn't. "Don't you agree? It makes sense, right?"

I didn't answer, still just staring.

"Tell me that makes sense," she ordered.

"That makes sense," I repeated back obediently.

She was studying me like she thought I might be mad.

On the contrary. I was ec-fucking-static. There was only one reason a woman would do that.

She was jealous. Possessive. And there was only one reason she'd be either of those things.

She cared.

And she wasn't hiding it from me. She was *showing* it to me.

I went to look in person at her fit of jealousy.

I studied the damage she'd done as she hovered behind me and made excuses.

I wasn't listening to her right then, I was too busying

having a rather profound revelation.

I wouldn't miss one thing about that room. I hadn't even been inside of it for months, but it was something I hadn't realized until just that moment.

The sex room, the complicated positions, the parade of partners, the threesomes, *all* the kinky shit had been there for one reason, to disguise one thing.

I'd been nothing so much as bored. Sex with random women was *boring*. Had been boring for a very long time. That's why I'd made it into a game. To get some sort of entertainment, something to replace the enjoyment I'd taken out of the robotic motions of getting off.

And now said unwanted room was a complete disaster, and it was making my day. "Did you have a book burning party in here, as well?" I asked her cheerfully.

"Maybe," she said sullenly. "You don't seem that upset," she pointed out.

I turned and looked her dead in the eyes. Tried to. She was too short. I pulled her to the closest staircase and set her two steps up.

Hands on my hips, eye level now, I stared her down. "About time you showed some guts," I said succinctly.

She exploded. "You're right!" It was a shout. It was the first time I'd ever heard her yell.

Usually she just quietly verbally decimated me.

"You're right." Quieter now. "I've been a coward. I was very, very hurt and scared of being more hurt, and I shut you out. I've been turning my back on the risks. There are no guarantees."

"I *guarantee* I'm better in bed than that virgin you've been dating," I couldn't help slipping in.

She giggled.

"I changed my phone number," I told her, still going down the checklist of things I needed to prove to her. "I wish I'd thought of it sooner. Also, before I did that I sent out a mass message to every single woman I know and told them I was happily married and expecting a baby soon."

Her eyes widened, her mouth opening and closing, before she finally said, "You're insane."

"Well, yes. What's that got to do with anything?"

Her face was solemn now and tender.

"And you love me," she said.

It was almost a question, stopping just short of it. "I love you," I agreed. "I'm crazy about you. It started way earlier on than I'd like to admit to. You've charmed my socks off from the start. I love everything about you, from the top of your head to the bottom of your itty bitty adorable feet."

She opened her mouth, and I knew what she was about to say. I covered it with my hand. "No. I do not have a foot fetish. Stop that."

I took my hand away. "Your turn. You love me too. Say it."

She was trying not to laugh. It was perfect. "You can't just tell me to say it like that."

"I did and I am. Hit me with it, cupcake. You know you want to."

Our eyes on each other were tender now. And she didn't have to say it, I knew now how she felt. She'd shown it in the form of the smoke we were both inhaling right at that moment.

But she did say it, thank God. "I love you, Turner. I love you so much."

I closed my eyes, soaking that up for a moment before I pulled her from the second step to the floor.

I took a ring box out of my pocket and went down on one knee. I grinned, an *I told you so* grin.

Her hands covered her mouth. She was so ruffled, I could hardly stand it. I wanted to drag her down and ravish her right that second.

Instead, I opened the box, took the ring out and said, "Now marry me."

I put the ring on her finger. "Nothing to say?" I asked her.

"Yes," she said simply. "I'll marry you. Yes."

"Good," I said briskly, standing. "We're going to get the paperwork done today, right now. We're eloping as soon as it is legally possible. I need that. I've spent too much time not married to you. Does that make sense?"

She didn't answer.

"Tell me that makes sense," I told her.

"That makes sense."

EPILOGUE

I made her call Aaron and dump him on the spot. I wanted to talk to him myself, to do the honors.

She had the unmitigated gall to do it herself and let him down easy.

I shamelessly listened to the entire thing.

He took it with affable good grace, the Boy Scout. Barf.

When she hung up I tickled her to the ground. "You complete me."

"Like a pin in a hand grenade," she agreed.

Just perfect.

"You love me," I told her just to hear it again.

"Yes."

"Obviously I know how irresistible I am," I continued.

"Insufferable when you get your way," she added.

I ignored that. "Now tell me when," I ordered her.

"When?"

"I want to know the exact moment you knew you were falling for me. Hit me with it. It was when I answered the door in a towel on that first day, wasn't it?"

She ignored that, chewing her lip, really thinking about it. "I think it was the night of your pool party, when you were acting like a maniac. The way you took care of me like I was your only thought, your only priority. I think that was when I started to get an inkling."

"Do you want to know mine?" I asked her.

"Let me guess. It was after I showed you Mischief and Mayhem, wasn't it?"

"A solid guess, I must say. Wrong, but a good try. I was in strong denial but I actually think you had me hooked from 'Dev is trite.'"

I'd left her speechless.

I kept going. "I'm not sure how you'll take this, but even though I was slow to figure out the love stuff, I still meant every marriage proposal I ever leveled at you."

We were married in record speed, which was saying a lot in Vegas.

We hadn't even pulled out of the parking lot to head home from the courthouse when I said, "Have the IUD taken out. I want to get you pregnant yesterday."

Her reaction was better than it could have been, to be fair. She just laughed. "Shut up, you wacko. We don't have to do everything this very second. Let's take a minute to breathe."

"I don't want to," I was driving, and I caressed her thigh with my right hand, then tried to cop a feel. "I want to fill you with cum with a *purpose,* and I want to do it this *instant.*"

She batted my hand away. She was programming the music for the car from her phone, and not ten seconds later the speakers started blaring out *You can't always get what you want.*

"Wife," I said it like an insult.

"Husband," she matched my tone precisely.

"Ball and chain."

"Albatross."

Ro's parents showed up at my house less than twenty-four hours after she told them about the wedding.

She was right. They were adorable, and when they were finished chewing us both out and sizing me up, they were delightful to have around. As different from my own family as it was possible to be.

Wholesome and somehow wickedly fun.

They adopted me on the spot, and I instantly enlisted them in my plot of convincing Ro to have ten babies with me sooner rather than later.

They were more than happy to, and they were very good at it. I saw quickly where Ro had gotten her irresistible charm.

Her mother's name was Ginny, and she was as funny as she was cute. Delightful and a little terrifying, just like her daughter.

She was a very kind, serene woman, but her sense of humor was acerbic and dry, a marvelous juxtaposition that reminded me of no one I had ever met aside from Ro.

I was wandering into my kitchen one morning sans shirt when her wry voice stopped me in my tracks.

"I must've forgot I ordered a stripper for breakfast," Ginny said with perfect, biting timing from the kitchen table. She sipped her coffee, set it down, and asked with pointed impudence, "Where's the music? Shouldn't *Pony* be playing?"

I pointed at her. "You can stop that right now. If your daughter can't get me to wear more clothing, no one else is going to manage it."

But I did put on a fucking shirt.

Her father's name was Arnold, and he wasn't as cute as his girls, but he was damned funny, a dad joke connoisseur.

"Sorry, we had some work," Ro told them one day as we

met them at the dinner table a few minutes later than we'd planned.

"Well, good work, then. From the looks of it, your work should make us grandparents in about nine months," Arnold said wryly.

Ro blushed down to her toes, and I smiled at him fondly.

It was rather like being in a house full of Ros, so much fun I could hardly take it all in.

Her parents were both retired, and I talked them into staying with us for two months and made them promise to come back in a month even as I dropped them off at the airport.

"I'll have her pregnant by then for sure," I told her dad conspiratorially.

It was hard to pull off with Ro in the passenger seat, obviously.

"I'm right here," she said huffily.

Ro's parents were very happy about the marriage in short order, but no one—except perhaps for Ro and I—was filled with as much unmitigated glee about it as Iris.

We told them over dinner at their house. It was just us, them, and their kids.

She and her children had danced around the table in a gloating celebration for about five solid minutes.

Dair just watched them, looking besotted.

"You *are* an evil mastermind," I told Iris begrudgingly when she sat down again. "Downright Machiavellian." I looked at Ro. "But sometimes, I suppose, it's justified."

Iris snorted. "That's the point now, isn't it? Of Machiavellianism."

I ignored that. Sass flowed around me like water these days.

I did talk Ro into the tattoos on our asses, and it didn't even take me long. Apparently marriage made that sort of thing 'more appropriate.' Who knew?

It was over a year later, and she when she published her first book, Mayhem the Unicorn Stands Up to Bullies.

I was so proud I could hardly contain myself. I did such a large blast on social media to my dedicated horror fans about the adorable, off brand for me book, that I got some disgruntled emails about it. I couldn't have cared less, in fact that only encouraged me.

Her publisher even set up a reading and signing at a large local bookstore. There was a pretty good turnout of little girls and boys and even some eccentric adults that were instantly taken with the sassy purple unicorn. I acted as her assistant for the event, our three month old daughter strapped to my chest in a baby carrier.

I bounced baby Avril and we cooed at each other while I got Ro absolutely anything she might need during the event. I was kind of an expert at it. She kept turning and beaming at me and our daughter between books. Every time she did it I went and kissed the top of her beautiful head, nuzzling into her silky hair.

Our family was so adorable that I felt sorry for anyone that had to look at us. We were disgusting. Highly exceptionable.

I was in absolute heaven

I was only sorry I couldn't deliver her a proper drink when we were halfway through and she made a tequila face at me. She was staying dry while she breastfed.

Oh well, there was always next time.

OTHER BOOKS BY R.K. LILLEY

STANDALONES
ARRANGED

THE LOVE IS WAR SAGA
BREAKING HIM
BREAKING HER
SAVAGES - COMING SOON

THE WILD SIDE SERIES
THE WILD SIDE -IRIS-DAIR
THE OTHER MAN
TYRANT
TEACHER'S PET - COMING IN OCTOBER

THE UP IN THE AIR SERIES
IN FLIGHT
MILE HIGH
GROUNDED
MR. BEAUTIFUL
LANA

THE TRISTAN & DANIKA SERIES
BAD THINGS
ROCK BOTTOM
LOVELY TRIGGER

THE HERETIC DAUGHTERS SERIES
BREATHING FIRE
CROSSING FIRE

THE GILDED CAGE
A COLLECTION OF EROTIC FAIRYTALES
THE GOLDEN QUEEN - COMING SOON
THE KING'S PET - COMING SOON

Made in the USA
Columbia, SC
09 September 2023

22660197R00173